"*Lost Girls* is a horrifying look at human trafficking wrapped around a compelling thriller. Shuman is one of my favorite reads."

—Gregg Hurwitz, bestselling author of
The Crime Writer

"A compelling human drama, told no holds barred by a dynamic storyteller."

—Bookreporter.com

LAST BREATH

"Shuman has written a story that is intricate, shocking, and terrifying, and filled with colorful characters that resonate."

—*Tucson Citizen*

"Shuman brings a chilling realism to his depiction of crime scenes and has a real gift for conveying fear."

—*Publishers Weekly*

"Part police procedural, part psychological thriller . . . engrossing."

—*Kirkus Reviews*

"A mesmerizing, gritty, gut-wrenching, gruesome tale that's distinctly not for the weak at heart."

—*Lansing State Journal* (MI)

"Shuman does an excellent job . . . the details of the investigation ring true. . . . A gripping, fast-paced and extremely creepy thriller. . . ."

—Bookreporter.com

18 SECONDS

LOST

GIRLS

A SHERRY MOORE NOVEL

GEORGE D. SHUMAN

POCKET STAR BOOKS

NEW YORK LONDON TORONTO SYDNEY

Pocket Star Books
A Division of Simon & Schuster, Inc.
1230 Avenue of the Americas
New York, NY 10020

This book is a work of fiction. Names, characters, places, and incidents either are products of the author's imagination or are used fictitiously. Any resemblance to actual events or locales or persons, living or dead, is entirely coincidental.

First Pocket Star paperback edition July 2009

POCKET STAR and colophon are registered trademarks of Simon & Schuster, Inc.

For information about special discounts for bulk purchases, please contact Simon & Schuster Special Sales at 1-866-506-1949 or business@simonandschuster.com.

The Simon & Schuster Speakers Bureau can bring authors to your live event. For more information or to book an event, contact the Simon & Schuster Speakers Bureau at 1-866-248-3049 or visit our website at www.simonspeakers.com.

Cover design by Jae Son
Image of woman © Glowimages/Getty Images.

Manufactured in the United States of America

10 9 8 7 6 5 4 3 2 1

ISBN 978-1-4165-5304-5

This book is dedicated to
Elizabeth M. Shuman,
a most incredibly gifted woman.
Your boundless energy, intelligence,
compassion, and creativity have touched
far more people than you may ever know.
You are truly one of God's home runs.
Thank you, Mom, for whatever fraction
of yourself was passed on to me.

FOREWORD

EXCERPTS FROM
Trafficking in Women and Children:
The U.S. and International Response
Updated March 26, 2004
Congressional Research Service
Francis T. Miko
Specialist in International Relations
Foreign Affairs, Defense, and Trade Division

Traffickers acquire their victims in a number of ways. Sometimes women are kidnapped outright in one country and taken forcibly to another. In other cases, victims are lured with phony job offers. Traffickers entice victims to migrate voluntarily with false promises of well-paying jobs in foreign countries as au pairs, models, dancers, domestic workers, etc. Traffickers advertise these "jobs" as well as marriage opportunities abroad in local newspapers. . . . The largest numbers of victims trafficked annually from the former Soviet Union and Eastern Europe come from Russia and Ukraine.

While there is no single victim stereotype, a majority of trafficked women are under the age of twenty-five, with many in their mid- to late teens. The fear of infection with HIV and AIDS among sex tourism customers has driven traffickers to recruit younger women and girls, some as young as seven, erroneously perceived by customers as being too young to have been infected.

Trafficking victims are often subjected to cruel mental and physical abuse in order to keep them in servitude, including beating, rape, starvation, forced drug use, confinement, and seclusion. Once victims are brought into destination countries, their passports are often confiscated. Victims are forced to have sex, often unprotected, with large numbers of partners, and to work unsustainably long hours. Many victims suffer mental breakdowns and are exposed to sexually transmitted diseases, including HIV and AIDS. They are often denied medical care and those who become ill are sometimes even killed.

The presence of sex tourists from Europe, North America, and Australia (in Latin America and the Caribbean) has significantly contributed to the trafficking of women and children. A growing number of sex tourists are going to Latin America, partly as a result of recent restrictions placed on sex tourism in Thailand, Sri Lanka, and other Asian countries. Favored sex tourism destinations are Brazil, Argentina, the Dominican Republic, Mexico, Honduras, Costa Rica, Trinidad, and Tobago. Brazil has one of the worst child prostitution problems in the world.

Raw winds hailed lacerating ice, stinging earlobes and ruddy cheeks beneath the climbers' black snow goggles. The storm had an under-growl that suggested it was both alive and malevolent.

It came out of nowhere as polar storms do, the clockwise rotation of Pacific highs meeting counter-clockwise Siberian lows, fusing to form a cyclone in ancient cauldrons of granite and glacier. Mountains the size of Denali virtually produce their own weather.

Allison Metcalf descended the headwall below the summit clipped to a fixed line, testing the ice with cram-pons on the toes of her boots. The well-trod western approach was quickly vanishing under their feet, transmuting into an alien environment of wind-sculpted ice. She took another step and then another, trying to quell the rise of panic. Only three hours ago they had stood on top of the Western Hemisphere. Now they were in a race for their lives to get beneath it.

The spatial world was no more. There were no more ups and downs, no rights or lefts. One could reach out an arm and not see the glove beyond the wrist. If any of the climbers were to unclip from the fixed line, even for a moment, it was doubtful they would find it again; more likely they would wander off the side of the mountain or fall into one of the hundreds of bottomless crevices of prehistoric ice.

"You okay?" Sergio's voice caught faintly on the wind. He was below her, but still close, only a dozen feet away. *Was he straggling to look out for her?*

"Okay," she yelled, but the words evaporated with a blast of chilled air. She tugged gently on the line tethered between them and a moment later she felt his acknowledgment. It felt good, this tangible connection to another human being.

If they could at least descend to high camp at 17,000 feet, they might survive the night in the uppermost cradle of the summit. The poor buggers above Archdeacon's Tower had yet to negotiate an exposed knife-edged ridge. They would not be so lucky, would not last an hour when the sun dropped below the horizon and windchills plummeted below minus sixty degrees. Allison could not imagine a night of terror in subzero hurricane winds, tethered to four other people in the open, any of whom might panic and make an error fatal for all of them.

Allison had met only two of the other climbers from the teams still up at the summit, both of them women from British Columbia. They'd shared stories of climbs in the Canadian Rockies and a stove for soup this morning as the sun began to rise. One of them was also named Allison. They'd laughed about the chances of that, but now she found that other woman's face etched upon her mind, could not dispel it.

Suddenly Allison's feet went out from under her and she began to backslide, frantically grabbing for the ice ax on her belt. Just before she went head over heels, she wielded the ax two-handed, driving its pick into the side of the mountain to break her fall. She hung there a moment on her side, both arms extended, hanging on to the handle, but then the ax let loose and she began to spiral away, chin raking the ice-sheathed granite until her boots struck something solid.

She tried to blink away the snow that covered her eyes, to see through the hail of white wind, and there was Sergio's purple snowsuit. He wrapped his arms around her waist and put his face to hers and it was cold.

"You okay?"

She tried to speak, but the words wouldn't come. Her mouth was filling with warm blood, her eyes welling with tears.

He helped her to stand, neither able to see the other's expression through the dark lenses of their goggles. She put a gloved hand over his heart and held it there and he nodded. Then he gave her his ice ax, turned and pointed down and grabbed the line, descending into the whiteout. Allison nodded as he disappeared. There was no time to reflect.

But Allison did reflect. She had spent last night in Sergio's sleeping bag. It was the first and only time since they had met—eight days before in the village of Talkeetna, where solo climbers came to buddy up with summiting teams—that he had even spoken more than a dozen words to her. Allison thought him arrogant at first, one of those handsome playboy types with infinite time and money on his hands. She had even goaded him about it on the mountain, trying to provoke a re-action until in an unguarded moment in their tent she saw an unmistakable look of despair on his face. It was then she realized there was more to Sergio than met the eye. He hadn't come to Denali to conquer the mountain. He had come here to run away. But from what—a lost love, a failed marriage, some deep incom-prehensible disappointment in his life?

They never got to talk about it and perhaps, she thought, they never would.

She remembered his lips pressed to the side of her neck in the cocoon of that sleeping bag last night. He had actually cried after they made love. He did not want to leave the mountain, he'd told her. His warm tears had been wet on her neck; he'd told her he did not want to return to who he was.

DENALI NATIONAL PARK

FIVE DAYS LATER

Harsh sunlight glinted off the big blades of the HH-60 Pave Hawk, creating strobe-like effects inside the he-licopter's cargo bay. Captain Metcalf, sitting opposite Sherry Moore, shielded his eyes from the rapid-fire bars of white light deflecting off her snow goggles.

"Glaciers." He leaned toward the edge of her helmet. "We're almost there."

Sherry nodded, her stomach queasy as the craft began to tilt on its side, darting toward the tallest mountain in the Western Hemisphere. Sherry was no stranger to helicopters. She'd spent much of her life being whisked from one place to another, knew the crew seats of the big corporate Bells and Hueys and Sikorskys, even the fleet of luxury VH-3Ds designated Marine One when the president of the United States was on board. But the Pave Hawk was like nothing she had experienced before; it was the difference between riding a flea and a bumblebee.

"Is it clear? The summit?" she asked.

"Blue skies. Hard to take your eyes away," Metcalf said absently. She felt him looking at her just then, knowing he was regretting the offhanded reference to sight.

Her own images of the mountain were formed from books she'd listened to on tape or disk, of blinding white snow and black granite walls, of ice-blue glaciers and bottomless crevices.

"I can imagine," she said softly.

The Alaskans called the mountain by its Indian name, Denali, meaning "the great one," though U.S. geological maps still call it Mount McKinley. It towered four miles above five glaciers, with more vertical face than Mount Everest, high enough to be seen from

Anchorage, a hundred and thirty miles away, on a good day.

There were no climbers on the summit of Denali today. No colorful string of snowsuits negotiating the Denali pass or the notorious ridge or the turn called Windy Corner.

All of the climbers known to have survived the storm had been found below 14,000 feet, near basin camp, where National Guard Chinooks were evacuating them as fast as they could assemble.

Above 14,000 feet, conditions were simply indescribable, or, as one Denali ranger told reporters, a wasteland of flash-frozen cornices. Of valleys pitted with hidden fissures wide enough to swallow rescue teams or helicopters.

The storm was the result of a low-pressure system that had inserted itself on the mountain last Sunday, generating what was known as a polar cyclone. The system laid upon Denali for five days, producing a dozen feet of new snow in gusts of wind exceeding 100 miles per hour. The storm virtually resculpted the upper third of the mountain.

Now it was Friday and twelve people were still missing above basin camp. One expedition of four had summited the morning of the storm and was making their way back to high camp when the storm hit. Their last FRS radio transmission before the communications system went down due to the storm was from the Denali pass, 800 feet above high camp. They had every chance of making it then, but five days later they could not be reached, and it was impossible to know where they had finally dug in to weather the storm. It was also unlikely their supplies had been sufficient to sustain them.

Other expeditions, one from Thailand and one from British Columbia, were only nearing the summit when the storm suddenly developed. Their last reports indicated they were going forward, only a few hundred feet to the top, before they would turn around.

The cyclone hadn't been predicted, but that was the nature of Denali. The sheer mass of the mountain created its own weather. Any beautiful morning could end with an afternoon storm and a climbing disaster.

Meteorologists, as always, wasted no time getting their warning out, but those on the upper third of the mountain needed days, not hours to make their descent, and that was under optimal conditions. Anyone above basin camp last Friday was there to stay.

From the television on board the private jet taking Sherry to Alaska, Sherry learned there was little hope for climbers above 16,000 feet. Teams attempting the summit would have cached much of their equipment and food below, leaving them light for the final two-day ascent to the top of the mountain. Which meant that time was their greatest enemy. Even if they managed to reach high camp, there would be little food and fuel for heat, certainly not five days' worth.

The park rangers set up a triage area in the permanent medical station on basin camp, doctors from Anchorage and Fairbanks dividing their attention between cases of frostbite and acute mountain sickness. There was no small number of broken bones too, and a tent was set aside for bodies retrieved from a rescue in the gully below the vertical headwall under Camp 6. Three had fallen to their deaths.

A fourth body, photographed by search planes, was dangling off that headwall by a line wrapped around his boot. He was hanging just below the 16,000-foot mark and his jacket, once bright purple, showed faint lavender under a sheath of heavy ice. Perhaps a carabiner or ascender broke, releasing him to the gale-force winds. Perhaps the winds themselves upended him and tangled the rope around his boot? Whatever the case, exposed to the elements as he was, he managed to make a signal mark with luminescent paint on the granite wall. The mark appeared to look like an arrow pointing upward with a circle on top. He was obviously trying to leave a message. To show rescuers there were survivors above the ledge. By altitude, he could only have been one of the team of four who had radioed they were trying to reach high camp the day the storm set in on the summit of Denali. Apparently they had descended to Camp 6 over the next two days, where they would have had to dig out a snow cave, but where above the ledge and under all that new snow should the rescuers look? Any original sign of a cave would have disappeared an hour after it was built, and finding it now, under new snow, was fairly impossible.

A spokesperson for the National Park Service announced they would not be committing teams to a random search above basin camp. It would pose too great a risk for the people and equipment it would take to get them there. More than a hundred people were on Denali when it hit, all but twelve having had time to descend to the ranger station at basin camp, or they were already below it. But even this group suffered countless casualties.

Landing zones above basin camp could no longer be presumed safe; it was late in the climbing season and glaciers were beginning to fracture, forming bottomless crevices, some as wide as a house. New snow above them presented the constant threat of avalanche and last, but hardly least, another storm was forming off the Bering Strait that would be upon them by midnight, obliterating the mountain in yet another whiteout. Rescue teams made it clear they would make no attempt to search the upper third of the mountain without clear evidence of life. The endeavor was not only risky but would divert badly needed personnel and helicopters already committed to evacuating known survivors. As for the body hanging from the ridge, his team was probably already dead. The marking he had made on the side of the mountain was not a sign of life, they reminded. It was only a sign, and how many days old?

It was all a little hard to digest, Sherry thought. She'd been following news of the disaster on Denali throughout the week. There was a sad recap of the story every evening as the storm prevented rescuers from getting to the mountain. But a mountain in Alaska was far removed in time and place from her living room in Philadelphia. She could not imagine a relationship to it.

Then, this morning, Garland Brigham, her neighbor and best friend, knocked on her door. It was six A.M. He had been awakened by a call from Washington state senator Metcalf. The senator's only daughter, Allison, had been with the team of four believed to have survived the first day of the storm.

There had been a break in the weather. Rescuers were gearing up to reach the survivors. Metcalf wanted to know if Brigham's famous friend would fly to the mountain and attempt to learn if there had been any radio contact between the survivors and his daughter's team before the communications systems went down. Sherry, he said, would be given access to the bodies of the fallen climbers. Could any of them have seen his daughter descending when the storm hit? He was grabbing at straws, Brigham said, and the senator well knew it. Still, it was only two A.M. in Alaska. She could be on Denali before noon if she left right away.

Sherry Moore would do anything for Garland Brigham, even if only to make a demonstration of compassion. By 6:30 A.M. she was in a military police car speeding for Philadelphia International. At 6:50 she climbed the carpeted stairs of a luxury Gulfstream jet and was handed a mug of coffee. She was the only passenger flying at .85 mach across the country.

She knew from what Brigham had told her that the rescuers had daylight in their favor. The Alaskan sun wouldn't set until midnight, providing nineteen hours of light. She also knew that the senator's son, U.S. Navy SEAL captain Brian Metcalf, would be meeting her in Anchorage, where she would transfer to a privately contracted helicopter from Washington State that would take them to Denali National Park and basin camp.

Sherry had dozed on and off during the flight, listened to cable news on satellite television, and spoken with Brigham by phone several times. He told her that Captain Metcalf had contacted him and wanted to know if she might attempt, with him, to reach a body hanging from a headwall. Metcalf was convinced it was a member of his sister's team. The man had apparently been trying to leave a message with signal dye on the side of the mountain when he died.

It wasn't a request and it didn't require an answer. Brigham was only warning Sherry what to expect when she arrived in Anchorage. But there must have been a conversation between the two men about her physical capabilities. Metcalf would not have raised the possibility of descending a mountainside with a blind woman unless Brigham had assured him that she was in good physical condition. Brigham wouldn't have told Sherry what he thought she should do—he never tried to lead her one way or the other—but he might have considered it a real option.

One thing she knew with certainty: He wouldn't let her do anything that might compromise her safety. She knew as surely as she knew her own name that if Brigham raised the possibility of such a thing, he had complete confidence in Metcalf's abilities. As for the biological side of it, all Sherry needed was a body intact, with the remnants of a neurological system and an inactive brain, to see a corpse's final seconds of memory.

Sherry felt the helicopter getting buffeted in the wind. She knew something about the Pave Hawk: it was a modified version of the army's Black Hawk, seventeen million dollars' worth of technology refitted for rescue work in hostile terrain. It was used not only in the mountainous extremes of Afghanistan but also in civilian rescues like those for Typhoon Chanchu and the Indian Ocean tsunami and Katrina in New Orleans.

There were three other men in the chopper, all navy SEALs, she'd been told, and they were strapped in harnesses on the benches to her right. Sherry's toe struck the duffel bag between them. It would be orange or red or yellow, filled with morphine and oxygen, heat packs and adrenaline syringes, and there would be CO_2-charged splints and neck braces and of course disposable body bags. Metcalf might have come to perform a rescue mission, but all rescuers knew that such undertakings often turned into a recovery. She knew Metcalf was thinking about that. Thinking about his sister.

She couldn't quite say how it had happened. One moment she was heading for the relative safety of basin camp to visit the bodies of three dead climbers. The next she was listening to Metcalf's argument for reaching the dead man, and donning heavy snow gear to descend the side of a mountain.

Metcalf was not a man of many words—he wasted none explaining their objective—but he was nonetheless convincing. She felt confident in his presence, and it was a contagious feeling that continued throughout the mission. She knew now why Brigham had let it get this far. You didn't always need eyes to size up a man. The perception of comportment was not exclusive to people with sight, nor were qualities such as competence and self-assurance. Metcalf was a Navy SEAL and that assumed certain abilities, but there was far more to Metcalf than ability.

The plan was extraordinarily simple, he told her. The pilot of the Pave Hawk would drop them above the headwall at 16,200 feet. Then they would belay off fixed lines—already attached to the side of the mountain— and rappel 400 feet to where the body was hanging. Recovering the dead climber's body was not an option— there was no time for rescue baskets and Metcalf could hardly divide his attention between a blind woman and a dead man once they were down there. But if the dead man had been part of Allison Metcalf's team, Metcalf might be able to make clear the meaning of the message the climber had been trying to write on the side of the wall. If they could decipher it, Metcalf could radio the information to his men up above and they could focus their search accordingly.

Sherry often went into these kinds of situations feeling doubtful. What a person was thinking about in their last few seconds of life was not always what her clients wanted to hear. No one knows the precise moment they will expire and what random thoughts might occupy their short-term memory when they did. This was especially true when death is inevitable but protracted. People preparing themselves for death run the gamut of emotions, all the while searching their mind for visual references of their journey through life.

The man hanging from his boot had surely frozen to death. He was probably thinking about loved ones in the end, most people did, but he might also have been occupied by the technical problems of his situation, how to regain the fixed line on the side of the mountain, how to right himself again.

Even if he could still focus on the message he was trying to leave, Sherry couldn't imagine him producing a mental image that might help them locate a team of climbers buried in a snow cave above them. In fact she could not imagine how he had hoped to find his own way back in a storm of the magnitude that had been described.

It occurred to her that he might never have had the intention of returning. That he might have known he was not coming back, that his message on the wall was an act of extreme selflessness.

"Kahiltna Glacier." The pilot's tinny voice came over the headphones. Metcalf tapped the side of her helmet and Sherry nodded to acknowledge that she'd heard. That her equipment was operating.

She pulled the microphone away from her mouth to speak to Metcalf privately. "You know the admiral?" Brigham had never mentioned Senator Metcalf before. She was aware that Brigham had friends on Capitol Hill, had even overheard a woman at one of those rare gatherings at Brigham's house comment on a birthday card with the presidential seal.

"Mostly by reputation, ma'am."

"Reputation?" she repeated lightly. Sherry had never thought of Brigham in terms of having a reputation.

Metcalf was silent again, even stoic. Except for the brief description of what he'd asked her to do on the side of the ridge, since leaving Anchorage he'd spoken only to his men and always in fewer than three words. He didn't like questions, or so it seemed. He wasn't used to them and they probably made him uncomfortable.

"So you've never met?" Sherry couldn't help herself.

"We've met," Metcalf allowed.

Sherry had always had a nose for people's discomfort. She knew that Metcalf had a lot going through his mind. His sister, alive or dead, was out there somewhere. One could only imagine the stress he must be under. She couldn't help but wonder why he was putting such energy into taking her along with him. It didn't quite fit the manner of the man. Was it Brigham's influence over the captain that had convinced him to meet her? Men like Metcalf would not be happy chauffeuring civilians around in times of crisis. They were far more likely to put faith in training and experience rather than some paranormal exercise. Metcalf just had to be thinking this was a waste of precious time, but then why was he doing it? Was it in deference to his father or the admiral's rank? Had the senator called Brigham or was it the other way around?

Sherry's ability to "see" dated back to an incident in her childhood, an inadvertent gesture of tenderness that linked Sherry to a dead girl's mind, flooding her with images of things that she had never known and could not possibly have seen. For all the skeptics who would follow, none were more critical of her interpretations than Sherry herself, and it wasn't until many years later that she realized she was actually seeing glimpses of memory, the final seconds of a person's life.

Much could be said about Sherry's documented experiences with corpses since then. The press had labeled her paranormal, but Sherry's ability was gaining credibility in the medical community and an impressive list of neurosurgeons and scientists around the world were beginning to draw parallels between Sherry and new research on how human memory is stored.

Each year researchers inched closer to the possibility that Sherry's ability to link short-term memory was based in science, not metaphysics. On paper it made sense. Millions of skin receptors and nerve cells were wired directly through the deceased's central nervous system to the cortex of the brain. If memory was but an encoding of the body's sensory experiences, then why couldn't the right kind of electrical stimulus tap into it? The wiring was in place. The brain was still there, and brains were computers.

She was curious about Metcalf, but not at the expense of alienating him, so she decided to let it lie. The day was half gone. The Alaskan sun would set before midnight. She would do what she came to do and then she would be back on the jet and heading for home. All of this would be behind them.

She heard Metcalf clear his throat. His head was near. He seemed to be leaning in toward her. He surprised her by speaking and this time it was with inflection.

"I'm sorry, ma'am. I didn't mean to be rude."

She hesitated a second. She wanted to get this right. For some unfathomable reason she wanted this man to trust her, to like her, even if he could not believe in her. She couldn't explain why that was. She usually didn't dwell on the misgivings of others, but Metcalf somehow mattered; she wanted to reach him on a personal level and it wasn't going to be easy. It was a little like trying to approach a wild animal, she guessed. It would require the use of round, harmless-sounding words. Say the wrong thing, use the wrong tone, and it was over. But she really wanted to understand Metcalf's relationship with Brigham.

"We met in the Pentagon once and several times at my father's home in Boston. I actually remember him from my teenage years. How about you? Have you known him long?"

"Ten years, a little more," she decided to say.

"So you're close then," Metcalf said. "Friends?"

Sherry smiled. "I can honestly say he has become my best friend, Captain."

Metcalf took a moment to digest that, seeming uncertain about the ground in front of him. When he finally decided to speak, he turned to face Sherry, covered the mike on his headphones so the pilots couldn't hear, and spoke loudly over the din of the engines. "A lot of people would go to hell and back for that man. Myself included."

Sherry was surprised by the emotion in his voice. It clearly wasn't an idle declaration. He really meant it. But what did that mean? Metcalf didn't sound old enough to have served with Brigham; by her estimation he couldn't possibly have been a peer, so what would he know about Brigham to qualify that statement?

"Whatever he told you, about what we have to do up here this afternoon, I want you to know you're in good hands. Nothing bad is going to happen to you, I promise."

Sherry nodded, but she wasn't thinking about the mission anymore.

"He's been retired as long as I've known him, Captain," she said.

"I'm forty-four, Miss Moore. I joined the navy straight out of college. I did three years under the admiral in the Gulf. He was my CO during Desert Shield."

Sherry pulled off her own headphones. "You served together?" she said, surprised.

"He never talked about the Gulf?"

She shook her head. "He never talked about the navy. I always imagined he was a bureaucrat. You know, life behind a desk."

Metcalf was silent again, but now Sherry wanted more.

"He told me he was stateside at the Pentagon." Sherry wanted to keep the conversation moving.

Metcalf grunted.

She was losing him. He was getting defensive again.

"He said he pushed papers," Sherry prodded.

Metcalf actually snorted.

"Well, tell me!" she blurted out, and immediately she regretted it.

There was a moment, a crossroads moment. Sherry knew she had either lost him or broken through.

"Did the admiral ever speak of DEVGRU?" he said at last.

Sherry shook her head. "No. What's it mean?"

"It's an acronym for development group. The admiral chaired the special warfare development group in the Pentagon. This was following the First Gulf War."

Sherry's expression was blank. Chaired, she thought, trying not to be cynical. He had probably "chaired" a dozen committees at the rank of admiral, which meant he delegated assignments to rear admirals and subordinate commanders. No big deal about that.

"What's so special about DEVGRU?" she asked.

"Let's just say there was nothing trivial about the kinds of papers he pushed."

"Tell me about DEVGRU. What kind of development . . ." she began, but Metcalf put a hand on her shoulder, leaning close to keep from being heard by the pilots. "Ma'am, I don't feel comfortable talking about Admiral Brigham behind his back. I was just trying to make conversation."

With that he put the headphones back on and Sherry knew it was over. He wasn't being unpleasant, but he'd reached his limit of conversation.

She sat quietly for a moment. Then she leaned into him, shoulder pressing against his bicep. "Thank you, Captain. I just want you to know I understand that this can't be easy for you. I know how odd you must think it is, my being here. Maybe even a waste of your time."

"Miss Moore," he said, abruptly pulling the headphones away. "I started this day with nineteen hours of daylight and a suggestion from Admiral Brigham that bringing you here was worth every hour doing it. That might not carry a lot of weight in the civilian world, but if Admiral Brigham also suggested you could fly this helicopter to Denali, I'd be strapping in next to you, so you see I do not take the admiral's suggestions lightly. Plan on doing whatever it is you came here to do and have faith that I'll keep you safe while you're doing it. When we get my sister off this mountain, you will have the most grateful man on the planet at your beck and call."

Sherry had to smile, but then she sensed Metcalf wasn't smiling, so she pulled her microphone back in place and shifted nervously in her seat.

There were goose bumps on her arms. Not because she was cold, but from the sheer gravitas of the man. He was, she thought, one of the most intense human beings she had ever met.

The obvious consequence of Metcalf's unwavering belief in Admiral Brigham's word was to assume an unwavering belief of his own. A belief, though he knew nothing independently about her, that she was capable of assisting them by doing something a reasonable person might think impossible. It wasn't logical by any stretch of the imagination. Faith wasn't a transferable entity when it came to matters of life and death. And rappelling off the face of a mountain with an inexperienced climber who was also blind was in itself a matter of life and death.

What was she getting involved in here? she wondered. And what kind of men were these who would stake their lives on the word of a long-retired superior? Why did she suddenly feel the ponderous weight of responsibility? As if she had a stake in saving this team lost on the mountain. She was becoming one of them. No longer a one-person show, but part of a unit going on a mission. Suddenly she needed Metcalf to know that she wasn't infallible. Any thinking person should know that, but Brigham had said something to him and now Metcalf was long past doubting her abilities, if ever he did.

This didn't remotely correspond to Sherry's experiences in the civilian world. Life for Sherry was a daily quagmire of uncertainty. Every year brought some new form of attack on what she did. Lawyers everywhere seemed bent on testing her right to practice what most people would call clairvoyance. It wasn't clairvoyance, of course, not by a long shot. But instead of science making her more credible, it seemed only to make her a more desirable target, at least in the eyes of the legal world. Suddenly there was something they could point to. A tangible concern was at stake. If she wasn't trying to defraud the public and was actually reading dead people's memories, then the law had better get out there and regulate dead people's memories, too. Someone had better ensure that the rights of the dead were protected. Or at least that's what the lawyers were trying to get on record in a courtroom. Sherry found herself having to hire lawyers to protect her from lawyers.

This was a refreshing change, she thought, men and women who spoke plain English. A group of people who believed that lies and strategies had two different meanings.

She had learned about this phenomenon of blue or green love, whatever you called the brotherhood of arms, from her late friend Philadelphia police detective

John Payne. But Metcalf took the concept of esprit de corps to a whole new level. It had only been necessary for Admiral Brigham to say it was possible for him to believe in her—that was all Metcalf needed, another man's word. It was mind-boggling.

The Pave Hawk began to descend into updraft turbulence. The metal floors hammered under her feet and she felt herself tense, fingers clutching the bottom of her seat.

Metcalf was moving around the bay, organizing things for their departure, or so she imagined. She tried for the second or perhaps third time to guess what he might look like, knowing that voices could easily fool you. Usually Sherry put an approximate face on casual acquaintances and that was good enough. Sherry assigned variations of speech and manner certain physical characteristics and had no doubt they were well off their mark. Not that it mattered. Face recognition was not part of Sherry's world. She was at liberty to imagine anything she liked about the people she came in contact with infrequently. When she did become close with someone, she cared more about his or her physical reality. When she became very close, she looked at his or her face with her hands. For some unfathomable reason she wanted to see Metcalf's face.

He was a big man. That much was obvious from the physical contact she'd had with him, especially in the limited constraints of the helicopter's cargo bay.

His chin, she thought, would be dimpled and square. His hair she imagined dark and buzzed across the scalp, his eyes were kind and blue, but for no other reason than . . . Suddenly she stopped, realizing she was fantasizing, and fantasizing was something Sherry Moore did not do.

"How high are we?" She spoke quickly into the headset.

"Just above sixteen thousand," the pilot said. "We'll be putting you down in a minute."

"You've done this before?" Sherry joked.

The craft began to make an arc. She could feel the tail coming around on its axis.

"Once or twice," the pilot said dryly.

Sherry hoped he was smiling, too.

"How many people climb Denali?" she asked, trying to keep her mind off the descent.

"About twelve hundred a year," the pilot said.

"Most make it to the top?"

"About half."

"Am I distracting you?"

"Not in the least."

"Any die?"

"Five or six a year. Fifty or sixty too broken to come back and try it again."

"How long does it take?"

"Fifteen to twenty days on average, but Denali can be a cakewalk or it can be hell. No one walks into a storm on purpose."

"It's impressive," she said, "that people can do such things."

"You know there have been blind climbers on the summit?"

"I've heard," she said.

And she had. Ever since reading about Erik Weihenmayer's summit of Everest in 2001 she'd become interested in the sport. Weihenmayer had gone on to become both a world-class climber and an athlete after losing his sight at age thirteen. He had told his interviewers after Everest that summiting was far more than a spiritual quest. Erik liked the feel of hard rock under his hands. He liked the technical challenges. He liked, he told reporters, to surround himself with competent people, the kind of people who would make him a better human being.

You didn't have to think long on that. To be blind was not a choice. How to live and the kind of people you determined to follow was.

There was some excited radio traffic over a cockpit speaker about an airlift off the Muldrow Glacier. Something was wrong with the lift arm of a rescue sling.

"Down there?" the pilot said.

Sherry felt Metcalf lean forward. She imagined him looking out a window in the door.

"You can work with that?" Metcalf asked.

"I can get you down," the pilot allowed.

Suddenly the vibrations in the floorboard smoothed

out and the Pave Hawk began to move laterally, approaching the top of the ridge.

"I never saw anything like it," the pilot said.

"The ice?" Metcalf asked.

"I've been flying this mountain for fifteen years and it's never looked like this."

"Tell me," Sherry insisted.

"Everything's glazed over. Like ocean waves frozen midbreak."

She saw the surf breaking in her mind's eye, a memory from her childhood in Wildwood, New Jersey, before the incident that took her sight at age five. Bluish white and elegantly curved, they would be dangerous for the rescuers to cross, she knew. This was not a place for amateurs, not a place for mistakes, and she thought once more that she was a potential liability to this man who was relying on her to save his sister. Once again she felt the obligation to qualify herself. She didn't want to endanger anyone who was trying to get her down the side of a mountain unless he was very clear about her limitations. In spite of Brigham's confidence in her ability, there were real-life issues to consider, the least being common sense and logic. What were the real possibilities that a man hanging upside down in a whiteout below the ridge would be lucid in the last few seconds of his life?

She pulled the microphone away from her face. "Captain Metcalf, I don't know what Admiral Brigham told you about me, but there are things I cannot do. I'm not a mind reader. I can only see what people were thinking about a few seconds before they died. I'm not always able to see anything relevant."

"I know what you do," Metcalf said evenly, "and what I need when we get down there is for you to tell me what you see. I don't care if you think it's trivial, I don't care if it makes sense to you or not. Don't filter it. Tell me everything he was thinking about."

Sherry nodded, but she clearly didn't understand. How could this navy captain be so certain this would work?

"How long do we have?" Metcalf asked the pilot.

"Eight hours, maybe a little more." The pilot tapped his watch. "I'll get a refuel and wait to hear from you at basin camp.

"You and your men will have until twenty-one thirty, but then we've got to fly," the pilot continued. "That's when the window starts to come down."

Sherry flipped open the hinged face of her watch. It was just after one P.M.

"Copy that, twenty-one thirty hours," Metcalf said to his men.

Sherry could hear a change in the engine's pitch.

"Suit up," Metcalf told her. "We'll be out in a minute."

Sherry zipped her jacket to her neck and Velcroed the collar, slipped on her two pairs of glove liners, then allowed Metcalf to push on the heavy snow gloves. Her ice boots were already biting into her shins.

The helicopter thumped on hard-packed snow, lifted several inches, and spun a ninety-degree arc with skids scraping ice.

The pilot hovered the craft there, keeping its full weight off the snow. The door opened and the machine rocked as a blast of cold filled the cabin. Howling winds forced them to yell to be heard.

Metcalf took her hand and tugged before they jumped into the snow.

"Brace yourself between steps," he yelled. "Imagine that you are walking in water, feet wide apart, and do not let go of the rope."

She took a wide stance. Feet apart and awkwardly testing the snow, she moved one foot then the other, crampons slicing noisily through the crust of ice.

"It's going to be hard going until we reach the edge of the ridge."

She nodded and he slipped a harness around her back and snapped it off at her waist. "Don't want you sliding off the edge of the mountain on your back."

Sherry, who couldn't have agreed more, said nothing.

The going would be twice as slow because of her. An experienced climber would have made the descent in half the time. But getting to the body was only part of the ordeal. The minute they were finished with the body, they needed to contact the search team above and get back up to the ledge. Metcalf would be bearing much of her body weight on the ascent. She couldn't imagine the complexities of what it took to do that, but her job was to maintain balance and concentrate on what she came to do. He would take care of the rest.

"Sandstorm, this is North Sickle One," he said, making a radio check to his men. "Do you copy?"

Sherry heard a voice come over the air. "North Sickle, you are loud and clear, over."

Metcalf tapped Sherry's arm gently as they began to approach the ledge. "We're going to clip to cleats and rappel off the ridge. One of my men will keep safety lines on us until we're over the wall, then we'll fasten onto the fixed line. Use the toes of your boots. You'll get used to them quick."

Sherry nodded, wondering what she'd let herself in for this time. It would have been an understatement to allow that she had spirit—she did—and she'd been in some pretty unusual places before, like belly down on the front line of an equatorial civil war or compressed into a metal cage and lowered into a coal mine. But Sherry did not consider herself to be reckless or an adrenaline junkie. She might have overcome the fear of not being able to see, but she respected life and feared whatever a prudent person might fear. She had no death wish.

Step by step, they lowered themselves. Crampon by crampon, their boots dug into the mountainside, negotiating toeholds that were beaded with ice, rounded corners of slick granite smooth as glass, the wind bumping them on the lines as they were carefully lowered, but at last they were under the ridge and Metcalf clipped them to the wall. Then they began the slow descent down the face of granite. It took almost an hour to reach the body and when they did, Metcalf went silently to work, chipping away at the heavy cast of ice around the dead climber's arm.

The experience had been like nothing Sherry had ever known. It was both terrifying and exhilarating at the same time, the physical challenges of identifying foot- and handholds on a brittle wall of ice, the nearly intoxicating rewards of personal achievement. This was nature and self-awareness at the extreme.

Metcalf's immediate concern was clearing the corpse's hand of ice and getting Sherry situated next to the body, making sure she was comfortable enough on her lines so she could forget about her physical situation and focus on what she came to do. Metcalf kept chipping away with the butt of his survival knife at the man's glove, which was hanging below his body. Once it was clear, he used a chemical pack to thaw and remove it. It took fifteen minutes before he was guiding Sherry into position alongside the inverted corpse.

Removing her own glove was tedious, but at last it was off, and she gently exercised her stiff fingers. Once more she thought about how the climber's end must have come. He would have tried to upright himself several times before the effort became too much. Then he would have relaxed into his fate, remembering, thinking, ruminating about loved ones. Perhaps, if Metcalf was right, he would also have been thinking about the people he set out to save. She hoped he would have considered them one last time before he drifted into eternal sleep, hoped that bringing her here was not time wasted. Still, she could not imagine what the dead man might have been thinking that would lead the climbers to a cave buried under a literal mountain of snow.

Metcalf rested on his lines, feet against the mountain wall, and wrapped his arms around her as she reached for the dead man's hand. She felt Metcalf's cheek brush against hers. His arms encircled her waist and pulled her body tight into his. She could feel him taking the weight off her line. Then he reached for the dead man's hand and pulled it toward them, guiding it to her hand.

There was a full moment when she was thinking about nothing but Metcalf's arms around her, his warm breath on her neck as he took the weight off her harness. She had to make herself concentrate as she worked the cold fingers with her own until the hand was pliable and soft, and at last she felt the familiar transformation taking place.

. . . *a woman's face, her lips were bleeding beneath patches of darkening skin. She was lying on red cloth, candlelight flickering on a brass zipper and all the white snow that surrounded her. A small electronic device was propped by her head, it looked cold and useless; now he looked up at the chin of a man and a tightly knotted necktie, olive skin and starched white shirt, gold cuff links on his wrists. His own little hand on the arm of a white wicker chair, the man was rocking him, they were on a green lawn above a crystal-blue sea; a woman now, a beautiful woman with hair pulled into a bun. She wore a two-piece bathing suit beneath a short cotton robe, turned to face a cortege of uniformed servants, one of them holding his hand; a man was sitting across from him, a black man with one white eye like a doll's, he was drinking something amber and smoking a long cigar; a procession of black limousines, a white casket buried under flowers, men in suits wearing sunglasses; bright-colored flags snapping across a vista of low clouds, a pretty girl with long dark hair, she was wearing a snowsuit and had sunscreen on her nose; numbers floating on a small disk of black space; the girl again, she was laughing, her lips had not yet cracked, were not yet bleeding; there were arrows on the black disk, one red pointed to a letter, an* N, *the other to three white digits, a one, a nine, and another one; looking down from the sky through the windshield of a helicopter, it was landing in front of a massive stone castle in a dense jungle. The building had spires and buttresses and was surrounded by tall security fencing. Guards were posted at gates and next to the landing pad.*

He was inside now, there was a circle of black men wearing black uniforms, the room was large and damp and windowless, the floors were dirt except for a small round wooden platform. There was a floor-to-ceiling pole in the middle of it with leather hand restraints near the top, there were a dozen women circled around it, facing it, stripped of their clothes and kneeling. The uniformed men stood behind them with automatic weapons pointed at their heads. Others, Caucasian and Latino men, crowded forward to see. He backed away from them all, followed a dark corridor toward a pale pink light behind a partially open door. He looked inside and the walls, like the floor and ceiling, were painted blood red. There was an examination chair with stirrups in the middle of the room, a young blond woman was strapped to it, face immobilized by a clamp over her head, her left hand and foot were wrapped in bloody bandages. She was facing a large television screen that was playing a video. The video was of a woman sitting in the same chair, a naked black man with white face paint was standing between her legs, he was penetrating her, his skin broken in bleeding lesions and secreting ulcers, his eyes were dead as if he were in a trance.

On a stainless-steel instrument table next to the woman were bolt cutters . . .

He was off the side of a mountain, canister of dye aimed at the rock wall, wind spiraling him as he fumbled with the clips on his harness, he reached down, trying to undo them . . . then he was upside down, watching the snow fall, as if from heaven. . . .

"Sherry?"

She jerked her head toward the voice.

"Sherry?"

"Okay," she said shakily. "I'm okay."

"What did you see?"

"Numbers." She nodded. "I saw the arrow he was making, but there were numbers on a compass, I think."

"It wasn't an arrow," Metcalf said matter-of-factly. His arms still around Sherry's waist, he was using his free hand to work a safety line through the dead man's climbing harness, securing it to the fixed-line pitons anchored in the granite wall. "They're numbers," Metcalf said. "The canister shoots a single stream of dye. He was leaving us the team's position in degrees. He must have been getting tossed around because they're not pretty. The nine is lying at a forty-five-degree angle on top of the one. If you weren't thinking about numbers, you might see an arrow with a circle on top of it." Metcalf finished tying the safety line off and let the body go.

"Something happened before he could finish it, maybe the wind was banging him around and he dropped the canister or maybe the line broke or released and he got upended. We know he wasn't finished writing because nineteen degrees points out there"—he nodded over his shoulder—"into space."

"The one and nine were followed by another one," Sherry said.

Metcalf broke another chemical pack and placed it in Sherry's hand. "Hold this," he said. "I'll help you with that glove in a minute."

He took the mike to his handset. "North Sickle, this is Sandstorm, over."

There was a crackle of static. "Go ahead, Sandstorm."

"Bearing one, nine, one, do you copy?"

"Copy, that's one, nine, one degrees, Commander?"

"Affirmative," Metcalf answered, then helped her with her glove.

"Are you ready?" he asked.

She nodded, thinking the moment would have seemed anticlimactic except for what she had seen in that castle and the red room.

"You did good, Miss Moore. You did very good."

"What will they do now?" she asked.

"This fellow's not going anywhere, I clipped on a safety line to make sure. We'll come back for him when the storms have passed through. My men up above will use the compass coordinates to search for snowbanks. You build snow caves into the side of an existing bank, not underneath it. Every bank on the compass line, they'll probe with avalanche sticks. Find something hollow and they'll dig."

"Why are the coordinates so important?"

"There's twenty acres up there. A three-degree variation would put them off mark a hundred yards for each quarter mile. Walk a mile and you're four hundred yards off target. That's the difference between here and the moon when you're trying to find a six-by-six-foot hole under the snow."

Sherry nodded.

"You ready?" He checked the lines and then her harness.

Sherry nodded again. "I'm fine." And with that they began their slow ascent to 16,000 feet.

The Pave Hawk made two lifts off the Denali mountain that evening, the first to Providence Hospital in Anchorage with three surviving members of the American climbing expedition. They had been found a mile and a half from the ridge, dug into the wall between two peaks. The climbers were near death; none were aware the storm had ended. None were physically capable of digging their way out if they had known.

To say Metcalf was euphoric was an understatement. His energy was palpable, and it stayed with Sherry for the longest time. She felt an unmistakable sense of camaraderie. She had become a part of something much larger. She had become kindred to these men for a day.

The inn on Parks Highway was abuzz with excitement when they arrived on the second lift, but it was soldiers who greeted them, not reporters. No one in the civilian world yet knew what had taken place during the last six hours and 2,000 feet above basin camp on Denali. No one even knew they were there.

Thirty miles away, at the Talkeetna Ranger Station, reporters were being briefed on the progress of airlifts from basin camp. No hope was given for the teams caught above them.

A day later a United States senator from Washington would surprise the American public with an announcement that his daughter, Allison, had been one of the three climbers rescued from a ridge on Denali and that he wanted to personally thank Alaska's Air National Guard, Denali park rangers, and the Army High Altitude

Rescue Team involved in bringing all of the survivors off the mountain. No mention was made of Navy SEALs or the pilot of the Pave Hawk. No mention was made of Sherry Moore.

Around the base of Denali, there were still days of mourning ahead, bodies to be recovered and identified, funerals to be held, but life went on, and new teams of climbers were already forming in Talkeetna, making plans for their summit assault. The disaster had diminished to back-page news articles, part of the chronicle of the mountain's recorded history.

Not so for Sherry Moore. To say she had been moved by the experience of clutching the side of a mountain would be a vast understatement. The enormity of where she had been was as vivid an image in her imagination as if she had stood, looking with good eyes, upon the summit herself. And yet it was impossible to enjoy that achievement, that memory—not without also remembering those women in the bowels of a castle in a jungle.

The memories of Sergio Mendoza were impossible to leave on Denali. They had become an obstruction in her life. The women would not give her peace until she came looking for them.

And she was terrified of where that might lead.

2

A queue formed at the double wood doors leading to the hotel's banquet facility by an etched brass placard that read SASKATCHEWAN ROOM. Linen-covered tables occupied by perky hotel clerks throughout the week had been cleared of programs and floral arrangements, leaving behind wilted petals and the handful of laminated name tags representing those who'd never made it.

Inside the room, you could sense the mood of a final day. Airline tickets poked from pockets of wrinkled sports coats, people with slumped shoulders shuffled around coffee urns surrounded by mountains of sugared pastries. The ones with hangovers grinned slyly at co-conspirators. The gym rats still damp from their showers drew common looks of disdain.

There was a table at the back of the room with placards that read, DUTCH, RUSSIAN, GERMAN, ARABIC, HINDI, FRENCH, where yawning interpreters fussed with headphones as they brushed doughnut crumbs from lapels and sipped coffee.

The attendees were of all races, all cultures. They came from major cities and frontier outposts, from icy tundras to desert wastelands, as different in language and dialect and dress as anyone could be and yet there was an unmistakable sameness about them.

You saw it first in their eyes. When you spoke to them, they were slow to answer. They didn't seek to interrupt or contradict or impress. They looked you in the eye and listened as if the act of listening required its own exclusive allotment of time.

The hotel's comptroller had commented to the general manager that there was something creepy about them. "They make you feel naked, eh? Like they know your dirty secrets?"

"Please, everyone, five more minutes." A woman tapped the microphone, provoking feedback, and the hangovers grimaced as stewards dashed to squelch the earsplitting howl.

The crowd around the coffee urns began to disperse, some to escape the noise, some for last-minute restroom calls in the lobby.

This time tomorrow they would all be back home. Back to their desks and a mountain of work because everyone knew that crime didn't take a holiday, that the world was a busy place for the most senior law enforcement investigators on the planet.

They'd run the gamut of topics throughout the week, from experts monitoring arms sales to rogue African states to breakthroughs in a Turkmenistan pipeline for heroin pouring out of Afghanistan. Lithuanian counterfeiters were moving euros to France and Spain, and biotechnologists in Miami were discovering new ways to detect chemical scents indicative of bombs. At Scotland Yard investigators were making strides identifying a source of radioactive isotopes that were being smuggled out of the old Soviet Union, including polonium 210, which had been used to kill former KGB agent Alexander Litvinenko.

There remained but one speaker to deliver a single topic this morning. More seats in the room would have been vacated by early departures but for Helmut Dantzler's reputation. He was a law enforcement legend, to say the least. His career began with an appointment to a branch office of Germany's Bundeskriminalamt— Federal Criminality Agency—where he studied intelligence responsible for capturing Andreas Baader of the Baader-Meinhof gang in the early 1970s. By 1977 he was a member of GSG 9, the world-class counterterrorist unit best known for secretly flying behind a hijacked Lufthansa jet to Mogadishu, where they landed, then stormed and liberated eighty-six passengers from RAF radicals. In the 1980s Dantzler commanded GSG 9 responses to hijackings, hostage takings, and bombings on foreign soils, and in the early 1990s he transferred to Germany's covert intelligence service to interpret the terrorist threat from abroad. It was during his time in intelligence that Dantzler had a first look at Russian migration into the Czech Republic and a new kind of crime, which, having nothing to do with terrorism, tore at his very soul.

Young women and little girls, mostly war refugees

from the former Soviet states, were being routed toward the Czech border, unaware they were about to become slaves to organized crime.

Criminals responding to the collapsing Soviet superpower had graduated from trading black-market arms to trading people, meeting the demands of Germany's burgeoning sex-tourism industry. Dantzler, appalled, was later quoted as saying that he knew at that moment what he had been preparing himself for all his life.

Dantzler put in his retirement papers and accepted a position with Interpol in France, where he had been granted permission to develop the first international bureau dedicated to monitoring human migration and exploitation. It would take a decade of intelligence gathering to convince the European Council to adopt a "Convention on Action" against trafficking human beings—even then a quarter of its members refused to ratify it—but by that time Germany had yielded its ignoble reputation as sex capital of the world to Southeast Asia, which in turn capitulated to South America in the twenty-first century. Brazil had become the sex-tourism capital of the world.

Dantzler stood in the back of the room by a glass wall overlooking the Saskatchewan River Valley. The river was gray. Above it spits of snow danced like chaff in the bright morning sunlight. He raised a shirt cuff and glanced at his gold Breitling, then drew the curtains.

The woman tapped the microphone again, gently blew into it, and smiled at the stewards waiting in the wings. Then she clapped her hands and gave them a thumbs-up.

"As you know, we've all had a long week. We've all absorbed a lot of information." She made a show of wiping her brow. Her red lips parted broadly; her painted eyebrows raised, she looked around the room. "No more housekeeping issues, I promise. I'm sure everyone is sick of hearing those two words."

There was muted laughter and sparse applause.

"Our final speaker, Helmut Dantzler, comes from Interpol to talk with us today. His topic will suggest different things to you, different images and emotions will come to mind, but it is truly a topic common to us, a topic of our time."

The woman looked down at her notes.

"Long before the United Nations could agree on a definition for human trafficking, you were waging the battle against it in your own cities and streets. From human toys shipped to the United Arab Emirates to sweatshops in New York City, you investigated these cases one at a time, tedious prosecutions where your victims, mostly illiterate foreigners, were expected to draw sympathy from jurors of so-called peers in a country they had only ever seen from a locked window. You had no international laws to draw upon. To this day, police resort to weak local and regional statutes that are all but impossible to prosecute. You charge a murder here, a kidnapping there, sometimes an immigration and naturalization violation, but rarely, ever so rarely, are the men and women who are actually in the business of human commerce prosecuted in the world's courts. Well, the world is getting smaller, ladies and gentlemen. Forty-one countries have now passed legislation to address human trafficking, from Pakistan to Sudan, from Miami to Bangladesh. The world is beginning to react to the reality and the horror of modern-day slavery. Last year there were nearly five thousand—not arrests, mind you—but"—she raised her hands and used two fingers to denote quotation marks—"*convictions,*" she said loudly, nodding vigorously, "and many within third-tier countries that have been selling their offspring since before recorded history."

There was brief applause. The speaker took a sip of water from a bottle on the podium.

"Helmut Dantzler, as many of you know"—she replaced the cap on the bottle—"has waged war on many continents as an officer of GSG 9, but his most recent, the one that compelled him to a new avocation, was fought closer to his home and heart, between the borders of Germany and the Czech Republic, where a new kind of crime was beginning to dawn on the world. Like many of you, he has stories to tell. Like many of you, he was caught between organized crime and the constraints of German law and international politics. Helmut is no longer in law enforcement. He has joined the ranks of elite intelligence officers around the world at Interpol, where he wages his battle against human trafficking through the exchange of information. Please welcome Helmut Dantzler."

Tall, rigid, elegant in his mocha-colored suit, he approached the front of the room as stragglers moved in from the rear. Dantzler paced through loud applause and stood at parade rest before the audience until it ended.

"In Brooklin, Canada, scientists are manipulating atoms in a field called nanotechnology. It is assured to be a trillion-dollar industry by the year 2015. They hope, among other things, to build molecule-sized robots they can inject into our bloodstream to fight cancer, increasing our life span by twenty years and then perhaps fifty." He paused. "In Bihar, India, mothers poison their newborn daughters with the sap of oleander to keep them from bleating for breast milk. This happens every day of every year. There is no food in the family to support another girl." He looked at his hands, paused, and looked back at the audience.

"We can only wonder that these things happen in the same century," he said. "That they happen on the same planet. Major Lamb in introducing me mentioned that the world is growing smaller. We know more about each other than ever before, and let me assure you, that knowledge is a good thing. Education is a step toward a greater humanity, toward a union of cultures."

Dantzler's thick German accent reverberated across the silent room.

"One day we hope that all people benefit from life-

prolonging advances. And we should hope through pro-
gressive law enforcement to protect all people from the
human malignancy that has too long hidden behind religion and politics. It is high time we direct the light
upon the transgressors and not the transgression. It
doesn't take a German to know that child labor is wrong
in Munich and it doesn't take an American to realize
forced prostitution is wrong in Los Angeles. These are
human issues, not issues of state."

He dropped his arms to his sides and looked at the
toes of his shoes for a long moment. "Ah," he sighed,
"but you're thinking I am an old man, an idealist. The
world is more complicated than that, you all know.
There will always be borders. There will always be corrupt leaders. There will always be organized crime. And,
you are thinking, there will always be laws that will con-
strain our efforts as investigators. So where does that
leave us?"

He looked up again, finding eyes around the room.

Dantzler took a folded document from an inside
breast pocket and held it up in the air. "I went over the
enrollment last night and performed some math in my
room. You are two hundred and nine people with an
average of fourteen years' experience. That means there
are three thousand years' worth of experience in this
room. I retired with only thirty-two."

Muted laughter.

"I didn't come here to tell you anything today. I came
here to listen. I want to hear your stories about human

trafficking. You all have them, your war stories, if you will. We all possess knowledge of things our prosecutors could never introduce into a court of law. We know the tidbits of intelligence that frustrate law enforcement officers all over the world, those things we know to be certain, but cannot prove to be true."

Dantzler pointed out at the crowd. "And I want the person sitting next to you and the person behind you and him across the room and her by the coffee urn to hear it, too, because while the world really is getting to be a smaller place, the criminal networks are getting larger. Now more than ever we need to communicate."

Dantzler stepped off the podium.

"You stare at your open cases for hours looking for the missing piece, when all along it is sitting in a jail cell in Lyon. The number of a TransAsia flight between Taipei and Phnom Penh, the key code for a Cadillac parked in Queens, New York, the name of a ship whispered softly in the alleys of Rome or Buenos Aires. In isolation these things mean nothing, but added to the sum knowledge of the investigator sitting next to you it might open new doors, so no, I didn't come here to talk to you today. I came to listen, to hear your stories. You might not remember each other's names a year from now, but you will never forget these stories. And that will be enough to get you talking to each other, burning up the phone lines as they say, making the world a smaller place in which to hide."

Dantzler stepped away from the microphone and

walked to the front row. He pulled an empty chair into the aisle, put a leather loafer upon it, and leaned on one knee, elbow pressing flat the razor crease in his trousers.

"I'll go first," he said. "In Germany there was a woman who operated a visa factory."

He spoke loudly, without the benefit of a microphone.

"It was a difficult time for us. Our government had just relaxed border constraints between Germany and the Czech Republic. No one bothered to look at the visas anymore, legitimate or not, they mattered little to our border police. We estimated at the time that one out of twenty visas represented a human slave from the Czech Republic or more likely from Ukraine to their east. One particular woman who produced visas selected her victims from ads placed on Russian websites looking for domestic help for wealthy Germans. She required photos and proof of date of birth. She met them in front of Theater Imago in Hamburg and introduced them to their new employers—it was always one of three men who then spirited them to a windowless building in Bielefeld, where they were stripped of everything they owned, beaten, and forced to watch snuff films in the very room in which they were filmed. The psychological impact of the films was sufficient to suppress thoughts of escape. Afterward they were introduced to heroin and forced to prostitute themselves in the Mafia-owned nightclubs. If they refused, they would become one of the snuff film's fatal stars. The woman's name was . . ."

An Inspector Singh of the Mount Lavinia police spoke next, telling the group about a man in Sri Lanka who owned a certain vessel that visited China and the coast of South Korea. Nearly a million people had been displaced in his country in the past five years, one-third of them under the age of eighteen. And they were eager for his help. . . .

Lieutenant George Basescu of the Romanian National Police described a warehouse in Bucharest converted to a human shopping mall. The defendants, all low-level criminals, displayed their human wares on a makeshift stage in a showroom with gaudily carpeted walls and mirrors. When the girls were not being paraded on display, they were housed behind another wall made of cinder block and soundproofing foam, in eight-by-eight-foot cells with toilets. They came from everywhere, but mostly from war-torn Macedonia and Bosnia and Herzegovina. What might be of interest to the others was that when the warehouse caught fire and police found the charred remains of the women still locked in their cells, there was a Rolls-Royce parked in a cargo bay. It was registered to a flamboyant Korean known only as Jong-pil. And Jong-pil suddenly disappeared from Bucharest's nightlife scene. His whereabouts remain unknown to this day.

A regional directorate of the Border National Police

Service in Bulgaria once had a narcotic informant who was present at a conversation about women being trafficked from Bulgaria to Haiti. A dark-skinned, one-eyed man bragged that he tattooed the women's faces with a voodoo image before he sold them into slavery in South America.

A nineteen-year veteran of Thailand's police spoke of reversing trends in Southeast Asian human trafficking. Wealthy Thai men, instead of exploiting the children of their native impoverished population, were buying Eastern European children for back-alley brothels in Pattaya. . . .

A Texas Ranger talked about adolescents' being recruited in Mexico by a phony employment foundation to work in New York City hotels as housekeepers. They met in a hotel parking lot in Nuevo Laredo and were trucked across the Texas border, where they were forced to work as prostitutes in a Houston brothel.

The stories went on for six hours.

3

Brigham swirled the port around the rim of his glass, laid the letter on his lap, and took off his reading glasses. "So what did you think of Captain Metcalf?" he asked.

"I'm sorry?" Sherry said, feeling heat rise from the back of her neck. Brigham watched her, amused; she'd asked one too many questions about the Navy SEAL since returning from Denali. He could see the color on her beautiful face. She fussed with her luxurious chestnut hair, twirling it around her fingers in a rare moment of awkwardness.

"The senator's son was quite taken by you, I heard. In fact, you were all he talked about once they got his sister back home."

Sherry kept her head down, binding the hair tightly around her finger.

"I mean, how well you handled yourself on the mountain and all, that kind of thing." Brigham watched her carefully. "You don't just go out and do things like that when you're blind. Metcalf admired your strength, he kept saying."

"Yes." She nodded. "Well, I thought he was quite capable himself, very, um, competent I guess is the word."

"Uh-huh." Brigham smiled, taking a sip of his drink. "Yeah, competent."

Sherry decided to change the subject. "He said it was very difficult for his sister to talk about what happened up there. I was given the impression she and the dead man might have gotten close on the mountain. Close, but she still didn't know anything about him."

Brigham was silent on the subject.

"I can't stop thinking about that, you know," Sherry Moore said.

She laced the fingers of both hands behind her neck. "I really can't, Mr. Brigham, and I'm trying. Honestly trying."

Brigham grunted. "You want to finish these or what?" He picked up the letter from his lap and flapped it noisily in the air. They were going through the week's mail, a ritual of sorts. Sherry and Brigham would often choose a handful of letters from her public PO box and debate the merit of answering pleas for Sherry's assistance. Sherry handled only a small number of cases a year, the most compelling usually from law enforcement, but occasionally she was so moved by a particular letter that she might contact the author. It was Brigham's role to play devil's advocate at those times.

"I want to talk about it again."

"We already talked about it, Sherry," Brigham said grumpily. "You know what kind of a world this is. You can't take it on single-handed."

"I'm not trying to. I was just thinking about what I

saw up there on the mountain." Sherry reached for her drink and stirred the ice noisily with a finger. "I think he was overwhelmed by it himself, Mr. Brigham. Why else would he remember such horrible things in the last few seconds of his life?"

"Maybe he didn't know they were the last few seconds of his life," Brigham countered her. "You're the one who's always pointing that out to people. Context, you like to preach. You can't take things out of context and put them back together again."

Sherry heard Brigham uncorking the port, a bottle of Graham's 1994. Try as she might, she could never acquire a taste for the stuff, but she delighted in stocking his favorites in the house.

"Are you done ridiculing me? "

Brigham sighed audibly, sat back, and raised his goblet.

"What is it that I'm missing, Mr. Brigham? You actually seem to bristle when I bring up this castle and those women. Do you know something I don't?"

"Leave it, Sherry, just leave it," Brigham said.

"Is it what I saw that's the problem for you?" she persisted.

Brigham sighed and set down his glass.

"It's not what you saw, Sherry. It's who he was. Who Sergio Mendoza was."

Aleksandra felt the eyes of the dead girl on her, staring out of a bloodless mask of skin and red hair. Twenty hours of gravity would do that to a face, when the heart stopped pumping, capillaries and veins begin to drain to lower parts of the body. Pockets of dark purple formed wherever blood was trapped, under forearms and thighs, sometimes the feet looking discolored as if the corpse was wearing black socks.

Her buttocks would be one of those places, though you couldn't see her buttocks in four inches of diesel fuel, vomit, and shit.

Today was the first day in a week they could see one another's faces. Today one of the ship's crew smelled the diesel fumes rising from the false hold and realized that a fuel tank had sprung a leak. Before today, in utter darkness, one of the girls might succumb to the fumes and pass out in a corner, might fall facedown in the muck, not to be found until it was too late. Two had died that way during the storm their first night at sea, drowned in their own waste.

Aleksandra stared up at the light.

The opening wasn't a hatch in the truest sense of the

word. It looked more like a section of flooring that had been cut out of the desk and then laid back in place. She knew they were near the engine room from the rumbling and pervasive vibrations in the walls surrounding them. She had heard of false holes welded into the hulls of freighters to smuggle illicit cargo and had no doubt they were sitting in one.

She looked at the young faces around her. Some looked as young as fifteen.

Before the "hatch" had been removed, Aleksandra would not have bet on any of their chances for survival. They would simply have exhausted all the oxygen in the hold and begun to suffocate, one by one. Now that they could breathe again, Aleksandra was encouraged to live. Aleksandra was resolved not to die without a fight.

She looked around the narrow hold, thinking they hadn't been the first to suffer this fate. The compartment had probably been constructed to move heroin or cocaine across the oceans. The space they occupied was no wider than her shoulders. They had to step over one another to walk to either end in hope of finding some privacy.

How many women had died here before them? Dozens? Hundreds? She'd known just how close a call they'd had on this trip when she saw the captain's face looking down at them. He was screaming at the crewman to extinguish cigarettes for fear of igniting the fumes.

The smell must have been unbearable coming out of

that compartment. Fuel, vomit, and shit and of course their filthy bodies, both dead and alive.

She was worried he might simply order them to flood the container with fire retardant and then seal it again. It would have been the safest thing to do under the circumstances. The price of a few bodies could hardly be worth the risk of fire at sea—an errant spark, hot ashes from a cigarette sucked into an air vent, lightning, static electricity, anything could follow the vapors to its source.

But he didn't. He just left them there, hatch open to ventilate the hold. She could only guess that they were nearing their destination and the captain wanted to be paid before ridding himself of his cargo. No one was going to pay him for dead bodies. Or maybe it was what he saw when he looked in that hold. Maybe he couldn't stomach the idea of more death.

The absence of a hatch gave them light and fresh air, but temperatures in the hold were near suffocating and the engines rattled violently. They were all light-headed and nauseous, all still vomiting.

Aleksandra looked at the young faces around her and wondered about their stories. They were Russian, Lithuanian, Romanian, Slovakian; all had somehow been lured to port cities on the Baltic Sea. The irony was that she, Aleksandra, who understood better than any of them what was happening to them, was not supposed to be among them. She was the mistake. She had never been part of the kidnappers' plans.

Aleksandra Goralski, Warrant Officer Class One of the Central Investigation Bureau, Polish National Police, was in the Baltic harbor of Gdansk to explore concerns about a corrupt chief customs commissioner. The commissioner had begun to exhibit sudden and extreme changes in his lifestyle, a lifestyle that included a teenage mistress, vintage cars, and a pleasure boat far beyond his means.

Because the commissioner was well connected to the Polish minister of interior, the assignment was conducted with great secrecy. Aleksandra conducted clandestine surveillance of her target in Gdansk, where she found his house and personal affairs in order. Nothing seemed amiss, or at least nothing that would explain a large infusion of cash in his life. He had received no inheritances, his bank statements corresponded with a salary of 48,000 euros, but the dacha, cars, and pleasure boat were worth more than a million three, and that meant he was acquiring large sums of cash.

Then Aleksandra heard a story about the commissioner and a Liberian-owned freighter that was in harbor. A delivery boy for a local butcher who carted meats to the docks supplying ships that were about to set sail said he knew the commissioner's Mercedes-Benz and had twice seen the man boarding the *Yelenushka* while it was in port. He had put a hundred pounds of beef on the ship himself. The crew said they were bound for Haiti.

Chief commissioners in Poland were still chauffeured

bureaucrats, the kind who preferred the aroma of caviar and Cuban cigars to that of salty brine and dead seagulls. Why would a chief commissioner be boarding a filthy cargo ship bound for Haiti?

Normally a ship the size of the *Yelenushka* would have a crew of ten, but not all of them would be on board that night. Tonight they would be out drinking, Aleksandra had told herself, out having a last fling on the wharf, saying their good-byes before they set sail. She'd wondered if it would be possible to look in the holds or break into the captain's quarters and rifle his desk, an idea that by Aleksandra's estimate was not out of the question. She had done crazier things in the armed forces when fighting the Taliban in their caves in Afganistan.

If cash changed hands with the chief customs commissioner, it might have something to do with the ship's manifest or what was in the holds. Perhaps there would be other incriminating documents or evidence of contraband, something that would explain the commissioner's odd visit.

The docks had their own kind of quiet at night—the sound of water cascading from the ship's bilges into the harbor, the metallic clanking of mechanics' tools, whining forklifts, and sparking welders. The noise was on a scale that made you feel puny, so many vessels towering hundreds of feet above the waterline.

Boarding the ship was easy; the shadows were plentiful, and the *Yelenushka* was in a remote area of the docks. If anyone had arrived early, she surmised they would already be asleep or she'd hear their footsteps long before she encountered them.

She wore dark clothing and avoided pools of light, reached the gangway stairs, and climbed them two at a time. Once on board she'd used the light from halogens over the superstructure to guide her way through a field of shrink-wrapped pallets on deck. When she reached the steel-encased doors to the ship's stairwells she kicked off her shoes and laid them next to a bundle of medical stocks bearing the symbol of the Red Cross and stamped PORT-AU-PRINCE.

She had just passed an open door to a steel stairs leading belowdecks, was just reaching the shadows of the superstructure when she heard a muffled scream. The sound could have been anything, made by seabirds or a rusty hinge, perhaps one of the containers straining against its bindings, but the second time she heard it she knew it was human and that it was coming from belowdecks. It would only take minutes to investigate.

Aleksandra returned to the open door, pulled the Glock Model 19 from her waistband, and crept down the metal stairs barefoot to the level below. There were dim floor-level lights along a steel corridor and she followed its course to a perpendicular hallway with doors off to one side. The floor was vibrating under her bare feet—the ship's generators were humming.

More light was coming from an open door down the hallway. She could hear the sounds of a coil spring mattress in motion and relaxed, a smile forming on her face. These were crew's quarters. Some young man must have smuggled a last lay on board before dawn.

She started to back out, feet silent on her return to the stairs, but then a metal door above her slammed and she heard boots strike the stairs. There was nowhere to go, only back through the corridor toward the crew's cabins. She tucked the weapon into her belt at mid-back, deciding to talk her way off the ship. There was no point in drawing attention to the investigation. No point in alerting the commissioner she had learned about his visits to the *Yelenushka*.

She messed up her hair, pulled her shirttail out over her slacks, and undid a button at the neck. If challenged she would claim she was leaving one of the men's cabins.

The boots continued to clank down the steel stairs; they would appear at any moment now. Five more steps, three, two . . . then she saw feet, bare feet, not boots, small feet, not a man's.

They belonged to a pale young girl wearing a trench coat over jeans. She was carrying a threadbare suitcase and there was a man behind her with a gun against her head.

"Well, well, what have we here?"

He was large and mustached, wore a navy knit cap and black leather jacket. Aleksandra turned to run, but there was a man behind her now, fat, wearing nothing but briefs and cradling a sawed-off shotgun.

A universal axiom among law enforcement officers was "Charge a gun and run from a knife." But the man on the steps was using the young girl for a shield. He would get many clear shots before Aleksandra could get past the hostage. The man with the shotgun, on the other hand, might worry about the noise of the weapon or the shot pattern in the small hall, which would undoubtedly strike his compatriot at the stairs. Perhaps his hesitation would be long enough for Aleksandra to knock him down.

She pivoted and ran toward the fat man, reaching for her Glock with one hand and using the other to meet the blow he was about to deliver with the shotgun, which he was now wielding like a club. She heard her hand crack when the barrel struck, fired a wild shot into the ceiling and then another that tore a ragged red line across the man's large stomach as her collarbone hit the floor.

The fat man was stunned, raking his belly with thick fingers until he was confident there was no hole, and he literally roared as he went for her throat, but this time Aleksandra didn't miss. The 9mm Hydra-Shonk hollow point round went through the fat man's stomach and blew a 13mm hole out his back. He never got to close his fingers around her neck.

Then the butt of the sawed-off shotgun struck her temple and she heard wood splinter. Aleksandra saw an explosion of white and tried to pull her knees toward her chest, to instinctively make herself as small as possible; her gun hand, the one that was not broken, barely extended from her chest, wavering around, but not knowing where to shoot.

The man in the leather jacket stepped on her wrist, crushing the weapon against her ribs. Then she heard a rush of air as the stock of the shotgun came at her head again.

There were few coherent moments after that. Once she was cognizant of warm fluid in her ear. Once she thought she heard a ship's whistle blow. Once she felt the weight of a man's body pressing upon her. When she finally came to, she was wearing someone else's clothing and compressed in a dark, narrow room with other women around her.

If there was such a thing as destiny, it had delivered her into their hands. Except that Aleksandra did not believe in destiny, could not believe in a destiny such as this.

She knew the others were thinking about what they could have done differently, knew they were lured here under some pretense and were thinking about the decisions they'd made that had changed the course of their lives.

It hardly seemed fair that such small things could impact for eternity and yet it was true. Change one thing and you changed the end of the story. Today, instead of being trapped in the hold of a freighter, she might be rowing a boat in Łazienki Park, planning the New Year's celebration with her lover.

The girls would all be thinking about their choices. Choices you had to live with, even the most innocent of choices.

Someone moaned in the shadows, but whether it was from physical pain or the pain of remembering was impossible to tell. Most of the girls had been raped in the cabins before the ship set sail. She had been raped, she was sure, perhaps by the chief customs commissioner himself. She was sure he would have been there to enjoy the send-off.

She stared up at the sheer steel walls rising above them and looked down at the dead girl once more. The little redhead had robbed the crew of the pleasure of exploiting her.

Aleksandra wondered if she might not have gotten off easy.

5

Café Bo Bo's was empty by the dinner hour, tourists departing for shuttles or embarkation ramps to one of the half dozen cruise ships in harbor.

The Bishop sisters faced each other across a tall bar table, heels hooked on wooden stools as they sipped their drinks from tiny straws. Jill, who would turn eighteen before their cruise ship returned to Miami, wore a pearl-buttoned peasant shirt and denim miniskirt, with heavy white athletic socks and Nike running shoes, and was drinking a virgin strawberry daiquiri. Theresa, the older sister by five years, was barefoot and blistered, wearing a Versace bikini and wrap and working her way through a second salty margarita. A pair of Anne Klein sequined sandals was heaped on the floor beneath her.

"Did you see Mom's bracelet?"

Jill nodded, rubbing the goose bumps on her arms, looking at pink ribbons fluttering from the dusty vents of ceiling air conditioners.

"It must have cost a mint," Theresa said. "Dad's still paying for taking that trip to the San Diego office last month."

"Why does he take those trips anyhow?"

"He likes to keep his hand in. It keeps him sharp."

Theresa adopted a tone of profound wisdom and nodded vigorously. "I have to say I get that," she added.

Jill rolled her eyes. "You get that," she mocked. "He's the CEO, Theresa. He could blow bubbles at his desk and everyone would applaud."

"And you should start getting some material of your own. Parroting Mom won't get you very far in life."

"Mom thinks he's going to have another heart attack."

"Mom thinks Oprah should be president."

"Screw you."

"No, screw you."

Theresa sneered, reaching into her Prada handbag—it was slung across her shoulder to keep street urchins from snatching it—for a pack of Marlboro Lights.

"Eeeuuuuw." Jill made a face as Theresa produced the cigarettes.

"It calms my nerves."

"Nerves," Jill said flatly.

"Yeah, nerves. You have no idea how stressful—"

"—law school can be," Jill interrupted, rolling her eyes.

"Fuck you."

"No, fuck you."

"We've got to be getting back soon." Theresa turned away from the vented air to light her cigarette.

"I told you I want a wrap to wear over my suit tomorrow."

"Then why didn't you get one? We've only been here for two hours."

"Two hours of visiting bars so you could drink margaritas. Does the word *blisters* ring a bell? You said we had to stop here because you couldn't walk another step."

"I couldn't."

"But you ran halfway up the ramp to get a drink," Jill mumbled, looking around.

Theresa's eyes strayed to something in the back of the room.

"What?" Jill started to turn.

"Nothing, don't look." Theresa clamped a hand on Jill's arm. "Just wait."

Jill exhausted a sigh and went back to her drink, emptying it until she was making sucking sounds with her straw.

The noise brought Theresa's attention back to the table. "Oh nice, what are you, three?"

Jill used the diversion to swivel in her seat to see a woman going down on a man in a booth behind a partition. She turned back as suddenly and sat red-faced, looking past her sister.

"I'm going back to the plaza."

"Don't do this, Jill."

"I'm not doing anything. I just want a beach wrap. That's why I came here in the first place."

"And I'm not waiting here until the last minute so I have to run to the ship on my blistered feet. You do this every time."

"Then go back now. I'll meet you there."

Theresa's eyes drifted back to the couple behind her. "I'll wait here, but hurry."

"Fine."

"Fine."

Jill scooted away from the table, tempted to turn toward the couple in the back booth again, but decided against it. "I'll pay you later."

Theresa shrugged and blew smoke at the ceiling while Jill hurried for the door.

The marketplace was still bustling, crowds inching their way through acres of brightly colored clothes. She found racks in a booth and was sorting through them when a woman tripped behind her, falling into and nearly pushing her to the ground. Then, to add insult to injury, their heads bumped as they stood to face each other.

"Oh, my," the woman said, looking dazed; she was young and pretty and dressed in an expensive gold top over white capris trimmed in gold. She was a native, Jill thought, her skin brown, her teeth dazzling, her luxurious black hair pinned back with tortoiseshell clips.

"I am soooo very sorry." She steadied herself against a lamppost to inspect the broken heel of a flimsy gold dress sandal. "I need to start keeping real shoes in the car." She grinned. "Marie." She stuck out a hand to shake.

"Jill," the girl answered, taking it.

Marie looked at her neck. "I have that very same heart, it's a Tiffany, right? It looks much better on you. I like it with your blond hair."

"Your hair is beautiful." Jill stooped to pick up a sarong on a hanger that had fallen to the ground.

"Like straw." The woman grabbed a handful and shook it self-deprecatingly. Then she tossed her sandals into a barrel of fly-covered trash.

"Wow," Jill said, staring at the Gucci labels.

"Who would repair them?" Marie shrugged. "Besides, they had bad energy, I wore them to please my ex. You're looking for a sarong?"

Jill nodded, replacing the hanger and continuing to flip through the racks.

"Occasion?"

"Pool party," Jill said. "I'm on one of the cruise ships." She thumbed over her shoulder in the direction of the harbor.

"I design them."

"Them?" Jill looked sideways.

The woman spread out her hands. "Sarongs," she said, "though actually I design most everything you see here. I'm a garment manufacturer in Santo Domingo."

"Get out." Jill grinned.

Marie shrugged. "We supply half of the booths in El Conde."

"Really," Jill said, impressed.

"The high-end resort boutiques as well. You know the Hispaniola Hotel. We have a shop there. The silks do well."

Jill nodded, raising her eyebrows. Her mother and father visited the casino there.

"You're so young." She stepped to another rack of wraps.

Marie laughed. "Not so young anymore, I just buy good makeup. It hides the wrinkles very well." She looked around, glanced at a diamond Omega on her wrist. "Oh, Lord. Speaking of hotels, I'm meeting my husband at Las Cañas, you know the place."

Jill shook her head.

"Overlooks the pool at the Hispaniola. Great way to end the day." Marie turned to leave. "Safe trip. Where are you from, by the way?"

"Chicago."

"Oh, I love Chicago," the woman said wistfully, a final wave before she walked away.

Jill pushed her way through more sarongs and a moment later heard her name being called.

"Jill?"

Marie was standing a dozen feet away, hands on hips.

"You know, I don't even know who I am anymore. Really, I mean I know it's hard to believe, but I was actually raised with manners. Come follow me"—she swept a hand in her direction—"I'll give you something worth taking back to Chicago, an original from my collection, pure silk and free for the pretty girl I almost knocked over."

Jill hesitated.

Marie made a face. "You can't be seen in one of these. I won't have it."

"I couldn't," Jill said.

"Of course you could, it's called kindness and it's the first thing I should have said, not the last."

"Are you sure? Don't you have to run?"

"The stock van's on the way to my car. I keep a box in the back in case one of my shops calls in. Just do something nice for a tourist when you get back home to America."

Jill smiled and ran to catch up, keeping step as they pushed their way through bodies from Parque Colón to Parque Independencia, dodging cars across a busy street, cutting through alleys until they reached one filled with teeming Dumpsters and windowless doors. Marie stopped at the side of a pink cargo van, unlocked a side door, and rolled it back on its hinges. Then she climbed inside and Jill could see a rack of clothes and cardboard boxes on the floor.

Marie pounded the top of one of the boxes with her fist, broke the strapping tape, and peeled the lid open. "Jump up," she coaxed. "Pick any of the smalls, you're going to love these."

Jill climbed in as Marie flipped through labels, then she heard footsteps charging up the sidewalk behind her. Jill started to turn but by then the door was sliding closed and a knife appeared at her throat.

"Not a word." Marie's voice was no longer pleasant. "Lie on your stomach and put your hands behind your back."

"No!" Jill yelled. "Please, no." She struggled.

Marie pushed her face into the clothes piled on the floor of the van and scratched the side of her neck with the point of the knife.

A man got behind the wheel and started the engine.

"Put your hands back," Marie hissed once more, and Jill did.

Marie taped her wrists, then her ankles, and last her mouth. The whole thing took a minute.

Marie got up and Jill arched her neck to see the curtain between the cab and cargo area swinging sideways with the motion of the van leaving the curb.

Marie went forward, leaving her in the dark.

The van sped through narrow streets, bumping curbs on sharp turns. The back of Jill's head thumped hard against the ribbed floor. She took deep breaths through her nostrils, trying to calm her pounding heart. Five minutes passed, then ten. No one had seen what happened. No one was chasing them. She had simply disappeared.

Her sister wouldn't worry for a while. Probably not until her next margarita was gone. By then it would be time to head back to the ship and even then she might not bother to look for her. She would probably pick up her sandals and limp on back for a shower before dinner.

What had happened? she kept wondering. Why her? Had they been following her? Did they know who she was?

She'd heard in school that kidnappings were commonplace in South America. Taking people off the streets was a new form of income for criminals. But they must know there was no way to reach her family. She had told the woman who called herself Marie that she was on a cruise ship.

She tried to quell the panic as the van rushed from the marketplace. The ride was a blur of ear-piercing merengue, city street sirens and angry horns as the driver jerked right and left, sending her rolling between the wheel wells and random boxes of clothes in the back of the van.

She was sure that at any moment the driver would pull over behind some tenement house and rob her and throw her out with her empty purse, but the van just kept on rolling and city blocks turned into city miles.

Where were they taking her?

Jill felt a trickle of warm blood from where Marie's knife scratched her neck. Her cheek was grinding into the dirt on the metal floor. Through a blur of tears she saw her purse lying near the curtain. Why wouldn't they have looked in it? It was just lying there, a brand-new leather Coach with four new hundred-dollar bills her father had given her when they left Miami. If the kidnappers wanted money, why didn't they take what was in her purse?

She lifted her head and looked behind her. Spanning the width of the back door was a steel rod thick with beach towels and flimsy sarongs on wire hangers. Next to her on the floor were open boxes and random pieces of clothing lying about. Were they really street vendors or was the van only a ruse? Only meant for one thing? Bait to lure someone like her into an alley?

She heard the sounds of blaring horns, clashing music, shouting people, the high-pitched whine of a motor scooter zipping by. Then the van sped away from it all; a ramp, a freeway, something was taking them away from the city, until at last there was nothing to hear but the dreary hum of tires.

She knew what would happen when her mother found out she wasn't on the ship. She would have a freaking meltdown. She would insist that the ship be searched. When they didn't find her her mom would insist the whole island be searched. She was never going to accept excuses from the police. She would call Uncle Adel. He was a United States attorney for the northern district of Illinois. Jill's father was a millionaire ten times over, but his brother Adel had clout in Washington. Adel, Jill's father was always saying, could fix anything.

Sooner or later she'd be told to make a call, either to the ship's mobile operators to reach her parents or to relatives back in the States. That's what kidnappers did.

She wished they hadn't taped her mouth shut. She

could have told them her cell phone was in her purse. Her father had bought SIM cards so that the girls' cell phones would work in the islands. He wanted them to be able to reach each other if ever they were separated.

Minutes later she heard a muffled noise, a familiar melody coming from the direction of her purse. *Her* ring tone, *her* cell phone!

Marie was moving out of the passenger seat and pushing aside the curtain to reach for the purse on the floor.

It could only be her sister or her parents, Jill knew. If it were Theresa she would be pissed. Wondering where the hell she was at. She hoped her sister would take the call seriously when Marie answered. She hoped she wouldn't say anything stupid or hang up thinking she was playing a joke.

Marie snatched the purse and unsnapped it on her way back to her seat in the cab. Jill strained to hear what she would say.

The phone continued to ring, third ring, fourth ring . . .

This was it, she thought.

Fifth ring . . .

They wouldn't have to go through the police now. Everything would be over and done with before anyone knew she was missing.

Sixth ring . . .

For God's sake answer it! Answer the freaking phone!

Then she felt a rush of air, a window was being lowered. A moment later the window closed and there was silence.

Jill felt at first like she was falling, like she had lost grip on a line tethering her to the world. For a moment she was confused about where she was, somewhere cold, somewhere she wasn't supposed to be. A bead of sweat ran off her scalp, tickling the back of an ear. She shivered, teeth beginning to chatter. She felt her chest rise and fall as she began to breathe more rapidly.

It was so wrong, so senseless, and yet so telling. If they didn't care about the money in her purse or reaching out to her family, then she had real reason to worry.

For the first time Jill began to think the unthinkable.

Minutes turned to an hour; the van eventually slowed to a stop. The driver was speaking to someone outside the vehicle. She heard the crinkle of documents, official but casual conversation. It was a border crossing.

There was only one border in all of Hispaniola, Jill was certain, the border between the Dominican Republic and Haiti. Jill could only visualize it as one thing.

A gate into Hell.

When the van began to move once more, she knew she was leaving a very important crossroads behind. She knew she would never be at this place and time again. She knew that with every new mile the unthinkable was becoming a reality.

The van soon stopped for gas, but then it drove on for several more hours. Jill began to become confused again; at one point she thought she heard her mother and father talking; she was a little girl in the back of their car. She lost all track of time. In lucid moments she noticed the roads had begun to deteriorate, they were beyond the boundaries of civilization. She needed to pee, she needed to relieve the muscle cramping in her arms, she needed to rinse the bad taste from her mouth, but most of all she needed someone to tell her she was okay. That everything was going to be okay.

The road twisted on for miles, dirt and stone under the tires. Then they slowed and distant voices brought her back to reality, someone was outside the van, muted laughter, creaking gates, a hundred feet, and the van came to a stop. The driver's and passenger's doors opened and closed.

The cargo door slid back and she looked up into the face of a gaunt black man. He was standing behind the glare of a spotlight. A pistol was holstered on his belt. He had one good eye, a brown eye; the other looked like a large white marble.

Marie climbed in next to Jill, cut the tape that bound her limbs, and pulled her up by the shoulders, avoiding eye contact as she nudged her toward the door.

Jill dropped her legs over the side and her sneakers hit the dirt. Her eyes were blinded by the spotlight. The woman threw her purse on the ground next to her, money still inside.

The black man handed Marie a thick brown paper bag, which she tossed to the driver and then she pulled the cargo door closed behind her. A moment later the van's taillights disappeared behind the closing gates.

Jill stood there alone, shivering in the midst of armed men.

They were at the foot of an immense stone building; it looked old and was tall, with spires like a church.

She could see coils of barbed wire inside the fenced compound. Two men wearing black shirts and jeans stood at the gates. One, with a hat, had dreadlocks. The other was older and fatter and he eyed her hungrily.

A military truck was parked next to them, a canvas tarp covering the cargo bed. A panel truck painted with fruit sat incongruously by a rusting fuel tank on legs emblazoned with a fading Texaco star.

The man with the glass eye nodded and two of the armed men grabbed her arms, pulling her to a set of bay doors that led into the foundation of the old building.

Inside was a catacomb of hallways. They took her to a large room lit by a string of bare lightbulbs. A row of wooden doors against one wall had small open panes cut into them, covered with wire screen.

She was led to the center of the room and the men stepped away from her.

She began to speak and the one-eyed man slapped her hard across the face.

Jill could taste blood as he grabbed the collar of her shirt and ripped it open from the neck to waist, scattering buttons like pearls in the powdery dirt. He pulled the pistol from his belt and put it against her forehead.

"Take off your clothes," he said.

"Money," she whispered hoarsely. "My father has—"

He pulled the hammer back on the gun.

She took off the shirt and let it fall to the dirt.

The pistol never wavered.

She felt dizzy, about to faint, but somehow she kept on her feet. She undid her skirt and let it fall to the ground, her top and bikini bottom. She was made to kneel in her socks and Nike sneakers.

And it began.

There was a moon on the ocean, lights ablaze over the superstructure of the gleaming white *Constellation*, the flagship of the Caribbean Star fleet, as it slipped from the harbor of Santo Domingo on a glassy black sea. The decks were crowded with tourists recently returned laden with sundries from the islands, beaches, and marketplaces.

It would soon be the dinner hour and a reggae band played poolside as guests filtered below, transformed from beachwear to tuxedos and evening gowns, rising to collect in cocktail lounges, waiting for their appointed seating in one of the ship's many ballrooms.

By 8 P.M. they were sitting at the captain's table, the room aglow with white candles. Golden champagne effervesced in delicate flutes. All around were smiling faces, teeth white and skin burnt red as they recounted their adventures in the Dominican Republic. It was a trouble-free place, this floating palace. The world was held at bay for thirteen days at sea. There were no frantic knocks upon their doors, no letters from the government or attorneys in the mail, no middle-of-the-night wrong numbers to set your heart aflutter. Temporary though it might be, for two weeks the ship was a sanctuary from the trials of an unforgiving world.

Or so Carol had thought. It would hardly have seemed possible for this ship to be the setting for the worst moment in a person's life, but that's what it had become. That's what it always would be.

"Mom?" Carol looked up from the dinner table to see her older daughter standing at her shoulder.

She admired her daughter's dress. "You look beautiful, Theresa." Theresa had four other dresses packed, so had Jill and her mother, all bought last April in Bloomingdale's or one of the boutiques along Oak Street, overlooking Lake Michigan.

Carol reached to touch Bob's arm, to direct his attention to Theresa's dress, when something on her daughter's face stopped her.

"What is it, Theresa? Are you okay?"

"Have you seen Jill?" Her daughter looked distraught.

Perplexed, Carol looked around the dining room, last at the captain, who was talking to a waiter in a tux. "She's not with you?"

"She left me in a bar by the marketplace in El Conde. She wanted to buy a wraparound skirt. We'd been looking at them earlier."

"El Conde?" Carol repeated. There was the slightest flutter in her stomach.

She forced a smile, taking a deep breath, convinced

she had heard it wrong. Theresa must have misspoken. Theresa had meant to say a bar near the ship's atrium. Jill was shopping for a wrap in one of the ship's stores and Theresa had been waiting for her in one of the ship's bars. That made more sense. And Lord knew it wouldn't be the first time Jill hadn't been on time. She could be so irresponsible at times. She could so easily get distracted.

"She could have gotten it tomorrow," Carol said, disappointed. "I told her this was important. Your father wanted you both here. So did I."

"Mom"—Theresa's eyes pleaded—"she never came back from the marketplace. I waited in the bar for an hour. Finally I thought I must have been confused about what she said. You know how she can be, so I came back and showered and I guessed she was out with you."

Theresa's lip trembled.

The flutter in Carol's stomach took hold and the icy fingers of providence marched up her spine. She turned away from the others at the table, tugging at her daughter's arm, pulling her close and bringing her lips to the girl's ear. "What do you mean she never came back to the room?" She tried to keep her voice under control, trying not to be overheard by the others, trying not to scare Theresa. "Never came back from where?" Her fingers were leaving white marks on Theresa's arm and she quickly let go.

"She left me in the village, in a place called Bo Bo's, a bar near El Conde. We were having a drink."

Carol was only able to nod at that point, her imagination running wild.

"She wanted to go back and look at a skirt," her older daughter said. "It was one of those street markets, just around the corner."

The sounds around the ballroom were suddenly dizzying. "Go on," Carol said. Her voice sounded strangely detached from her body. Her linen napkin fell to the floor. She snagged a nylon trying to extricate herself from her chair. Bob, chatting with the captain, now turned and started to rise, but she put a hand on his shoulder, pushed him down firmly, and led her daughter a few steps away.

A young blond woman had taken a position behind the Italian captain, touched him lightly on his shoulder, and stooped to reveal faultless breasts. She smiled as she was introduced around the table. Carol saw Bob reach to take the woman's hand, then turn to look at her, winking when he saw Theresa.

"She was supposed to come back to the bar," Theresa repeated. "I'm sure that's what she said, but she didn't and then I thought maybe I had it wrong, that she told me she'd meet me in the room or something. I was going to look around the plaza, but then the ship whistle blew and I came right back."

Carol wanted to reach out and shake her daughter, to get her to repeat what she'd said earlier and to put it in some context that made sense. But the girl looked distressed enough.

"I was sure she'd be back in the stateroom, Mom. You know, getting ready for dinner." Tears began to pool in her eyes. "When she wasn't in the room I thought she must have already gone to meet you. I called your room, but no one answered; you were already gone, so I didn't know where to look for you. I got ready for dinner."

Carol's eyes glassed over. "We were having drinks with Ed and Marge. . . ." Suddenly her voice trailed off; she was feeling the effects of the champagne, probably it was her empty stomach or maybe it was something cerebral, some knowledge that her world was changing and that it would never again be the same. "Call her," she said frantically. "Call her cell phone, for Christ's sake."

"Mom, I've been calling her for two hours."

"Call the bar, the place you had drinks, what was that place?"

"I did that too."

Carol looked down at her feet and saw a scuff mark on one white shoe. "She didn't get on the ship?" Carol's voice was husky, her eyes looked helpless. "That's what you're saying." She looked back to the table and to Bob and the captain. "Excuse me," she said, stumbling toward them. "Bob?" she called out. "Bob, I need to talk to you."

A few minutes later the ship's captain was reassuring them that this kind of thing happened all the time. That her daughter was surely on board the vessel. "Young

girls meet young boys." He smiled, hands clasped over
his gleaming silverware as if cheering, looking up at the
young blond woman at his shoulder. "Sometimes the
heart drowns out the wisdom of the mind and, well,
there are escapades and rendezvous and most
likely . . ."

Carol leaned down and put her lips against the captain's ear. "Get out of your fucking chair," she whispered
icily.

Jill Bishop woke in cool sweat, heat radiating from the walls of the cell that confined her. She was groggy and nauseated by the searing pain below her waist. Vomit had dried around the corners of her mouth.

There was a door made of wood and a slot in it at eye level. Behind her on the wall was another small opening through which she saw daylight, an air vent.

She could smell the stench of body odor and vomit and raw sewage. She could feel the grit of dirt and sand under her bare legs. Someone had put her underwear, shirt, and skirt back on, but she did not see her shoes. She tried to lift her head, but the motion triggered a skull-splitting spike of pain through the center of her forehead; she began to have flashbacks of a room painted red, a gynecologist's chair; she had been strapped to it and her head had been placed in a viselike device so that she could move only her eyes. An old black man with white hair gave her a shot between her toes with a hypodermic needle. There were bottles of dark liquids on a metal tray beside him and a camera on a tripod in the corner.

Other men lined up facing her. A large television on the wall played loops of a woman being raped with a rodlike object. Each time it was inserted, the woman's back came off the chair and she screamed as if being electrocuted. It was the very same chair in the very same room.

They told her if she disobeyed she would be raped by a zombie, a man infected with AIDS.

She vomited again, then rolled to her side and heaved until there was nothing left in her stomach.

Being gang-raped hadn't been the end of it. She remembered the drugs taking hold on her mind, how the red room had been painted to make you lose orientation. She remembered the old man leaning over her face, the dirty thick lenses of his glasses, the surgical gloves on his hands. Even as they raped her he took a hot iron rod to her face and burned the skin from beneath her right eye. It was the last thing she remembered.

She reached now to touch her face and found a patch of gauze. Why they had tortured her she couldn't imagine, unless of course they were terrorists. Unless they had made a film of what they'd done? She didn't dare think what it would be like for her parents, sitting in the recesses of some embassy or police station and looking at that film.

She started to peel away the gauze patch when something moved in the dark behind her and she lunged for the door, screaming as a hand came toward her. It was a small hand, its fingers clenched in a ball, reaching slowly toward her.

Jill pushed her back to the door and began to whimper.

She heard soft words in what sounded like Russian, then German, then English, before Jill nodded that she understood.

"It's okay," the woman soothed, hand lightly on her forehead. "It's okay." She stroked Jill's hair. "I'm a friend."

Jill looked at the woman blankly.

"Where am I?"

"Haiti," the woman answered.

Jill began to cry and the woman wrapped her arms around her.

"I am Aleksandra, from Poland."

Jill cried until she no longer could. Then she turned her head to study the woman's face. "Why are we here?"

"They are traffickers," Aleksandra said quietly, continuing to keep her arms around the teenager.

"I don't understand," Jill said. "What did I do?"

"Nothing, honey." Aleksandra stroked her hair.

"But what do they want with me?"

Aleksandra didn't say anything. "Why don't you rest for a while?"

"Traffickers, you mean like drugs?"

"People," Aleksandra said. "They trade in people."

"Do you mean they are going to sell us?"

Aleksandra just looked at her.

"No," Jill cried. "No!"

Jill had had nothing in life until now to compare this to. She had never even known anyone who had been date-raped, let alone kidnapped, gang-raped, and locked in a cell to be sold—at least, according to this woman. It was almost impossible to accept and, even if it was true, Jill was still sure somewhere down deep inside that her kidnapping had been a mistake. This must have been a mistake. The people who snatched her must have thought she was someone else. She just happened to have been in the wrong place at the wrong time.

Her father had told the girls for as long as she could remember that no matter how impossible something seemed, you only needed to get to the right person and anything could be resolved. Jill was sure that if she could only talk to whoever was in charge of this compound, she could straighten everything out. She needed to tell them who her family was. She needed them to understand that in good health, she was worth money, far more money than any amount they could get for her on the black market.

Not that Jill doubted she was in real trouble. This was way more than going to the wrong side of town and ending up at the wrong kind of party. Still, she didn't fit into whatever was going on here. These men had nothing to lose by letting her go and everything to gain. She wasn't going to press charges or cause them any harm.

It could only benefit them to let her go before the police came looking, and if Jill knew anything about her family, they would most certainly come looking. Bob and Carol Bishop would never stop looking for their younger child. They would have made that crystal clear to whatever authorities were in charge of this island and she knew they would pay for their daughter's return with no questions asked. They would leave a way out for the kidnappers.

If that didn't work they would hire the kind of people who could find her. That was what would persuade the kidnappers the most.

This woman Aleksandra might not have had the same options. Probably no one was looking for her. She had been abandoned and by now forgotten.

Money would straighten this all out. She would even negotiate to get Aleksandra out with her. She started to bang on the door. She started to yell out for the guards. She wanted to know who was in charge.

Aleksandra pulled her back, pinned her to the ground, covering her mouth with a hand.

"Don't," the woman whispered. "Don't make a sound."

Jill's eyes bore into Aleksandra's. She wriggled under the wiry woman's arms, unable to rise.

"The man in charge is the man that did that to you. The one-eyed man runs this camp. You fight him and he will take you back to the red room and there are things worse even than rape."

This place was an indoctrination camp, Aleksandra told her, for women being trafficked into South America. The authorities in Haiti were corrupt, she said. The police, the prosecutors, the judges, they would all turn their heads.

"Here we are to learn discipline," Aleksandra said. "If you resist in any way, they will make an example of you to the others."

Jill stopped fighting, but she wasn't convinced. She had certainly heard of human trafficking, but had never really given thought as to who was being trafficked where or why. The victims were always shadowy images in her mind, not the crisp, clear, up-in-your-face kind on screens at Live Aid concerts of children brushing flies from their eyes.

In fact, the whole concept of human trafficking was a little hard to get your head around, harder, say, than AIDS or ethnic cleansing, more in the realm of black holes and quantum physics. It was something people believed to be true but no one could really articulate. It was a reality, just not her own.

There was also a certain stigma suggested by the word *trafficking*, a stigma that implied consent and complicity. When you heard the word *trafficking* you had to wonder if most of the victims weren't somehow involved in their own demise, that they were co-conspirators in victimless crimes like gambling, drugs, and prostitution. She would have conceded there were probably third-world populations displaced against their will, tribes of one class moved across geographical lines and made subservient to another. That kind of thing had probably been taking place since the beginning of time. And sure, there must be an occasional woman lured off the streets to work as a prostitute, but this wasn't Russia or Africa or China. This was the Caribbean, not even a thousand miles from the coast of the United States. This kind of thing didn't happen here. People didn't go shopping in paradise one moment and end up a slave in some jungle the next.

Lying in this cell and hearing Aleksandra suggest she was to be trafficked into sexual servitude for the remainder of her life was an unacceptable proposition. And considering she'd been fooled once already, who was this Aleksandra woman anyhow? She was filthy and ragged and had this vulgar tattoo on her face of a grinning skull wearing a top hat. The tattoo in itself was telling. Serious people didn't disfigure their faces. Aleksandra, whatever else she might be, must have been into hard-core something in her life, she'd had to be, which was probably how she ended up here in the first place.

Jill knew the type. They were in every school. Aleksandra was one of those girls turned woman who went around asking for trouble. She was different from Jill, which was why Jill should be trying to speak with these men.

Then, as she lay in the dirt, looking up at Aleksandra, a seed of realization began to sprout. She stared at the woman's thin face and then into her eyes and back and forth and something vile wriggled out of the pit of her stomach, creeping up her neck and into her face. Her fingers reached to lightly graze the patch beneath her right eye, but before she touched it, she stopped and reached instead to touch Aleksandra's face and gently traced the outline of the tattoo.

Jill saw it all then. She saw it in the Polish girl's beautiful brown eyes. She hadn't been burned or tortured with any instruments strapped to that table. She had been tattooed. There would be a grinning skull wearing a top hat on her own cheek, just like the one on Aleksandra's.

Tears formed in her eyes. She had been branded for market. These men had no intention of ever letting her go. This was more than words or money could fix.

She broke down then, simply lost it, hugging herself and rolling in the dirt, choking on her sobs. She moaned and the moan became a long buzzing drone to block out the sound of Aleksandra's attempts to comfort her. How could this be? How could this happen to her of all people? She didn't party. She went out of her way to help people. She was a Goody Two-shoes, she didn't drink or smoke or use drugs of any kind. She even hated caffeine.

"Am I going home soon?" she blubbered. "Can't we go home now?"

Aleksandra cradled her head, stroking her hair until finally Jill cried herself out and fell asleep in her arms.

That evening she woke when the guards brought their food. She ate listlessly, numbly staring at the ceiling, not sure what to feel.

She knew her parents would be back in Santo Domingo by now, just miles away, though it might have been a million. She knew how crazy her parents would be. How stressed her father could get, and his heart worried her plenty. She wanted him to know she was okay. She wanted to tell them she was sorry. That she felt responsible. How stupid could she have been to crawl in the back of a van anywhere, let alone some foreign country?

Then she felt angry, angry at her sister who had blisters on her heels and who couldn't walk back to the marketplace with her. She felt angry at the men who raped and sodomized her. She was angry at the spectacled man that shot her full of drugs and tattooed her face and angry even for the guilt she felt for thinking she was above all this because she was an American from Oak Park, Illinois.

The anger subsided in time, replaced at first by exhaustion and then by hopeless resignation.

The first week was hardest. You were still a believer the first week. You still thought there was a chance you would be saved. Every noise, the sound of running feet, the beat of a low-flying helicopter outside the vented grates, meant you were going to be rescued. But when you weren't you began to let go.

Every night the man with the spectacles—the guards

called him *Docte*—would examine their bodies, looking for drug reactions or self-inflicted wounds. Jill knew what to expect by now. Jill knew that his soporific syringe was full of heroin. Heroin was a cheap and ever so effective restraint.

Aleksandra said the *docte* would keep increasing her doses until the day she would think of nothing but his nightly visit. Aleksandra said she was already there and Jill had no doubt it was going to happen to her. Everything else that Aleksandra had told her had already come true. The doctor drew blood from her. Later he performed a procedure in her vagina without anesthesia. Aleksandra said that inserts were wired into her fallopian tubes, a procedure performed on all the girls. In three months she would be sterile. Permanently sterile.

She mustn't fight them, Aleksandra told her. She must offer her body willingly in the hope there would be another day, another opportunity to be rescued or to escape. The alternative was to be sold on the market and turned over to a new master with his own kind of syringe.

The light in the cellar was the same, day and night. Their toilet was a seat screwed over a wooden box. The guards brought them a bucket of water for drinking and cleaning themselves. Once a day they were led to a room with showerheads.

Opposite the row of eight-by-eight cells the large cellar stretched into cobwebbed shadows. There were hundreds of sacks of old rice bags marked UNICEF. Pallets stacked with bags of lime, loose rifles, broken furniture, and old tires. In the center was a round wooden platform on which they were made to kneel for countless hours. In the center of the platform was a pole to which the women were tied if they committed an infraction. The guards sometimes tormented them with electric cattle prods while the others were made to watch.

Otherwise life was about waiting, waiting for their food, waiting for their shot of heroin, waiting to be taken upstairs to service strange men. Praying they would not be dragged to the platform or, worse, to the red room.

Aleksandra told her about the women who had been brought to the cellar with her. How some had died on the ship coming over. Those women had come and gone as had two other truckloads since. Jill saw the last group with her own eyes. They came in the middle of the night. The women were herded into the cellars and made to kneel on the platform as guards stood behind them with rifles. Each was stripped and raped in front of the others. Later they were taken one at a time from their cells to the red room. All night long you could hear their screams.

"Why don't they take us away?" Jill had wanted to know.

"They don't take you because you are rich," Aleksandra told her. "Rich people would recognize your face. There is probably a great price on your head.

Think about it, it's only been a little more than a month since you went missing. The Dominican Republic will still be swarming with cops. Maybe even your own FBI is on the other end of the island. They will be putting great pressure on the Dominicans and Haiti to allow them to search for you. If your parents are as rich as you say, there will be a reward for you, no? What would they pay to get you back, a half million dollars? A million? It would be a dilemma for the traffickers. None of these other women you see are ever missed. No one is looking for them and no one ever will. That is why you are never taken upstairs. It is also why you are safe from harm, my little friend. Safe for the time being."

"But if I'm worth so much reward money, why wouldn't they sell me back to my parents?"

Aleksandra shook her head slowly. "You don't know what kind of money is out there in the world. You hear the helicopters. You see the women come and go. A million dollars means nothing to these people. The less heard about you, the better for them. They don't want the attention."

"So they will kill me?"

Aleksandra reached for Jill's shoulders. "No, not unless they feel threatened. They will keep you. You will live to see tomorrow and any tomorrow could make you free."

Jill looked doubtful. "And why haven't you been sold, Aleksandra?" she asked.

"I am also a curiosity." Aleksandra laughed tiredly.

"The one-eyed man thinks I am a challenge. He likes to show me he is the one in control by not killing me. I will never leave here, though. Not as long as he is alive."

Jill had never heard of Aleksandra's kidnapping before, but then policewomen gone missing in Poland would hardly make Western news.

It must be hard for Aleksandra not to feel resentful at times, she thought, to know the search was still fresh for an American who disappeared on vacation rather than for a policewoman who had been missing three times as long, a policewoman who had just been doing her job in some bleak European harbor.

Jill, who had now seen women come and go from the cellar, could see that they were common people. They were dressed poorly, probably had little education. These men preyed on the weak. Their victims had few alternatives, had surely been driven to their demise by some hope for a better life.

Jill was thinking plenty about alternatives these days.

Contestus, named for the saint, was a mountain cathedral, built by slaves upon the stone and marble quarry from which it was made. Slaves had to be imported from Africa by the French to harvest sugar and coffee because the Spanish who preceded them had already decimated the indigenous Indians.

It was said that the dark mortar used to fuse the marble into floors and walls was stained red from the African blood with which it was mixed. The blood of its priests likewise stained the rocks of Monts de Cartache, when they were thrown screaming from the towers a hundred years later. That uprising of 1791 would lead to the first free black republic on the face of the earth.

Contestus fell to ruins over the next century. In time the spires were little more than a curiosity for island explorers and a landmark for early airplane pilots charting the Caribbean Sea. In 1927 it was purchased by mulatto coffee millionaire Christian Rousseau, who restored the magnificent stone and marble ruins to produce a hybrid that was part medieval castle—complete with ramparts and suits of armor—and part country manor, with its ancient cathedral spires rising tall above the jungle. The manor loomed magnificent over the glittering Windward Passage between Haiti and Cuba.

The quarry behind it had been abandoned and the foundations squared to accommodate stables for the horses and large food stores for the guests and staff.

Then a meek country doctor came to power and Haiti entered its darkest age. For the next fifty years the Duvaliers would terrorize the people, destroying the land of generations, raping the natural resources and an entire nation's economy. François "Papa Doc" Duvalier—and later his son, Baby Doc—would leave a bloody legacy, which would come to recall Contestus when slavery was resurrected.

There was never a rational moment when it came to Papa Doc Duvalier. Three years after the doctor seized power in a military coup, he suffered a massive heart attack that left him in a coma. After he was unconscious for nine hours, his own advisers agreed he had suffered irreversible brain damage. As Papa Doc revived, he claimed to have been possessed by the voodoo god Baron Samedi, spirit of the dead, portrayed by Haitians as a skull wearing a top hat. Duvalier immediately com- missioned a portrait of himself with Jesus Christ stand- ing over his throne and resting a hand on his shoulder. He began to affect the look of Baron Samedi, wearing a top hat, and spoke in a nasal voice on camera. He en- couraged the myth of zombies wandering the land.

In 1961 he disbanded the country's military—fearing a coup—and replaced them with secret police fashioned after Mussolini's Black Shirts of fascist Italy. He granted the secret police immunity from crimes yet to be committed and offered them not salary but spoils of enemies of state.

They found many.

In 1964 Papa Doc executed his secret police commander, fearing he was growing too powerful, and along with him the royal guard and countless civilians. The year he declared himself president for life he named Jean Bedard—a university graduate from the slums of Port-au-Prince—his new commander of secret police, designated the Silver Militia, but history remembers them only as the Tonton Macoutes—"Uncle Knapsack" in Creole—named for the legendary bogeyman who came to collect bad children in his knapsack at night.

The Macoutes' first order of business under Commandeur Bedard was to eradicate the mulatto aristocracy that ruled the land and seize their assets for the new "president." Bedard went about his job with chilling efficiency.

The Macoutes, numbering ten thousand, spared no one, not women, not children. They went from city to city, parish to parish, burning, raping, looting, and when they got around to seizing Contestus—the coffee magnate Rousseau had long since fled to France—Bedard had it surrounded with machete-wielding Macoutes, wearing their omnipresent sunglasses and zombie-like smiles, and declared it home.

The views from Contestus were truly staggering, pastel green seas extending west across the Jamaica Channel, ships' masts and superstructures crossing the Windward Passage to the north, rolling foothills of the many Mornes falling away like the brown and green ripples of a peasant's skirt. Better yet, the face of Monts de Cartache rose 2,000 feet and was accessible by a single mountain road, making Contestus all but impregnable. This was the beauty of Contestus to Bedard. He was literally king of this world. And here Bedard would begin to amass a great fortune.

By the time he was thirty he had seized the country's plantations and monopolized produce exports. For a pittance, he purchased a fleet of oceangoing freighters forfeited by Jean Claude Jasmine, who had ties to two young up-and-comers in Colombia, Pablo Escobar and Thiago Mendoza. Jasmine, in his enthusiasm to emulate the flamboyant Escobar, had the misfortune to bring informants into his inner circle and ended up with a life sentence in an American prison.

Bedard, who wanted nothing of publicity, aligned with Mendoza instead, buffering his business holdings with puppet corporations and armies of accountants and attorneys.

Bedard swore he would never forget the lesson of Jean Jasmine's demise. Officers of record took the risks for his corporations, men who reported only to him, men whose fortunes and lives, even the lives of their families, depended on him. To cross Bedard was a death warrant and one that the former Macoutes would carry out no matter if Bedard were dead or alive. Bedard demanded loyalty. There were no in-betweens.

Bedard's freighters moved in and out of Haiti's major seaports with impunity, subject to neither inspection nor regulation. His many spies were in the Haitian National Police, he had jail guards and he had chiefs on the payroll, and when the American DEA interfered in Caribbean waters, he even had someone in the narcotic interdiction office to monitor the incoming and outgoing calls of the drug unit's commander, an American-trained Haitian named Colonel Deaken.

The narcotics business near the turn of the century had evolved into a model of corporate efficiency. Thiago Mendoza, providing the crop and refineries, could not export enough of the stuff to meet demand. Bedard's unfettered pipelines from Haiti to Europe supplied distribution centers managed by men and women with marketing and financial degrees, none of whom had ever set eyes on a processing lab, who all shared profits and risks in the ever-growing economy of addiction. As Thiago Mendoza became a billionaire, Bedard's own fortune grew rapidly, modest by comparison, but he had already outpaced his own president's wealth.

The Americans would eventually turn up the heat on their war on drugs and Pablo Escobar declared war on them. On December 2, 1993, that proved to be a fatal error. Pablo Escobar was gunned down on a rooftop in Medellín.

Thiago Mendoza, on the other hand, isolated himself

in the remote mountains of Sierra Nevada de Santa Marta, where communist rebels loyal to him protected his poppy fields and processing plants.

Then Mendoza began to diversify, importing small arms shipments out of Belgium, low-grade uranium and cesium-137 hidden in engine blocks out of the fractured Soviet Union, women at the rate of a hundred a month out of Russia to be sold as prostitutes in Southeast Asia. Jean Bedard in Haiti facilitated this by hiding human contraband in his ships, using the same false holds welded between freshwater tanks for transporting Mendoza's cocaine to Eastern Europe.

The arrangement between Thiago Mendoza and Jean Bedard would net $60 million a year and with none of the scrutiny his cocaine trade received. Law enforcement agents around the globe were confounded by their very own absence of laws. There were no international sanctions, no crimes per se in the people trade. Even the misdemeanors it presented were difficult to prosecute; an employment scam arrest, a harvester charged with pandering, a violation of fair labor . . . All the while great fortunes were being made and new opportunities were presenting themselves in Eastern Europe.

War and poverty were a trafficker's two best friends. Widows and daughters displaced from their homelands were ripe for the picking, and Mendoza charged Bedard to employ more and more harvesters.

Many of the women from battle-ravaged cities came willingly to sell themselves and their daughters into domestic bondage, believing they could buy back their freedom in time. Some came as prospective employees for corporations that did not exist or were lured as would-be models, actresses, singers, or musicians. Some were Russian brides for men that did not exist, some were granted work or travel visas with unexpected ease. Some were simply kidnapped off the streets.

Bananas, coffee, mahogany, and cocaine heading east; guns, nuclear waste, and women heading west. Bedard had even begun to freight humanitarian relief stores out of Europe bound for Haiti, the poorest country in the Western Hemisphere. Tons of grain and seed and medicine and machinery afforded him new opportunities to make port in the harbors of Germany, France, and Italy, where his ships were given priority and seldom boarded by ICE or drug interdiction agents.

He unleashed even more harvesters upon them.

To be sure, Mendoza's influence on trafficking women was only a fraction of the world market in the beginning of the twenty-first century. Then an Indian Ocean tsunami reduced Southeast Asia to rubble in 2005 and Brazil, not Thailand, became the sex-tourism capital of the world. Business quadrupled.

He really couldn't have planned it better. It couldn't have been easier money for the truly unremarkable risk. More ships brought more women, profiting the harvesters who lured them off the streets, profiting Bedard in nearby Haiti, who initiated them to discipline and then conveyed them to Mendoza's men, who moved them through South America to Brazil to the tune of hundreds of thousands of dollars each. The women, made to work impossible hours for their merciless masters, paid for themselves in a year's time and reaped profits for several more. But trafficking, like narcotics, was a self-perpetuating enterprise. The women had a shelf life. In four or five years they lost their appeal and were devalued, sold on declining markets until they reached the bottom rung of the ladder, the mining town brothels and backwater saloons, some in the end sold to drug gangs and jungle camps of leftist rebels.

It was usually a five-year free fall from the glitter of Rio de Janeiro to cow towns in Brazil or Argentina or Colombia or Peru. None had imagined such a beginning or end. None had guessed they would be spending the last years of their lives addicted to heroin and craving it for their wages. None would have believed that heroin would become their single reason for living, their only friend until the day they were deemed unserviceable, and that in the end even that would be taken from them.

Of course there were unavoidable risks in any business. An occasional shipment was lost at sea to oxygen contamination in the poorly ventilated holds. Sometimes one of the women had a breakdown and could not be controlled. When that happened Bedard had bodies on his hands, or more apropos, he had physical evidence to get rid of.

Bedard didn't worry about ships' crews testifying against him; dozens of straw corporations insulated him from the day-to-day business of his freighters. More important, every captain and crew member had a family in Haiti and an understanding of the consequences of betraying Jean Bedard. In a country with an 80 percent unemployment rate, men lined up to sell their souls and willingly risked their families as well.

What kept Bedard up at night was evidence. You couldn't threaten the evidence. Policemen in the superpowers had a near mystical ability to connect disjointed pieces of crimes and conspiracies. From voice recognition of incriminating conversations to microscopic pollens or undigested food cooked in your kitchen, you never knew when you had misspoken or were suddenly contaminated by something that connected you to something else. He had read about a case in the United States where a man was found guilty of murder because the cops proved DNA of dog shit found on his shoes matched the murdered man's dog on a remote farm. It was proof he had been where he said he had not.

It was always the little things that got you and the older you got, Bedard thought, the more dog shit you had collecting on your shoes.

Which was why Bedard had been concealing the bodies of his victims in the ancient quarry behind the foundation of Contestus for thirty years. It simply wasn't prudent to trust their bones to a capricious sea.

Bedard's link to narcotics trafficking was no secret to

the American DEA. His ties to Thiago Mendoza—
including a mansion in Mendoza's backyard, Santa
Marta, Colombia—suggested only one conclusion. But
Haiti was a morass of crime and corruption; even past
presidents profited directly from cocaine. Bedard might
be one of Mendoza's many exporters of cocaine, but
with all his layers of protection he never quite made the
top of the DEA's most wanted list. And Bedard's compound continued to go unnoticed under the protection
of Haiti's anti-American government.

But times were changing. Thiago Mendoza, now deceased, had been suffering this last year from incurable
cancer. His son and successor, Sergio, a man Bedard
had met only weeks ago, also lay dead from a mountain-
climbing accident in the United States. Haiti was doing
its best to look like a democracy, trying to distance itself
from its ugly past, and some thought Bedard, the former commander of Papa Doc's secret police, was an
enormous blemish on that history.

Bedard wasn't worried about being deported. His
main residence in Colombia was all the home and protection he would ever need. But he was worried about
the evidence of his crimes. He did not want forensics
people trampling his castle so they could put him on
trial in his last years on earth.

In the end, it was all those things and Jill Bishop that
motivated his timing. The shock waves following the
American's kidnapping in the Dominican Republic were
still reverberating throughout the capital of Haiti. The

Americans had already approached President Préval to allow their search for the girl to extend across the Haitian border. Should the FBI one day convince Préval to let them search Contestus, they would find far more than dog shit on his shoes and Bedard was not about to let that happen.

Bedard decided it was time to cash in. He was seventy-two years old. He couldn't spend what he had in banks throughout the world, and there were no children in his life. He decided to sell off his shipping lines and export businesses. There were plenty of buyers waiting in the wings. But first he would hire a blast engineer, an explosives expert who could bring down the ancient cathedral and bury a half century of history.

Now that he had made his decision to quit Haiti and get out of the business he would also act on Jill Bishop. She had been too hot to handle until now, was worth far more in reward money than he could sell her for on the open market. If he let her live, someone would try to cash in on her and that would come back to haunt him, which left him with two alternatives.

Keep her or kill her.

He decided to do both.

He decided to send her to his compound in Colombia.

Aleksandra could see the confines of her world through two small slits in the cell. The one in the wooden door allowed them to see when one of them was being punished. You might not want to watch, but you couldn't escape the sound of their screams. From the air vent behind them, they could glimpse the mocking blue sky or jetliners blinking across a field of stars at night. The vent had become as unintentionally torturous as the hole in that door.

Right now her cheek was pressed against the wooden door, her voice barely above a whisper. *"Anmwe! Anmwe!"* she called out to the man.

There was a long moment of hesitation before he looked her way, his eyes darting up and down the corridor before he turned to study the door.

"Souple anmwe," she'd begged.

The man in the green pants was walking toward her, squinting as he put his eye to the small window of her cell.

It had never occurred to her that she might go numb if he actually did walk up to her, but now he had and for one long moment she found herself speechless.

"Ki yès sa?" the operator whispered hesitantly.

She tried to collect herself, not to stammer as he put his eyes to the slit and looked in on her. Along with a flood of relief she felt, in some small way, embarrassed. This was not how she'd wanted to be seen by anyone, not ever. But here he was and there was no time for that now. She'd have to use the moment wisely.

"Souple, van mwen kreyon paye." Paper and pencil, she'd begged. She knew few words of his language so she wanted to write it down. She needed to get it right. She needed him to take her message to someone on the outside.

"Souple, ban mwen"—please give me—*"paye kreyon. Prese, prese!"*—pencil and paper. Please hurry!

There had been no way to gauge understanding by the look on the man's face. He had the look of a witness of a terrible accident when he stumbled away from her cell door. His expression was of pity and revulsion all wrapped up in one. She couldn't blame him. She could only imagine what she must look like by now, half naked and living on a bare dirt floor, face disfigured by a grinning skull tattoo. Not to mention the little blond girl balled up in a corner behind her. Jill had begun sucking her thumb. They must look worse than pathetic, the two of them.

And had she said it right? Had it made sense to him? She only knew what little Creole she had learned from listening to the guards speak, in combination with French she'd learned in the university in Warsaw.

But perhaps the bigger question was, Would he dare to do what she asked? Would he come back again or would he tell Bedard what she'd said?

Which was why she had been terrified when the man walked away without responding; it was like watching hope itself walk away, every step making it harder to hold on to. With every step she worried she might never see him again.

The man in the green pants had first come to the castle a week ago. He was with Bedard at the time. They were in the room opposite her cell, a map spread out on the wooden platform that was used to display and discipline them in front of each other. The man in green pants tapped on the ancient walls with his hammer. Then they left. Two days later he returned and the drilling started. The man in green pants began making fist-sized holes high in the walls at regular intervals.

She pressed her eye to the slit in the door and watched him as long as she could. The guards were off drunk as usual, probably on their second or third bottle of rum for the day. She had heard them laughing earlier; they rolled dice and smoked ganja when Bedard was not around and Bedard had not been around for more than a week, not since the day he brought in the man with green pants.

He was not supposed to be here now without an escort, she was sure. She could tell by the expression on his face he had not known what this place was used for, had not known until he heard her calling out to him that there were actually people behind these wooden doors.

Something had definitely been different about these last days in the cellar. First the trucks that used to regularly bring girls to the compound had stopped coming. Then Bedard began spending more and more time away from the castle. And the man in green pants was the first civilian she'd seen since arriving here. She knew the moment she saw him that she had to take the risk.

She scraped the grime of sweat and dirt from her face with the heels of both hands. She closed her eyes to a wave of vertigo that accompanied the beginning of an ear infection and sat down, hugging her knees to her chest. The temperature in the cells soared by midmorning. She opened her eyes and looked up through a dusty shaft of light from the air vent; it was like a laser slicing the cell in two.

She'd marveled of late how simple this whole human trafficking business was, so simple and yet beyond the grasp of most educated people. It was a paradox if ever there was one.

Where criminals had advanced—or declined, as many would see it—to trade in human beings, one would expect a sophisticated, rather than trite, display of resources. But there was nothing sophisticated about it. In fact, there was something primitive, base about the whole thing, something that brought cattle to Aleksandra's mind. Cattle didn't end up as your Sunday roast at the hands of sterile men in starched white smocks. Cattle stood in their own shit waiting to be rendered unconscious by a metal rod fired into their head so they could be hung by their legs and bled to death. It was a lot more about gore and men in rubber suits than green pastures and sterile deli counters. It was a lot more like that in harvesting humans too. There were no big thinkers here.

It began with lies and rusty freighters, stripped-out airplanes and filthy cargo trucks. You spent your days in dark holds and cages. Then you were beaten and raped and addicted to heroin. When you were finally—and thoroughly—broken, you were ready for market. Then you spent the rest of your life servicing strange men.

Any idiot could have done it, any idiot with no conscience.

She heard the roar of a jet through the vent, a military jet. It was the third such jet she had heard this week. This was something different, she knew, different altitude, different time of day. It was a different sound from the commercial jets beginning their approach to whatever airport lay nearby. Something was going on out there, someone was finally taking a look at this god-forsaken country.

Brigham sat at the head of the table in Sherry's dining room. Sherry sat in the middle, facing the man Brigham introduced only as Graham. She didn't know where Graham worked and no one was going to tell her, Sherry understood. It was a conversation of courtesy and one that never took place.

Brigham had been reluctant about opening dialogue over Sherry's vision from the moment he'd learned who the dead climber hanging off the side of Denali was.

He reminded Sherry that she wasn't bound by any legal or moral edict to "act on every damned thing she happened to see in a dying man's head." It was like she was looking for trouble when there was already more than enough trouble waiting out there in the world. Not to mention the phone calls and letters she received each day beseeching her to become involved in this or that.

"Can't you just stick to serial killers and sociopaths?" he'd said jokingly, but he really wasn't joking. "You don't need this," he'd told her. "You really don't need this, Sherry."

"I have to know," she'd said stubbornly. And at last Brigham had conceded.

And told her that she had tapped into the last memories of Sergio Mendoza, son of Thiago Mendoza, head of the most powerful cocaine cartel in the world.

And now this man Graham was sitting across the table from her.

It was surreal in a way. It wasn't the kind of conversation one might have about things found in the newspaper today.

"So Sergio was not part of his father's cartel, is that what you're saying?"

"Never even visited Colombia until last year," Graham said. His mother wouldn't permit it after the divorce. She'd lost two of Sergio's older brothers to drugs before she left her husband, one killed by a bullet that was meant for his father in the city of Medellín."

"What did Sergio do as a child? Until he turned thirty?"

Graham seemed amused by the question. "His father was the twenty-second richest man in the world. He grew up in Monte Carlo and played polo around the Mediterranean. What else would he do? Yachts, women, casinos, he was a kid in life's candy store."

"And he was an adventurer. He climbed mountains," Sherry said.

"Two in Tibet, I'm told. Two before Denali."

"So what brought him out? After all those years of avoiding his father's lifestyle?"

"His mother died of myelogenous leukemia two years ago. Sergio was living in Monaco when Thiago was diagnosed a year later with cancer of the pancreas. Sergio decided to come home. I guess he was looking for roots and his father was all he had left. We knew that Sergio stayed with his father in Colombia the whole time he was undergoing chemotherapy. They were flying him in and out of Dallas that year."

"Wasn't Thiago wanted by the FBI?"

"He was dying, Miss Moore, we knew it because we saw the medical reports. There were more interesting things to learn by watching him in his final months than placing him under arrest. Actually, that was how we first identified Sergio. As you know, the press hasn't even picked up on him. The paparazzi had lost interest in the boy years earlier when his mother remarried. By the time he came to South America he was an unknown."

"Thiago died two months ago?"

Graham nodded. "Funeral was in Barranquilla."

"And the boy from Monte Carlo suddenly becomes heir to the biggest drug cartel in Colombia."

"A gift I wouldn't wish on my worst enemy," Graham said.

"Because he wasn't prepared for the lifestyle?"

"Exactly. He had no history, no support system. He had just become an assassination target for his competitors, men long intimidated by his father's political connections in Bogotá. Sergio did not have his father's power or respect. He only had the land and money and that would not have kept him alive for very long in Colombia."

"Was he close to his father in the end?"

"I can't say he was close, but he was certainly getting involved in the business. The old man's inner circle closed around him. They had to be worried for their own safety and were probably trying to get him in control as fast as they could."

"Sergio thought he could continue his father's legacy?"

"We had no doubt. At least at first."

"And this building, this castle I told you about, the things that I saw, what could it possibly have to do with the Mendozas and cocaine?"

"Ah, yes," Graham said, "a very good question, Miss Moore. I guess the simple answer is that the cartel, like any corporate model, was paying attention to markets and trends. The black market conduits were already in place. It only made sense to evolve into human trafficking. It would have been foolish to send empty ships home to South America. As for opportunity, they knew they were well ahead of law enforcement. Until 2002, we were still trying to figure out what traffickers were guilty of when customs caught them smuggling a shipload of people."

Brigham got up from the table and she heard him open the French doors to the living room, bottles tinkling in the liquor cabinet.

"The castle or whatever. Do you have any idea where it might have been?"

"As the admiral pointed out earlier, it may have nothing at all to do with the cartel, it could have been from any place or time in Sergio's life. The boy had seen a lot growing up. He was worldly. What you saw is exactly the kind of thing he might have encountered in Thailand or Indonesia. We can't know for sure, but this memory, as you call it, could have been many years old."

Sherry smiled inwardly. How uncomfortable this man must be talking about a "memory" seen by a blind woman. Retired admiral aside, Brigham must carry quite some political weight to bring conversation to the table from intelligence analysts or CIA agents or whatever Graham was.

"But it was more likely a recent memory," she said. "He thought about it as he was dying. Perhaps it was the memory itself that drove him to the mountaintop."

"I understand your theory, Miss Moore, and yes, it's possible."

"So?" Sherry asked. "Do you know where in recent weeks he could have been?"

"Sergio was photographed with members of the cartel in Venezuela right before he went to Alaska. We also know he traveled from Colombia to the Caribbean with his father's accountants and bodyguards. It was impossible to account for his every move, but it seems he remained exclusively in the Western Hemisphere after his father's funeral. Actually, up until the day he died."

"How did Sergio end up in Alaska?"

Brigham reentered the room, took a seat at the table, the sound of his glass on the table.

"Two weeks ago on a Monday, all hell broke loose at the Mendoza compound in Colombia. Cell phone calls, cars, in and out, helicopters, even military vehicles."

"They lost him. He slipped away."

"Uh-huh."

"His head must have been reeling from what he learned about his father's cartel. About where all that money came from that had supported his lifestyle as a boy," Sherry said.

Graham remained silent a long moment.

"I think it is obvious, Miss Moore, that your theory is correct and the boy was running away from his legacy. I also think it is possible you are describing a location in the Caribbean, an indoctrination camp where they ready women for the market. That is common in the business. I really can't tell you more."

"Will you call me if you learn anything new?" Sherry asked. She appreciated all that Brigham's friend Graham had told her, but she was still left with the visions from that mountainside. She didn't want it any longer.

"I know I have only given you the abstract of the cartel, Miss Moore, but yes, there are people in DEA and Interpol who have a more intimate knowledge of the Mendozas and who certainly know more about human trafficking than I. I'll do this for you. I'll place a call to a friend at Interpol. I'll tell him exactly what we spoke of today and I'll let him make his own decision about calling you. If he rings one day, fine. If not, I have told you what I could."

Aleksandra turned away from the slot in the door, hearing light snoring behind her, and reached down to pet the head of Jill Bishop. The girl's hair was soaked with sweat, as hot as the walls that radiated around them. She had been sleeping a great deal lately, if you called whimpering and shivering sleeping.

Aleksandra had entered law enforcement after serving in the Polish army, where she attended Land Forces Military Academy. She was educated in the effects of prolonged stress in battle and knew about the body's common biological responses. The terror of battle raised blood sugars at the same time it debilitated the body's ability to digest. When the spleen began to expedite red blood cells to produce more oxygen, high levels of cortisone and adrenaline were pumped into the circulatory system. If the encounter ended quickly, the body's countermeasures stood down. If the encounter was protracted, the body's biological responses, some fourteen hundred altogether, would mutate to meet the undue stress. Over time those transformations would begin to take a physiological toll; the person would begin to experience involuntary muscle contractions, nervous tremors, fatigue, intestinal maladies. Eventually he or she would forget things, lose problem-solving abilities, confuse what was vital with the trivial.

The sleeping girl was almost there, she thought. The sleeping girl was shutting down.

Aleksandra wiped her hands on her T-shirt and stood again, put her eye to the hole in the door, and looked around the cellar. Then she heard footsteps in the corridor, one person, coming toward her.

The girl behind her rolled over, moaned, then gasped loudly for air. A second later her breathing returned to normal, and the slow smooth snoring resumed.

The footsteps were getting closer. Aleksandra's heart began to pound.

She tried to control her emotions, head pressed tightly against the wooden door.

Aleksandra thought once more about destiny. If there really was such a thing, then what was to be her destiny today?

She sometimes envied the sleeping girl behind her, would not have minded curling into a ball and sucking her thumb for a day. But then she thought of a young redheaded girl on a ship all those months ago, buried now not far away in the recesses of the castle's foundation. She didn't want to end up like her. She didn't want these despicable men to decide her fate.

She heard boots scratching dirt—they were only a

dozen meters away, would be visible in a moment's time—and then suddenly the man with green pants was at the door and she felt her heart pounding in her chest.

Destiny once again flickered through her thoughts. To believe in destiny was to admit that all that had happened was preordained, that every victim in life was born to suffer their fate, born to come to ruin on a particular day and time. It was such an unfair scenario, and yet could it be that destiny worked in opposing directions? For both good and bad? If destiny had brought her here, could it also have brought the man in green pants to her rescue?

His hand went to the slit in the door and through it he pushed a small cylinder. Then he turned and walked away.

Oh my God, oh my God. Her lips formed the words without sound.

She kept her eye on him until he was gone, then she slid back to the door, until she was sitting in the dirt and facing her spent cellmate. Aleksandra reached for the cylinder and unrolled it, heart pounding, tears welling in her eyes.

It was a single cigarette paper wound around the stub of a lead pencil.

It was almost too hard to believe. They had a real chance now. They might yet come out of this alive, she thought.

She knew she had no control over what the man did with the paper once he left here. Who he saw and what he did with it was completely up to him. She could only pray that he was as wise as he was compassionate. That he would know whom to give the note to. That they would call the phone number in Warsaw that she would write.

She held the pencil stub in one shaking hand and tried to think of what to say. She had never really prepared herself for this moment, never really believed something like this might happen. Now that it had she could only wonder how to reduce these months of hell to the size of a cigarette paper. What words to use when your life hinged on every one.

She actually smiled for a second, realizing she didn't even know what language to write in. She could express herself in three languages, but not well enough to risk making a mistake. Not with something as important as this. Probably it wouldn't matter if it were in Polish. Probably it was more a matter of whom the man in green pants gave the note to rather than what it said. The right person would know how to get it translated.

Water struck the fragile paper and she realized she was crying. She held the delicate paper away from her face and blew upon it gently. She mustn't destroy it. There would be no other chance.

When she got herself together, she put it on her knee and started to write.

Nazywam się Aleksandra, I am Aleksandra. . . .

It was silent and eerily so, a thousand-foot stretch of runway cut out of the dense mountain jungle. There were no buildings, no lights, no windsocks. Only this strip of tarmac that was old and cracked and hot as a frying pan under her feet.

Tangles of vines and withering palm fronds lay on glimpses of old fencing; once there had been deer and wild boar to worry a taxiing pilot, but the wildlife was all gone from Haiti, decimated like the island's forests and plantations.

Two white-necked crows scanned the runway for vertebrates. A Haitian man poked his machine gun like an angry finger in her face.

The truck that brought her here had disappeared in a blur of black and green vegetation, a gate or hole or section of open fence that was beyond her line of sight.

If Aleksandra had been here she would have told her to remember where the truck entered the jungle. To run for that place if anything happened.

But Jill wasn't thinking about running. Even walking was difficult, as she was shaking badly. The move from the cellar was entirely unexpected. It was the trip she had been dreading all these months in confinement.

She knew that something bad would follow what Aleksandra had done. She knew that Aleksandra would be taken to the red room and that something terrible was going to be in store for her as well.

She missed her brave friend and wished she were here now, she wished that they were going away together now. She couldn't imagine how she would have survived the past month without the Polish girl, how she would have managed alone with her thoughts, always ignorant of what was happening around her. She wondered if possibly Aleksandra was dead.

Dead like the man in green pants whom they shot in front of the cell door. It had taken an afternoon for the man to finally die. He just lay there and moaned, crying out and speaking names in a language she did not know.

It was the first time she had ever seen her friend Aleksandra cry, the first time Aleksandra had been shaken to the point of losing control.

Then Bedard came for her and he took her away. And Jill could hear her friend's screams all the way down the corridor.

This morning the guards had come for her, but instead of the red room they brought her to this airplane. She would never see her parents again. Not if she left this island, she knew.

Looking back, Jill's life had been easy until now, her sacrifices few. She had taken the time to volunteer, feeding the homeless, decrying war and poverty and discrimination. But in the end she was just like the rest of her contemporaries. She thought she could identify with suffering, when nothing was further from the truth. She had been deluding herself. Up until now she had not the slightest idea what kind of suffering went on in the real world.

The airplane was small, an old commuter. You could still make out the traces of the red and blue logo across the tail, the snags of once colorful carpet clinging to rivets on the aluminum steps that led up to the ominous outline of an open door.

The interior was dark but for a single ray of light escaping the cockpit. A black man wearing a dirty white T-shirt sat behind the controls.

Philippe, the oldest and fattest of Bedard's security guards, mopped his brow with a filthy kerchief, occasionally wringing out the sweat, which sizzled on the hot tarmac. His machine gun was cradled carelessly over the crook of his arm, and he scratched unconsciously at his crotch and under his arms.

Aleksandra had always said that Philippe was the weak link among the guards. Aleksandra said if she were ever alone with him she would kill him and go hunting for Bedard with his weapon. Jill never doubted that she meant it.

Something popped like a firecracker and everyone jumped. Philippe swung his weapon toward a puff of black smoke lingering over the right wing. A moment later there was another pop and the propeller turned a half rotation, then it caught and the engine ratcheted to life. Jill watched it turn until it was only a blur and the plane began to vibrate on its bald rubber tires.

This was a big crossroads, she knew. This was the last place she would ever have been seen, here on this island shared by the Dominican Republic and Haiti.

Philippe said something and she turned to see him leering at her. He extended the barrel of his machine gun and pressed it against her breast. Then he grinned, exposing a gold tooth, and nodded toward the stairs of the aircraft.

"Move," he commanded. "Move, move, move."

Jill knew that Aleksandra wouldn't have wanted her to set foot on that plane. Aleksandra had always said that their best chance for escape would be when they were being moved from one location to another. Jill knew that Aleksandra would have been pleased to see that Philippe was their guard. She knew that Aleksandra would have seen this as a chance to escape. Aleksandra always thought she had a chance to escape.

But Jill was not Aleksandra.

"Move," Philippe barked again.

Jill looked once more toward the jungle, toward the spot along the fence where the truck had disappeared. Then she took a deep breath and held it.

Philippe raised the barrel of his machine gun until it was level with her head. There was a moment of uncertainty before Jill released her breath and the muscles in her face relaxed. She looked at the plane a long moment, then nodded her head in resignation, taking a step forward.

Philippe relaxed, pushed the kerchief against his neck, scratched his crotch.

Jill had spent these last few months thinking about her childhood. Thinking about all the years leading up to this nightmare. Any girl in her position would have: all would have tried to put this into context.

Why, they would have wondered, had it happened to them of all people? Why not someone else, why not the girl standing next to her in that market square? Perhaps some saw it as part of their god's bigger plan.

Jill, who had been raised Catholic, thought not. No true god would permit such an outrage. No true god would permit men to disgrace what he created.

It had at last become easy for her to empathize, to imagine the horror of poverty and starvation and slavery. She understood the agony of being torn from family. She understood the hopelessness of an uncertain future. She knew that every day that separated her from her old life she had changed as a person, was moving away from who she once was. And you couldn't go back, you could never go back. Even if you were rescued you could never become that person again.

She put a foot on the step and climbed toward the door, strands of blond hair sticking to the sides of her face. Her mother was near. She sensed it. Carol Bishop would never have stopped looking for her daughter. She would never have taken no for an answer from the Dominican government. For all Jill knew, they were already in Haiti and hours away from finding her. Perhaps that was what prompted the guards to move her from the castle.

It didn't matter now. All was for naught. She would never again be this close in time and place to her parents and what she considered the last day of her life— the day the cruise ship *Constellation* left her in Santo Domingo.

She neared the door and felt the stairs bounce under her feet. Philippe was behind her, still yelling something unintelligible.

The pilot was starting the other engine.

The hull of the plane stank of dead rodents and moldy carpet. The seats had been removed but their outline was still visible where they had once rested against the filthy metal walls. Near head level, where cargo would have been stored, were open bins filled with fruit rinds, mango pits, and rusty tools. Threads were left hanging from rivets beneath a line of badly scratched windows.

She was made to sit on the bare metal floor. The craft rumbled, shifting to the right and turning on the runway. The roar of the engine was deafening in the sweltering cabin; muffled shouts rose between the pilot and the guard and then the door was pulled closed.

Jill looked down at her hands. Philippe sat opposite her, machine gun on his lap. He eyed her hungrily. Never had she been alone with any of the guards before.

The plane began to inch forward, tires dropping in and out of ruts in the tarmac. The engines provoked a spine-numbing vibration throughout the hull. The plane picked up speed making its run, and Jill could feel the craft grow light under its wings. Moments later they were airborne and the plane banked steeply, causing her to pitch forward in the direction of Philippe.

Jill craned her neck to look through the cockpit and caught a glimpse of green mountains before they entered blue sky.

Jill rested her head facedown between her knees and saw the initials JMS scratched on the metal floor between her thighs. The initials were followed by a question mark and the year 2002.

Who was JMS, she wondered, and where was she now? Would she be alive or would she be long dead? And if she was alive, what had she been made to do?

Jill wasn't a virgin before the family cruise to the Dominican Republic, but neither was she experienced. She did it with a boy one Sunday afternoon on the rec-room couch in her parents' house. She could still remember the smallest details of the day. They had just returned from the movies and found a note from her parents telling them they were out with friends. Money for pizza was clipped to a Domino's coupon and left by the telephone. They turned on a movie, a horror movie, but he was soon kissing her and his hands were on the buttons of her blouse.

Try as she might, she could not speak, mesmerized by his fingers, willing each to find another button and then another. Only when he began to lift her bra did she utter a sound, but the sound was not a no and she groaned when he put his mouth on her.

It was laughable now, the dreams she'd once had, just fucking laughable. She had imagined finishing college and volunteering in some third-world country. She and the imaginary boyfriend who would accompany her to some impoverished village, they would work in an improvised hospital by day and make love in their tent by night. They would return to America and then they would get married and buy a home in Oak Park near her parents and write papers and get published. She would have a room for an office to organize her philanthropic endeavors. There would be candles in the bedroom, a husband's cologne on the pillows.

She'd made a frivolous vow to herself one night in the cellar. That she would give up men for the rest of her life if ever she got out of here. She would do anything not to be touched by one again, even join an order, in spite of her distaste for religion. She would have kept the vow, too, but none of that was ever going to happen. By the time she'd be old enough to drink alcohol she'd be secondhand goods, and that was if she was lucky enough to survive.

A boot kicked her sandal and she looked up at Philippe. His wiry hair was going gray around the temples. He was sweating profusely, khaki shirt ringed at the neck and underarms. He was talking to her, rolling a joint between long filthy fingernails. He put the joint in fat worm-colored lips and lit it with a yellow Bic. Then he put the lighter away, patted his forehead again with his dirty kerchief, and lifted the machine gun off his lap with his free hand and waved it in her direction. He spoke to her in Creole.

"He wants you to undress," the pilot said.

Jill glanced at the cockpit and saw the pilot turned in his seat.

The cabin was filling with the pungent aroma of marijuana.

"He says he wants you to undress and if you don't he'll throw you out of the plane."

Jill stared back at Philippe in horror.

The guard locked eyes with her, and waited.

Jill kept her eyes on him, never blinking, until he looked away. Then she put her head down on her arms and closed her eyes.

Philippe took a deep hit off the joint and laid down his machine gun, stood, and walked to the door. Sunlight glared off the pilot's windshield, the plane leveled off, the sound of the engine diminished. Philippe grabbed the stainless-steel latch and yanked the door back.

Sunlight blinded them as air rushed into the cabin, sucking everything loose from the floors and pitting their bodies and faces with sand and dirt. Clothing, paper, Philippe's roach all flew out the door; it took a full minute before the cabin cleared and they could lower the hands that were shielding their eyes. There, beyond the open door, was an azure sky and fresh sweet air, far below it a diamond-studded ocean.

Philippe spoke again, pointing at her once more, grabbing his shirt and pulling it up over his fat belly, wanting her to mimic him, to strip. She looked at the open door and stood.

Slowly she moved her hands to her waist and grabbed the bottom of her blouse.

Philippe watched her eagerly as she undid the buttons and dropped the shirt to the floor. He pointed, laughing, as he nodded toward the pilot. Jill unzipped her skirt.

Philippe made kissing sounds, put his lips together, smacking them.

Tears streaked down Jill's face as her skirt fell to the floor.

She stood there, hands balled in trembling fists. Philippe was watching her closely, his eyes sliding up and down her body.

Jill fought for balance as the plane pitched through

turbulence; the pilot was turned in his seat looking back at her through the cockpit door.

Jill's long blond hair whipped about her face, rising from her shoulders in the rush of warm wind. She looked down at her body and for the first time in a month she smiled. Then she stepped toward Philippe, reached behind her back, and undid her bra and dropped it in his lap. Then she sidestepped him and walked out the door.

A Bertram sportfisherman rolled in calm waters off the coast of Jamaica. Rolly King George, wearing only sunglasses and a pair of black swimming trunks, looked across the portside rail of his boat with powerful binoculars. His huge black arms were beginning to dry the chalky white of sea salt. One of several dive tanks was strapped to his buoyancy compensator and regulator and dropped carelessly like the flippers and mask at his feet. Two stiff wahoos lay against the wall of the transom, dark holes trickling blood from their silvery sides and pooling on the fiberglass floor, eyes wide and glazed, staring toward his bare feet as he contemplated what he had just seen.

Rolly King George, senior investigator of the Jamaica Constabulary Force, was on holiday and spearfishing in the shallows south of White Bay when he first heard the airplane's growl. It was an old plane, a Douglas DC-3, and it was flying south in cloudless skies. Heading toward the mainland of South America when he first saw it. Pushing one of the wahoos over the side of his boat, he'd slipped back in the water, put a shot of air into his buoyancy compensator to keep him afloat, and used a hand to shade his eyes from the sun as he watched the plane's approach.

Unmarked planes were hardly unusual in the Caribbean; plenty of islanders maintained personal planes on private airstrips, not to mention that DC-3s were the favorite of drug runners—old and gutted of their seats, they could be bought cheap at thirty or forty thousand dollars and disposed of once their job was done.

But something about the plane kept him looking up and treading water as it came overhead, and then he saw the black outline of an open door and suddenly a body came out, arms flailing, legs kicking as it plummeted to the sea.

It seemed to take forever but at last he saw a small spray by green shallows.

The plane banked hard, circling low over the place where the body had dropped, then it changed direction and headed southeast. He followed it until it disappeared into the horizon.

It didn't seem possible and yet it had happened. Now he was back in his boat with his eye on the place where he had seen the body hit the water.

He pushed the throttles with shaking hands and twin Cummins diesels screamed as the boat rose out of the water.

Minutes later he reached a sandbar, pulled back on the throttles, and tossed the binoculars on the dash, then trimmed the inboards to prevent the propellers from dulling in the bottom furrows. He killed the engines and vaulted over the rail into thigh-deep water.

She was lying facedown, young and trim and wearing only red bikini panties. Her long blond hair floated lazily about her head. Blood wiggled like red threads from both of her ears.

He looked around. There was nothing else in the sky, nothing on the ocean's horizon. No one had seen what happened here, only he.

He turned his attention to the girl, examined the back of her head, then her torso and legs. He pushed down on one of her shoulders, rolling her over in the water, and he groaned when he saw the damage to her face. He put a finger on the carotid and raised her eyelids with a thumb. Then he used the thumb to stroke the tattoo just below her right eye, a grinning purple skull wearing a black top hat.

"Lost Girl," he whispered, heart pounding in his chest.

She had been beautiful, he thought, young and beautiful, but now her skin was a maze of fractured blue lines. Rolly King George had seen trauma like hers to a body only once before, when a young Italian boy leaped off the cliffs over Treasure Beach in Jamaica. Her skin was like a road map of her circulatory system, veins bursting just beneath the surface.

He examined her scalp and torso, the hollows beneath her knees and armpits, any place that might conceal a knife or bullet wound. There was nothing. She had apparently been uninjured before she came out of the plane.

A wave washed over her face as he rocked her in his trembling arms. Then he looked up and replayed in his mind the image of what he had seen. First the plane was heading west, but after it circled where she fell, it turned southeast. Had the plane flown here specifically to murder this girl or had something gone terribly wrong? What had happened up there? Why had the plane changed direction?

He grabbed her by the ankle and pulled, using his free hand to guide her toward the back of his boat. Then he rolled her onto the swim platform and pulled himself out of the water, lifting her over the stern.

The trip back to the northern coast of Jamaica would take just under an hour. Under any other circumstance he would have called the ministry and had constabulary investigators meet him in Port Antonio. The parish could have taken the case from there. But this was not normal and Rolly King George, most senior investigator of the Jamaica Constabulary Force, knew there was little time to waste. He must place a very different kind of a call.

He climbed the ladder to his flying bridge and took a seat at the console. All around him shadows of lumbering clouds looked like stepping-stones through the shallow mint sea. He scrolled through numbers in a cell phone until he saw the listing "I-24/7."

And dialed.

A few minutes later he was connected to an international operator and then to the National Central Bureau of Interpol in France.

"Helmut Dantzler, please."

He was put on hold for nearly a minute, then connected to a second operator, an older man. "He's not available," the man said dryly.

"Do you have a number for him? A cell phone?"

"I'm afraid he's in a dark spot, monsieur, may I take a message or perhaps I can help you."

A dark spot could mean anything. Maybe he was in some remote region of the world or maybe he was in the basement having tea.

"I must reach him right away," the inspector said. "You will tell him it is very important."

"He checks his messages frequently," the man allowed. "Who shall I say is calling?"

Rolly King George gave his name and cell phone number. Then he disconnected and nudged the throttles forward, turning the boat into deep water, accelerating, bow rising out of the water, propellers churning wake in a placid sea. He turned to look southeast once more. Eighty miles away lay the mountainous coast of Haiti. Was the plane heading for Haiti? Perhaps it had come from Haiti as well? He looked at the body lying beneath him by the transom. It had been over a year since the conference in Alberta. A year since he'd heard about the

Bulgarian informant and a story about women with skulls tattooed on their faces.

In the year since the symposium in Alberta someone must surely have made progress on the Bulgarian informant's story. Any organization that tattooed women's faces could hardly remain hidden.

Inspector George had a boat slip in Port Antonio, but the marina there was full of tourists and parish police. He didn't want to arouse curiosity, not even his fellow policemen's curiosity right now. Anyone who saw the girl's face would know she didn't drown. Would know that she suffered some great trauma. Worse, they would see the tattoo on her face, and the last thing he wanted, until he talked to Interpol, was someone leaking word of that tattoo to the press.

He headed the boat toward the inlet at Frenchman's Cove. The cove was familiar territory to him. He had kayaked these waters as a boy with a grandfather who once lived in Boston Bay. His grandma ran a jerk stand just above it on the side of A-4.

Someone would see him take the body off the boat there, he couldn't do much about that, but he didn't have to let them see her face. In a small marina he could control the transfer of her body from his boat into the bed of his pickup.

This inlet had been the beginning of his love affair with the sea, a place of magic for a young boy's imagination. The cove was famous for its history of pirates and buried treasure. He remembered his grandfather's tales of ghostly apparitions toiling on the beaches beneath Fairy Hill or at the bend in a path called See-Me-No-More. Ghosts dragging the weight of their booty and herding kidnapped slaves to launches that they would row to their mother ships at sea.

He knew that those "ghosts" were once flesh-and-blood human beings. He knew that more flesh-and-blood human beings carried on their tradition smuggling rum and marijuana and then cocaine and heroin between the islands and South America. The night waters of the Caribbean were alive with activity and they had been for as long as the islands had a history. And in that long history there had always been stories of Lost Girls.

You might not think you could make someone disappear on a tropical island, but then you didn't think of tropical islands in terms of mountain jungles rising to twice the altitude of Denver, or of islands the size of Connecticut, with remote irregular coastlines. The smugglers knew these coasts intimately, were equipped with jet boats and pontoon planes and catamarans and motored sloops that slipped tirelessly from cay to cay. And Jamaica was a cakewalk compared to the backcountry of the Dominican Republic or Haiti or, even worse, the mainland countries like Nicaragua or Colombia, where the mountains rivaled those of Tibet, where jungles were as dark as the Congo, and law, if it be found, fell to warlords and drug kingpins and rebels.

These were countries whose governments didn't care who went missing from some foreign land. These were countries whose bigger problems were war and poverty and drugs.

Simply stated, there was more uninhabited, unpatrolled, unassailable land south of Miami than any government could hope to tame, and the indigenous populations were as inescapably tied to the fortunes of their smugglers and drug lords as they were to the wind and the rain. If someone did go missing backcountry and in one of these poor nations, you could hardly expect that there were resources to go looking for them.

Peddlers young and old began to wade toward him.

"Ga-lang-bout-yu-business," Rolly King George said, nosing the Bertram alongside the dock at the Villas in Frenchman's Cove. George sometimes found patois less intimidating when trying to communicate with his countrymen.

He looked back to ensure that the woman in the stern was completely covered with a tarp.

"No-badda-me!" he snapped, putting the transmission in neutral and stepping off the side of the boat. He slipped lines fore and aft over pilings and looked around.

A handful of tourists watched curiously from the open decks of the Villas. An old bearded Jamaican man with gray dreadlocks raised a conch shell and blew a mournful note from the demarcation rope around the Villas' private beach.

Rolly King George called a teenage boy who was raking pawpaw leaves, showed him his badge and a ten-dollar bill, and held up the keys to his Toyota pickup truck, parked in Port Antonio. "Yuh drive, bwoy?"

The boy nodded.

He told him where the truck was parked and put the money on the dash of the boat next to an automatic pistol.

"No lick it up, bwoy; mi know every ding."

The boy reached for the keys, nodding enthusiastically as he dashed off in bare feet. The police inspector settled in for a wait.

The boy would have to hitch a ride to Port Antonio, twenty minutes one way. He must have been fortunate, for in only an hour he was back, and George was moving the wrapped body from the boat to the bed of his truck, where he secured her under a canvas. He wasn't worried about the forensics or transfer evidence by now. The ocean had done its damage. If there were evidence to be found, it would be *in* her body, not on it. The food in her stomach, the chemicals in her organs, tissues, blood, the fillings in her teeth, foreign DNA, the inks used to tattoo her face.

Two hours later he was sitting in traffic on the outskirts of Kingston when his cell phone rang.

"Helmut Dantzler." The German's accent was crisp and formal.

"Mr. Dantzler." Rolly King George was stopped in traffic behind a taxi that had hit a pickup truck carrying crates of chickens. People were shouting from their cars, feathers floating on the air.

"Inspector Rolly King George from the Jamaica Constabulary Force. I was in Alberta at the summit last year, we shook hands by the elevator before you left. You asked me if I knew Prime Minister Simpson-Miller and I did give her your respects."

"Yes," Dantzler said curiously. "I remember you."

"We heard a story at the conference from a Bulgarian policeman about women being trafficked to South America. A black man with one eye was bragging that he tattooed their faces with a skull. You were going to have your people at Interpol check on the ships that were in harbor at the time."

"Yes?" Dantzler said cautiously.

"I have one."

"One?"

"She is dead, one of the tattooed women. There is a skull wearing a top hat on her face."

There was a moment of silence before Dantzler spoke. "Where are you?" he asked.

"In Kingston. I am taking her to a safe place."

"How did she die?"

"She was thrown from an airplane into the sea."

"You saw this?" Dantzler said incredulously.

"Yes. I was in my boat, off the southern tip of Jamaica," the inspector said. "The door was open on the side of the plane when the body came out of it. The plane circled her once, then headed south."

"Markings on the fuselage?"

"None."

"Who knows about this?"

"I was seen putting her body in my truck so I had to notify the Ministry of Justice. I told them she was a drowning victim and that I am taking her to the morgue."

"That is unusual?"

"I am the senior investigator in major crimes. They will accept it for now."

"Nationality?"

"She is a white woman with blond hair is all I can say."

"Where exactly is this safe place you speak of, Inspector?"

"The University of the West Indies Hospital in Kingston has a teaching morgue. I know the administrator. He will keep her locked away from the press. But soon the ministry will want to know about my drowning victim. Can you send somebody?"

"You understand we are not a law enforcement agency, Inspector. We have no police powers. We only share intelligence."

"I understand who you are, but what of the informant in Bulgaria? Someone has been working this case."

"The informant in Bulgaria was found dead," Dantzler said. "The investigation went no further."

"But the ships that were in harbor at the time, you were going to check on them."

"And we never found proof."

"Here is the proof," Rolly King George shouted. "Do not treat me like a civilian." He slammed a fist upon the steering wheel.

Dantzler hesitated again, then spoke more softly.

"The Bulgarian informant was killed a month after our summit in Alberta. The nationals think he was fingered by the Russian mob. We looked at the records of ships in port at Burgas at the time and only one freighter sailed west beyond the coast of Africa. It was a Liberian-owned freighter and it was bound for Port-au-Prince, Haiti. By the time we actually located it and got policemen on board, it had been twice sold and was dry-docked in Singapore being refitted to barge coal."

"There is no evidence. That is what you're saying."

"They cut up the hull. If there were even traces of contraband they were long gone before we arrived."

"What did the ship's owner say?"

"The ship's new owners are attorneys. None had ever seen or set foot on the ship. Her manifest listed humanitarian aid and tractor engines."

"Crew?"

"The records were lost when the ship changed hands, or so we were told. There are no records of the crew."

"What about satellite images?"

"Everything we could access was pointed at Iran at the time. This was 2007, remember."

"What do they say in Haiti?"

"The port authority has no record of the ship, nor is there a record of a crew coming ashore."

"They are bought," George spat, turning the wheel to avoid a police car that had wedged itself between his truck and the taxi. The traffic was beginning to move once more. "They are bribed."

"That is our world, Inspector George, but you already know that."

"What am I to do with the dead girl?" George asked, looking in the rearview mirror. "I don't have resources to investigate what happens in international waters."

Dantzler hesitated, then spoke gently.

"We never doubted the Bulgarian's story was true, Inspector. Colombian cocaine being trafficked east into Bulgaria, Ukrainian women being trafficked west on the same ships. It only makes sense."

"And Haiti is south of us," George added.

"Haiti is well known as a hub for South American cocaine and close enough to Brazil to facilitate human trafficking," Dantzler said. "But we haven't found anything concrete. We have no intelligence."

"The tattoo is of Baron Samedi," George said. "Baron Samedi is the skull wearing a top hat."

"Yes," Dantzler said, "a symbol of Haiti. I get the picture, Inspector."

"It is voodoo," the inspector said. "Do you have people inside Haiti?"

"Our resources are poor in Haiti to say the least."

"What about surveillance?"

"The American DEA is quite active in the Caribbean, but their considerable efforts are focused on what is leaving South America, not going toward it."

George grunted.

"Your plane may belong to one of these traffickers, Inspector George, and it might have been headed for Haiti or it might have been flying over it to the Dominican Republic or to Puerto Rico or Grenada. I do remember you from Alberta, Inspector George"— Dantzler's voice went uncharacteristically soft, almost kind—"and I did speak with Prime Minister Simpson-Miller. She told me you gave her my respects, thank you. She also told me you are a man of intelligence."

Dantzler hesitated a moment.

"I want you to stay by the phone, Inspector George, while I make a call. Perhaps there is someone who can assist you."

14

An electronic tone sounded. The belt under Sherry Moore's feet began to decelerate; it was the last of forty minutes, in which she'd run four and a half miles. She grabbed a hand towel from the rail and dabbed her face as the treadmill slowed to a halt. The phone had rung twice in the last thirty minutes. She snatched a bottle of water from a mini fridge and walked across the solarium to a lounge chair and the phone. She picked up the handset and pushed a button for messages.

The first recording was of a disconnect. The second was from a man with a German accent. He left a number with the country code 33—France, she knew. She had friends in Rennes who called frequently.

It was November and snow was just around the corner, normally not Sherry's favorite time of year, but Sherry considered this a good year, perhaps even a healing year. She had promised herself that as the holidays approached, she would find opportunities in which to enrich her life. What good was shunning four months of every year, after all? It was like throwing a third of one's life away.

She smiled at the thought of embracing snow, thinking that if her old friend John Payne knew she was in search of the holiday spirit he would have turned over in his grave.

She dialed the number and waited.

She had entered herself in a Thanksgiving 5K in Philadelphia to sponsor the United States Association of Blind Athletes. She'd agreed to address a graduating class at Temple University's Health Sciences Center, a favor to her confidant Garland Brigham, who taught marine science at the university twice weekly. Since her experience on Denali she'd also considered a weeklong adaptive downhill skiing program for the blind, in Vermont, but that wasn't until January, so she still had time to test the holiday waters before she committed herself to make a deposit. By far her most outrageous plan was to buy a Christmas CD for her stereo, something by Il Divo, she'd decided. If anything would shock the people who knew her it would be the sound of holiday music emanating from her speakers.

What, no humbug! her neighbor Garland Brigham would tease.

"Interpol," a woman answered.

"Sherry Moore," she said tentatively. "Your number was left on my answering machine?"

"Yes, Miss Moore, you'll be holding for Mr. Dantzler. Just a moment, please."

Sherry pushed the record button on her answering device.

A moment later the German gentleman came on.

"Thank you for returning my call, Miss Moore. I hope it is not an inconvenience."

"Not at all," she said curiously.

"My name is Helmut Dantzler, Miss Moore. We have mutual friends, I understand."

Friends, Sherry thought. Graham and Brigham? Brigham had not acknowledged that he knew anyone at Interpol, as well.

"I know a man named Graham told me he had contacted Interpol, but I must say I didn't expect to hear from you." Sherry said it pleasantly. It was not a riposte. "To hear from you so soon, I mean."

"Actually, I'm surprised myself," Dantzler said flatly. "Your story about captive women was intriguing, Miss Moore, but hardly unique. I wouldn't even know where to begin trying to portray the extent and reality of sex trafficking; the stories are universal and beyond horrifying. What got our attention was the tattoo you mentioned on one of these women's faces. We'd heard a similar story told by a drug informant in Bulgaria, just over a year ago. Women were supposedly being trafficked out of Eastern Europe to South America and the buyer was tattooing their faces with skulls. The informant was dead before we had a chance to interrogate him ourselves. Other details of his claim could not be verified. Then a week ago the story resurfaced."

Dantzler took a pause. Sherry could imagine him deliberating on the other side of the ocean.

"I am told you are a serious woman, Miss Moore, a

woman who understands the nature of our work. Graham tells me I can speak candidly with you. That I can trust you to keep secrets."

Sherry only listened.

"I said mutual friends in the plural earlier; I understand you are also acquainted with a Madame Esme."

"Madame Esme?" Sherry repeated, and this time she was really surprised. It was a small world indeed.

"Yes, Miss Moore, and Madame Esme asked me to convey to you that she would have joined our conversation but for a matter most urgent. Unfortunately, the events unfolding no longer permit a delay."

Sherry was immediately reminded of Esme's voice, memories of Africa invading her thoughts. Madame Esme was founder and president of World Freedom, a nongovernmental organization that provided humanitarian relief to tens of millions around the globe. Sherry had been called upon by Esme to do work for World Freedom in 2002, when Janjaweed rebels attacked an envoy of UN peacekeepers guarding aid workers bringing food into Darfur. The rebels killed the military escorts and stole the food stores, kidnapping one of World Freedom's executives, who had just arrived on the continent.

After a week no one had claimed responsibility for the kidnapping. No one asked for a ransom and in Darfur it was difficult to tell what leader of what faction of the Janjaweed rebels might be responsible. Time was working against the hostage.

The bodies of rebel soldiers killed in the raid in Darfur were transported to Kenya. World Freedom, being a humanitarian organization, were neutralists in a hostile land, but Madame Esme was anything but. Esme, heir to the Chalmers diamond fortune of South Africa, was one of the richest women in the world. She had friends in very high places and was said to have a penchant for manipulating events as needed.

Sherry had been flown by United Nations military units to Kenya and was escorted—hood over her face—to a makeshift morgue where the rebels' bodies were being stored. Through the memory of one of the dead soldiers, Sherry was able to describe the leader of the attack, who had been riding a particularly striking horse—a white Arabian decorated with a strand of putrefied human ears around its neck. Armed with this information, the government in Khartoum successfully identified the tribal leader and brokered the release of Madame Esme's emissary.

"I need not explain that World Freedom's charter forbids the organization from interfering in criminal acts. I'm sure you've heard all this from Madame Esme before, but I must repeat it now."

"I will keep your secrets," Sherry said, "and Madame Esme's as well." Sherry had to admit she admired the character—embellished or not—that Madame Esme portrayed. She was purportedly able to manipulate whole governments to do her will. Things just seemed to happen when Esme was around. Perhaps it was coincidence or perhaps it was her clever machinations, one never quite knew with Madame Esme.

"What happened a week ago?" Sherry asked.

"One of World Freedom's aid workers in Haiti befriended a young girl in the village of Tiburon. The girl's father was trained as an explosives engineer by Reynolds Metals before they pulled out in 2000. When the company left, this man moved his family out of the city and began to do freelance work. There are still a few people with means in Haiti and government construction projects come and go with foreign aid.

"Anyhow, the girl overheard her father telling her mother that he had been in the cellar of a building he was working on and saw women locked in a cell. The girl didn't know where her father was working, but the village of Tiburon is on the extreme west coast of Haiti, so our assumption is that it was in that region of Haiti. Anyhow, the father tells his wife that the women in the cell had been tattooed with a likeness of Baron Samedi on their faces. Samedi is a religious symbol in Haiti, the keeper of the underworld. He is represented by a grinning skull wearing a top hat."

"Ahhhh," Sherry said, deflating in her chair, the images on Denali now occupying her mind.

"Two days later the girl's father was thrown dead from a car in front of his house. He had been shot in the stomach and a pencil and paper stuffed in his mouth. A poppet was pinned to his chest."

Sherry heard a phone ring in the background.

Dantzler excused himself and closed a door.

"There are few secrets in Haiti, Miss Moore. Only the rich can afford secrets. The pen and paper left in the man's mouth were a warning to anyone in the village that the man might have confided in. That especially included his family."

"The wife knows who he was working for?"

"If she knew she wouldn't tell the aid worker."

"But it could have something to do with the drug cartel. The Mendozas?"

"The cartels use many means to disperse their product throughout the world. Countries like Haiti become important because their harbors and airports are open to the traffickers. Haiti's very own leaders profit from cocaine. There are only so many fingers to plug the holes in the dike and the same is true for human trafficking. The borders of South America are both isolated and vast. We know that many European women end up in Brazil, but no one can control a coast that is twice the distance between New York and Miami. Islanders have been smuggling in the Caribbean for centuries. Cigarette boats and airplanes can easily penetrate the South American borders and meet truck caravans that move the women into Brazil. Haiti provides a hub from which to do that. It nullifies the efforts of legitimate customs inspections in South America's seaports. All of which is to say it is possible that the Mendozas are involved, yes, but these women you imagine to have seen were probably in Haiti."

"What about the Haitian police?"

"They came and looked at the body and left. They wrote it off as a drug casualty. The police in Haiti are often both corrupt and self-motivated. If there is nothing in it for them, they will stay out of private matters."

"So it was Madame Esme who called you."

"Yes and we in turn contacted a colonel in the national police known to our friends in French intelligence. He is in charge of Haiti's drug task force and was trained by your DEA. He's little more than a figurehead in the police department. He provides low-level intelligence to the French, mostly the political climate in the palace, and heads-up for French investments in the country. Other than that he is a self-admitted token to appease the American government. He says the police are entirely ineffectual in stemming the cocaine trafficked through Haiti. He doesn't even trust his own people."

"I'm sorry," Sherry interrupted. "But you said DEA-trained. Haitian police are trained by DEA?"

"Select members of a narcotics interdiction team were trained by DEA in the late twentieth century in exchange for U.S. economic aid. Something like forty million in U.S. aid to reform Haiti's police organization."

"Go ahead."

"The colonel has limited assets, a helicopter and a handful of men, but even one helicopter is more than we can get into Haiti right now. We are appreciative."

"What exactly is he looking for?"

"Anything that would require an explosives engineer on the site: government or private construction projects, working mines, land being cleared."

"Do the Mendozas own anything in Haiti?"

"Not by name."

"You mentioned a poppet. I'm afraid I'm not familiar with the term."

"A doll," Dantzler said, "a voodoo doll. These are a highly superstitious people, Miss Moore."

"What does the doll signify?"

"Someone wants the family to believe the dead man's soul is in jeopardy. It is believed in Haiti that the dead can be turned into zombies to serve new masters for all of eternity. To the descendants of slaves there can be no worse fate. Wizards, or bocors, as they are called, are paid to make magic into images of one's enemies."

"What about the paper and pencil in his mouth?"

"We had the aid worker mail them to us. Our lab people found writing on the paper along with DNA of the dead man. The writing wasn't much more than a name, *Aleksandra*. It was written in Polish."

"She was one of the girls the dead man saw where he was working," Sherry said.

"Probably, if the story is true."

"And a week ago you considered sending me to Haiti, to see if I could get near this dead villager's body?"

Dantzler laughed. "Absolutely not, Miss Moore. I

wouldn't have thought of calling you a week ago. There is little one can do in Haiti but get hurt, and while the dead man's story was compelling, your presence would have endangered not only yourself but the wife and little girl and Madame Esme's aid worker, as well."

Sherry grunted. "I might have been able to get in and out of the country unnoticed, Mr. Dantzler. Maybe tell you where the dead man had been working. Now the body is buried. The opportunity has passed."

"To begin with, it is impossible to connect what you believe you saw on Denali with the dead man. We have no proof the Mendozas have interests in western Haiti. Anything might have precipitated the man's murder, even drugs, as the police there like to believe." Dantzler paused.

"Miss Moore, I'm only trying to offer you some background here. If I thought sending you into Haiti was prudent I wouldn't hesitate. For that matter the dead man hasn't yet been interred. The voudons believe the soul lingers on for nine days. The ninth night of the wake is called the *denye priye;* a ceremony is held to discourage the person's soul from wandering the earth. Then and only then is he or she buried."

"Go ahead, Mr. Dantzler."

"Something came up this morning, something no less urgent but far safer than sending you to Haiti. The question is whether you are interested in getting involved. A body was found in the Jamaican channel and there will be a window of opportunity to examine it before it officially becomes a murder. A window in which you could get in and out of the morgue unnoticed."

"Tell me," Sherry said.

"An inspector from the Jamaica Constabulary Force was fishing off the coast of Jamaica this morning when he saw a body fall from a small plane. He managed to reach it within minutes and discovered a young white woman dead in the sea. The plane turned south and disappeared. There was a tattoo on the dead woman's face under one eye. A black top hat on a purple skull."

"Baron Samedi," Sherry whispered in awe.

"Yes," Dantzler said. "Call it what you will, coincidence or providence, but this police inspector happened to attend an international law enforcement conference in 2007 where I was speaking on the subject of human trafficking. He knew the story I shared with you about the Bulgarian informant and the tattooed women supposedly being trafficked to South America."

Sherry sat back in her chair; the recorder on the answering machine snapped off as it ran out of memory. She ignored it. "So he called you to ask what to do and you could not tell him what happened in Haiti a week ago because World Freedom was the source of your information."

Dantzler made a sound of acknowledgment. "Yes," Dantzler said. "At least for the time being, Miss Moore. You must understand that Interpol, like all intelligence agencies around the world, relies heavily on their confidential sources of information. The relationship between Interpol and Madame Esme is a very old and delicate one. More is at stake than meets the eye."

"I can appreciate that," Sherry said. "But you have shared it with me."

"Which is why it was so important for me to know I could trust you, Miss Moore. Before I acted on your request to Mr. Graham that I call, I tried to learn as much as possible about you. Frankly, I was surprised by what I read. Even more surprised after I made a few inquiries. I am even ready to allow there are things in this world that no one can label or understand. It was Graham who convinced me in the end, however. Graham says that Admiral Brigham all but asserts you can walk on water, Miss Moore, and Graham says no one takes the admiral lightly. If you are willing I would like you to bridge that gap between Jamaica and Haiti. Madame Esme has only asked that I convey to you her wish that you will use the utmost discretion with what I shared with you today."

"You have my word, Mr. Dantzler, but tell me about Bulgaria, please. Exactly what was known last year that didn't pan out?"

"In a nutshell, the Bulgarian's informant said a large number of women were being trafficked out of the Black Sea port Burgas, to South America. The informant described the buyer as a dark-skinned black man with a white glass eye. As I said, this man bragged about tattooing the women's faces with a human skull before he sold them."

"Interpol found the ship?"

"Interpol found a ship, but by the time they got to it, the information was several months old. The ship had been twice resold and she was dry-docked in Singapore being refitted to barge coal. The paper trail it left was as useless as the information about its owners, a law office in Liberia."

"So," Sherry continued, "you want me to go to Jamaica, to see the body that was thrown from an airplane and then tell you if the woman had memories of where she had been before her death."

"The plane was not marked, Miss Moore. There will never be another way to connect this woman to Haiti, if in fact that's where she came from."

"What's going on in Jamaica now, because of this woman's body, I mean. What am I walking into down there?"

"The Jamaican police inspector was very discreet about what he saw. We know he filed a report with the ministry that he discovered the victim of a probable drowning. He made a show of sending coast guard vessels out to look for signs of a boating accident. Nothing more. He couldn't keep the press from reporting a body was found. The inspector was seen transferring the body from his boat to his vehicle. But all they have been told is that she was found in the water and that she was Caucasian and blond. Soon, however, they will want a picture and a name to go with the body. If they don't get a name they will begin to get suspicious. You remember how it went on another island in the Caribbean several years ago."

"Of course," Sherry said. "And if it leads to Haiti, Mr. Dantzler?"

"Then we will talk again, but please, Miss Moore, one thing at a time. I made a promise to contact you if anything came up relevant to what you saw. I have done that. Perhaps what you see in Jamaica will be enough to lead our police colonel friend in Haiti to a specific location. We wish we could approach the Haitian government and ask them about the dead man in Tiburon directly. We wish they would be cooperative about the unidentified airplane seen heading toward their country, but the police in Haiti are far from cooperative. Please understand, Miss Moore, that Haiti is not without its good people, good politicians, and good policemen. Men like the colonel I spoke of. But those with the best intentions are caught in the reality of Haiti's corruption. Haiti is like Doctor Dolittle's Pushme-Pullyu creature with two heads going in opposite directions, neither being able to take a step forward or backward. We are concerned for the safety of the dead man's family in Tiburon. We are concerned for the safety of Madame Esme's aid worker. General inquiries might only lead to more deaths. Haiti is a country of extreme poverty and civil unrest. They don't have the time, money, or talent to investigate or prosecute organized crime. They will not be moved to pursue unverified sightings of captive women from dead or anonymous sources. They do not care about bodies that fall from airplanes in international waters. And, on top of it all, a third of Colombia's cocaine travels through Haiti on its way to the United States and Europe. If they won't intercept whole shiploads of cocaine, why would they help us locate a few women?"

"Point taken," Sherry said.

"I do not want this girl from the airplane to have died in vain. If we do not learn something specific about where she came from, the investigation is over. Perhaps it is already over. Perhaps the traffickers are destroying evidence even now. But we must try. I can arrange for you to fly to Kingston this afternoon and have the police inspector meet you. I will brief him about what you are supposed to do. I would also tell you the obvious. A tattoo suggests the buyer deems the women disposable. If there are others out there anywhere in the Caribbean, they are in grave danger."

"And exactly what is it that you will tell the police inspector about me?"

Dantzler muffled a laugh. "Of all the things I'm not sure of right now, that one weighs most heavily on me."

KINGSTON, JAMAICA

Rolly King George sat in a corner of a waiting room in the basement of University of the West Indies Hospital, flipping through magazines and tapping his foot impatiently on the stained linoleum floor. He had just delivered the young woman's body via an underground ramp to the hospital's basement loading dock. A cell phone call to a friend produced attendants who moved the body to a cold chamber in the hospital's teaching morgue. The young woman would be safe there from prying eyes until she could be examined by the chief of pathology and scheduled for autopsy.

An old woman sat across from him, her pale green eyes set in skin like burnt parchment. She watched him carefully as she pared a coolie plum with a pocketknife, most likely waiting for someone in X-ray. Radiation was just down the hall from the elevator that went to the morgue, and it had been another bloody night in St. James Parish. Inspector George was avoiding the reporters roaming the halls looking for relatives of the shooting victims. The old woman must have wandered into the waiting room taking refuge from them as well. If she was one of the relatives, she showed no outward sign of grief. But expressions weren't always telling in parish ghettos. For many, life and grief were interchangeable terms.

Inspector George was thinking about his phone call to the Ministry of Justice. His superiors were far more concerned with where in the ocean the woman's body had been found than with what had happened to her. They would give him some freedom to do as he wished with the body as long as he asserted she had been found in international waters.

George knew that last night's triple murder pushed

year-to-date homicides beyond all previous years and there were still three months to go. It was a nightmare for Prime Minister Portia Simpson-Miller. She already had her hands full with corruption allegations and now the drug gang wars were drawing attention to Jamaican street crime. If there was one thing that would exacerbate Jamaica's delicate economy it was a decline in tourism, a fact the World Bank had not failed to point out in a report to the United Nations. Crime would do the island irreparable harm, and the prime minister, in handling the economy, could not afford to lose the respect of cabinet members.

Inspector Rolly King George knew that the prime minister would not want the story of this woman's murder to bring more attention to Jamaican crime. Anything he could learn that would continue to distance the victim and her murderers from the island would be in the government's own interest. He had already assured his own commissioner there would be no record of this woman on Jamaica—no hotel register, no flight record, no cruise ship, no entry through customs. And because of his assurance he had been allowed to delay the official report.

The inspector's cell phone rang and he answered it while getting to his feet. The old woman watched him head for the door, laying a slice of plum on her pink tongue with the blade of her knife.

"Hello," he said, breaking left down the corridor for an exit sign.

"Rolly King George?" Dantzler said with his stiff German accent.

The inspector found a door to the hospital's court-yard and made for a park bench surrounded by peach-colored hibiscus. He took a seat and looked up to see a jet's billowing vapor trail connecting the towers over both wings of the hospital. Air conditioners rattled in windows, dripping water that evaporated before it could pool on the yellow grass. He had been up since dawn and hadn't eaten since last evening; his stomach growled.

"Yes," he said.

"I have a favor I wish to ask of you that will require a degree of faith on your part. I would like you to allow a friend of ours access to the body. If you agree to this, I will ask her to fly to Jamaica this afternoon."

Inspector George looked up at the sky and shook his head as if to clear it. The vapor trail between the towers was beginning to dissipate.

"You said her. You are sending an investigator? A scientist?"

"Not in the truest sense of the word, but let me ask you, Inspector George. Do you believe there are people who can commune with the dead?"

15

Sherry Moore sat with the telephone receiver on her lap. There was an overnight bag kept packed by her front door. She thought about it a long moment before she dialed. She had never asked Brigham to travel with her before, but her friend had seemed listless these last few months. She wondered if he wouldn't appreciate a diversion, a variation in his routine.

She picked up the receiver after a moment and dialed the number.

"Hello?" he barked.

"Mr. Brigham," she said merrily. Sherry had always been uncomfortable calling the retired navy admiral by his first name, Garland.

"Sherry," he said pleasantly.

"I heard from Interpol this morning and was thinking I might ask a favor since you don't have classes tomorrow."

"Do tell," he said. She could hear the sound of a television in the background.

It wasn't like Brigham to be watching television during the day. It wasn't like him to be inside the house, for that matter. Even in winter he was constantly tinkering in his yard, burning leaves or playing with his log splitter, hauling cartloads of firewood behind his little tractor.

He'd seemed bored lately. Bored of his university classes. Bored of his Thursday-morning breakfast club or whatever they called themselves. Bored or just in a rut, she thought. Sherry knew how easy it was to smile your way through life without ever letting on you were not well on the inside. She had managed to hide it for the better part of a year when she was coming apart at the seams over the death of John Payne.

"Jamaica," she said cheerily. "I'll know in thirty minutes or so."

"A pleasant island as long as you stay out of the cities. We'll be sunbathing, I take it? Somewhere by a tiki bar."

Sherry wondered if her neighbor hadn't been into his bottle of port this early in the morning.

"Here's the deal," Sherry said, wanting to keep it light. "We land in Kingston, take a quick cab to a hospital, I'm in and out of a morgue and we are on the way to Ocho Rio for a night on me."

"Sounds fabulous, can I think it over?"

Brigham knew, of course, she was going with or without him.

"It's a very worthy cause, Mr. Brigham."

"I'm thinking," he said.

"You have thirty minutes and I'm calling a cab."

"I'm in," he said abruptly.

"Damned right, you're in," she huffed, "and Mr. Brigham?"

"Sherry?" he answered.

"Thank you for always being there."

Sherry replaced the receiver and sat in silence. She would never wish on anyone what she had gone through last winter—that darkest chapter of her life and a depression so prevalent that it had threatened to kill her. Only Brigham had saved her. Saved her life, for that matter.

She would make it a point to keep an eye on her friend from now on. If he was slipping into a funk and needed some diversion, she intended to be there to do something about it. She intended to save him this time.

16

The sun was setting on the beach at Boca Chica. Carol Bishop sat cross-legged drawing circles in the wet sand. Robert, her husband, was in Colorado Springs, or so their daughter Theresa had said on the phone last evening. Bob was spending more and more time on the road, even though the CEO could easily have remained at the home office in Chicago.

He was breaking down, she thought. He was tasking instead of enjoying the fruit of his labor. He was giving up on the life they had worked so long and hard to achieve. She thought about their Oak Park home, their dream home with the empty pink room where their younger daughter once slept. It wouldn't be long before he gave up on her, too, she knew. It had been a month since she'd been back to the United States. Not that there was anything she could do about it. Jill was somewhere on this island. She couldn't bring herself to leave Jill behind. Their lives, so fundamentally family-oriented before Jill had disappeared, had begun to dissolve before their eyes.

A Dominican radio station playing salsa wafted across the hot beach. Somewhere in the background another radio station broadcast weather and news from nearby Jamaica.

Carol was tanned nut-brown from a summer in the intense Caribbean sun. Her fingernails and toenails, once meticulously manicured, were clipped close, split and dirty with sand. She did little else these days but walk the city streets and marketplace where her daughter went missing and the shorelines along the beaches, in her threadbare sandals, showing flyers with her daughter's picture, speaking to anyone who would give her the time of day.

They called her *madre de la muchacha perdida*, the Lost Girl's mother.

It had been a season now since Jill disappeared. She would never forget that night. Not for as long as she lived.

The captain had arranged a quiet exploration of the ship. The crew made subtle announcements over the hundreds of speakers onboard. Staff cabins were searched by officers, retail shops were checked to see if Jill Bishop's guest card had been scanned, digital images were downloaded from cameras at embarkation ramps and restaurants and decks and casinos, assembled for future investigators to study. But three days later, not a trace of Jill remained beyond the morning she was filmed leaving the ship for Santo Domingo.

The FBI boarded the ship in Miami, but a day and a night of cold questioning left Carol still wanting real answers. She boarded a plane back to Santo Domingo and had not left the island since.

She heard laughter but did not look up.

Her daughter had been right here, right in this city of two million people, and no one saw her disappear? The answer was still here, she thought. Not back in the States or onboard the *Constellation*, where the charismatic Italian captain would be charming his current round of passengers.

". . . found in the waters off the eastern coast of Jamaica is reported to be that of a young Caucasian female. Sources inside the Jamaica Constabulary say that while the cause of death has not yet been determined, they are treating the case as a drowning. In other news, a gangland shooting in Spanish Town left . . ."

Carol looked for the source of the broadcast and saw an Asian couple fussing over a boom box between toddling children.

She got to her feet and looked around, unsure of what to do next. Then she started to run.

Tam-Tam Boy brushed flies from cloudy eyes with gnarled fingers that stank of fish and rotten eggs. He dipped them into a rusty Campbell's soup can, crouched over the body, and painted a yellow line down the center of the dead man's forehead, then across his nose and mouth, bisecting his face. He dipped the fingers again and continued down the dead man's chest across his stomach to his abdomen, where he painted a yellow circle around a black bullet hole. Tam-Tam Boy patted the ground until he found a sardine tin of coagulating blood and used it to make red fingertip dots inside the circle.

The dead man was naked except for a pair of gray briefs. Tam-Tam Boy set down the tin, picked up one of the dead man's hands, and threw back his head, eyes staring vacantly toward the stars. A man opposite Tam-Tam Boy beat on an old goatskin drum. Three hounsis began to rise and dance, shaking their bodies, white dresses billowing, scarves knotted on top of their heads. They stamped about barefoot in the sandy dirt around the fire, heads rolling from side to side. One shook a gourd-shaped rattle filled with dried corn.

"Do you see him?" the woman sitting next to Tam-Tam Boy asked. "Is he going to come tonight?"

She was wearing a green Nike sweat suit and red-and-white Reeboks. She wore cheap costume bangles on one wrist and a fake gold chain around her neck. The old houngan ignored her, placing one hand over the circle of red dots on the man's stomach, pressing fingers into the bloated skin. Firelight reflected off his oily black face as he concentrated, eyes creamy white and opaque. His free hand clutched the hand of the dead man.

"Pioche lukin atchu now," Tam-Tam Boy said. "Him tell mi seh yuh look for a picture of a statue."

"Picture?"

The old man cocked his head to one side, as if straining to hear. "Pioche is looking at a picture. A man in front of a statue, " he said slowly.

The woman looked confused. The only picture of a statue she knew about was the one of Pioche's father, Amaud. The statue was Christopher Columbus and it stood in the harbor of Port-au-Prince before being torn down and thrown in the harbor by mobs in 1987. But why would her dead husband care about a picture? Why now?

The woman in the sweat suit looked on helplessly. "Who did this, Tam-Tam Boy? Who killed my husband? Why did they desecrate his body?"

"Di white ooman she call out to im. She is in a cage. She want im to take a message for er. She want im to help er escape. Pioche try to help her escape. Di ooman with Baron Samedi's mark on her face."

Tam-Tam Boy removed the hand that was rubbing the dead man's stomach and held it out.

"Pioche gave the ooman some ting, but di one-eyed man is coming, di one-eyed man see im," Tam-Tam Boy cried out in a strange high voice, "run, run." The old man shook his head. "But Pioche not run. Him say lef di ooman alone, but di one-eyed man he point di gun and Pioche be shot dead."

Tam-Tam Boy shook his head violently, eyes growing wider; he squeezed the hand harder and tears formed as he spoke. "Now Pioche see a young girl, di child with di long white pin in er hair. She is standing in front of a blue shantee, wit bricks all around on di ground."

"It is our daughter, Yousy," the woman in the Nike sweat suit said.

The woman began to bawl, but Tam-Tam Boy suddenly put a finger to his ear. "Shhhhhh!" he silenced her, grabbing her arm and pointing across the fire. "Pioche want to talk to you!" he cried out. "Pioche is here!"

One of the hounsis froze mid-dance, clutching her stomach exactly where Pioche had been shot. A moment later she stumbled forward, pivoting her hips until her torso was nearly horizontal with Pioche's widow's face, pointing down at the ground in front of her.

Pioche's widow looked up, tears running down her cheeks into the neck of her sweat suit.

"I wait with Papa Ghede by the gates of the cross-roads." The voice of the hounsi was deep and sounded something like her husband, Pioche, had sounded in life—before he was shot dead and his body dumped in front her house in the village. Pioche's widow looked up at the spirit of her undead husband and his eyes looked just like Pioche's eyes looking back.

"What mean you say about the picture, Pioche? What mean you say about your father, Amaud?" she cried out to the hounsi.

"Me waiting by the crossroads." The hounsi wagged a finger at her. "Me waiting with Papa Ghede."

The widow swooned.

Tam-Tam Boy picked up a cloth bag and sprinkled salt over the dead man's stomach. Then he spread his spindly arms and stood. "It be done for tonight," he said.

"What does he want?" The widow got to her feet, wiping dirt from her sweatpants, running to catch up to the old houngan. "What does it mean?"

The old man turned. "Where is the statue picture?"

"Over our bed. Pioche's father, but he is long dead," the widow said.

"This is what Pioche wants you to see," the houngan said, shaking his head and setting out across the path once more.

Tam-Tam Boy nodded. "Look behind the picture and tell no one what you found, not for a year and a day or it be gone away from you."

He turned and looked at her.

"Pioche will be back four more nights but then he must make the journey with Papa Ghede."

He held out a trembling hand, the distant firelight reflecting off his cloudy eyes.

The widow fished gourds out of an old kerchief, pushed the money into the houngan's hand, and blew her nose noisily, stuffing the kerchief back in a pocket. "Thank you." She squeezed the old man's hand. "Thank you."

Wild dogs slinked through shadows along the path between sloped shanties. The smell of dead animals mingled with sweat and a splash of Old Spice someone gave to the houngan as payment for a remedy. The houngan shuffled along the dusty path to a rickety shanty. Pioche's widow went the opposite way, down a steep hill to a narrow dirt road.

A young man and long-haired girl waited for her by a rusting white Toyota. Behind it a sprinkle of lights marked the village of Tiburon on the coast.

It had been five days since her husband's body had been tossed in front of their house. She remembered the morning the crowd gathered around her door, slowly parting for her to see the body in the street. Pioche lay on his back in the decaying palm fronds, flies swarming the slippery entrails protruding from his stomach. A small pencil and paper were stuffed in his mouth. A poppet in the shape of a man had been pinned on his chest. The casing of an expended bullet had been pushed into the fabric of the doll's stomach.

Hettie had kept her daughter in the house all that day. Policemen did not arrive until late the second day. They seemed nervous and wore ill-fitting uniforms. By then Hettie had brought Pioche into the house and removed the paper and pencil from his mouth, undressed him and cleaned the dirt and blood from his body.

Neither of the policemen touched the body or examined the bullet wound closely; they didn't seem to care about the pencil and paper that Hettie had taken from his mouth. They didn't touch the voodoo doll with the bullet casing in its stomach. There would be no arrests. Pioche, like all Haitians it was presumed, had invited his own death.

Hettie waited another day before she got up the nerve to leave the house, before she could convince herself that whoever had done this to Pioche was not coming back to kill her or her daughter. That was when she asked her cousin's boyfriend, Etienne, to put Pioche's body in the back of his pickup truck and take it to the old houngan Tam-Tam Boy. Perhaps, she'd thought, Pioche's body could be cleansed of the desecration and that way she might protect his soul after death and his body from being exhumed as a zombie.

Hettie remembered the aid worker from World Freedom who came to see her that night, offering her condolences and asking if Hettie knew where Pioche had been working when he was killed. Everyone in the village knew that Pioche went away to work in the mountains, sometimes for days at a time. Work was very difficult to come by in Haiti, virtually impossible for men without skill, but men such as Pioche were sought out now and then to work in the remote mountain enclaves that belonged to the rich. There were many rich people in the mountains; the homes of former plantation owners had been turned into weekend retreats for the latest government officials and there were estates of textile manufacturers who operated sweatshops in Port-au-Prince and drug barons with their hidden airstrips and convoys of trucks that rumbled along dusty roads to meet the go-fast boats at night along the coast. Pioche was even called to the cities on occasion, to help with bridges and demolish buildings for the government.

People in Haiti didn't brag about where they worked or how much they earned. Talk was dangerous in Haiti. You went about life minding your own business and in doing so spared yourself and your neighbors from harm. Which was why Pioche had been adamant that Hettie not speak of what he had told her about the women he saw and why Hettie had kept her mouth shut even though the World Freedom aid worker seemed so insistent to know.

Four more nights and Tam-Tam Boy would give her Pioche's body for burial. And every night until then she would ride with Etienne to the houngan's temple on

Morne Mansinte. She needed Tam-Tam Boy to convince Pioche's soul to enter the holy ground.

Hettie was angry with Pioche for trying to help the women. Why would he risk his life and those of his family over someone he didn't even know? Why couldn't Pioche take his own good advice about minding one's business?

Nothing seemed quite clear to Hettie since Pioche's body was found.

She got into the pickup and strained to pull the rusty door closed. The frame squeaked on the axles and road dust filled the cab through holes in the floorboard. One of the truck's headlights was centered on the narrow mountain road, the other shot up against the bank, illuminating the tangle of roots eroding beneath a half dozen dilapidated shanties.

She thought about Pioche's father. Pioche never spoke of him, but many times she had seen him take the picture of his father down and cradle it in his lap. She didn't intrude; she often reflected on her own mother's picture at night when her husband and daughter were asleep. She'd thought that Pioche must have simply been doing the same. Now she had to wonder if the picture meant something else.

Etienne dropped her and her daughter at their house before midnight. He would be going to the market in Port-à-Piment the following morning to sell plantains. Tomorrow her daughter, Yousy, would go with him, her first day back at the Jesuit school since her father had been killed.

Hettie entered the dark house and felt its emptiness. Something about it had changed.

The picture of Amaud wasn't a very good one, a yellowing Polaroid taken on his sixtieth birthday in Port-au-Prince. Amaud had worked as a domestic for a wealthy Canadian family. He'd died from a stray bullet during the riots, the same year the picture was taken. The frame around it was several inches too large, crudely made of bamboo and glass. A patch of old cloth was tacked across the cardboard backing. It was the thickness of it that Hettie noticed first. The padding between the glass and cardboard was wide enough to hold fifty pictures of Amaud.

But it wasn't pictures she found inside. It was money, nearly five thousand dollars. Pioche had been rich! She was rich!

She turned to look out the window: purple sky above Morne Mansinte. It was darker at night than it had ever seemed in her childhood. The poor were now too poor even to burn firewood. All the trees, even the fruit-bearing trees, had been cut for the few measly dollars' worth of charcoal.

In the mountains, however, the rich owned generators large enough to light a whole village. Haiti was like that, a country of contradictions, the rich as unproportionally rich as the poor were unproportionally poor. One in every eighty thousand lived in opulence, which seemed wrong enough without adding to the fact that they felt entitled to murder the poor.

Pioche hadn't had to die. All those years Pioche had been sitting on a fortune. Why would he have worked so hard to live in such squalor, to eat fish and fruit off the trees when they could have lived in Les Cayes in virtual splendor?

She turned and looked around the little house, at the image of President Préval on the wall where it could easily be seen. It wasn't really a photograph but was cut from the front page of the *National Catholic Reporter*, one that Yousy had brought back from the marketplace in Port-à-Piment.

She turned the picture of Amaud over and put the money back in. Then she laid it on the bed and sat next to it.

This had been her own mother's home, destroyed by countless hurricanes over the years and rebuilt by the fishermen who had been regenerating this village since slaves won their freedom from Napoleon. The collective memories of those fishermen, her mother, herself, were all a bittersweet muddle of happiness and pain. Haiti was as wondrous as it was cruel, its people the same. In the corner on an overturned bucket was a stack of Yousy's schoolbooks. Hung from a string on the wall where her daughter slept was a poster from USAID. Yousy's dream was to attend college in the United States. It had been her dream ever since she had begun to attend school with the Jesuits in Port-à-Piment.

USAID offered a scholarship program to Haitian children turned sixteen.

Hettie looked at the poster until she could no longer see for her tears. Then she smiled.

Pioche had been thinking about Yousy.

He had been saving the money to send Yousy to America.

There were two meetings in Contestus that evening and the staff was visibly shaken. Men with strange accents spent the afternoon walking the floors, moving from room to room with countersurveillance equipment. Some watched monitors on laptops supported by neck straps. Others used wands to sweep air-conditioning ducts, electrical plugs, lamps, telephones, and panels over light switches. An equal number was combing the grounds with portable microwave dishes.

Bedard had found plenty to worry about this last week. He was thinking he had already stayed at Contestus too long.

He refused to have a conversation with anyone, even the most trusted of his staff, until the castle was swept for listening devices. One could never be sure if one of his staff had left a little present from some intelligence agency with a spy satellite or an offshore fishing trawler crammed with eavesdropping equipment. One could never be sure of anyone's motives for doing anything these days. Not in Haiti. It was a dog-eat-dog world.

Perhaps the incident at sea with Jill Bishop was an accident. Perhaps no one had intentionally plotted to draw attention to him. Perhaps he was unnecessarily paranoid and his fear that the Americans were always just around the corner was all in his mind.

They had gone over this months ago in a meeting at his estate in Colombia. Thiago Mendoza was lying dead in his casket in Barranquilla and the cartel was introducing Mendoza's son Sergio to the principals of the organization. There was nothing to suggest that Bedard's operations were receiving more or less attention from law enforcement in the last year. No unusual boardings or heightened inspections of his cargo ships around the world. Nothing even to suggest there might be subterfuge in the ranks, a condition he credited entirely to the alarming reputation of his chief of security, Matteo, and soldiers, all former members of the Tonton Macoutes. But there was tension in Colombia following Thiago Mendoza's death, and Bedard had the castle swept twice before Thiago's son Sergio set foot on Haitian soil. The young man had wanted to see this aspect of his father's business as well. How and where the cartel's women, trafficked from Eastern Europe, were being introduced to the West.

And Bedard wanted to make certain that Mendoza's Colombian rivals didn't take advantage of the opportunity. Bedard wanted to ensure he didn't go down in history for hosting the event that killed the world's twenty-second-richest man.

A steel door swung open and Bedard walked in. For all his years Bedard could instill fear when he entered a room.

He still wore the black accouterments of the Tonton Macoutes and a pearl-handled Colt .45 on his hip. He removed the thick-framed opaque sunglasses so long associated with the Tonton Macoutes—it was no lie that Papa Doc had wanted his secret police to wear sunglasses day and night to fuel rumors that they were dead men brought back to life as zombies; that behind the dark glasses their eyes had no light.

Bedard laid the glasses on the table. He wanted these men to look into his eyes. He wanted them to see his anger. His dark hands trembled with it. A pale scar, which halved one cheek, began to slide back and forth as he clenched and unclenched his jaw.

Matteo, Bedard's bodyguard, pulled the door closed behind. Bedard, tall and menacing, looked down at them with his one good brown eye. His white eye, the glass eye, never moved. At last he took the seat at the head of the table. The smell of his sweet cologne settled around the room.

The pudgy middle-aged man sitting nearest him was sweating streams from his brow that coursed behind his ears to drench his collar. He was nervous and the smell of Bedard's skin made his stomach sour. He reached for the water pitcher, hoping he wouldn't get sick, but then thought better of it, retrieved the hand, and placed it on his lap. To have water might be construed by Bedard as a sign that he felt at ease, and this evening Philippe felt anything but.

A plasma screen on the wall came to light playing a taped news broadcast showing a reporter standing in front of an old brick building in the streets of Kingston, Jamaica.

Matteo turned up the volume with a remote. ". . . Sources from the Jamaica Constabulary have confirmed that the body of a young Caucasian woman was recovered in the Jamaica Channel this morning. Jamaica Defence Force launches have been sent to check the area for possible wreckage due to a boating accident. Police say a photograph is forthcoming. Meanwhile, Scotland Yard will take a second look into the murder investigation of soccer coach Bob Woolmer, found in his hotel room at the Jamaica Pegasus last . . ."

The screen went black.

Bedard's nose glistened with oil. His ears were sharply pointed and seemed too small for his body.

"Someone speak!" he shouted. Veins continued to pulse along his neck and raised the temples on either side of his forehead.

"She jumped, patrón," the man sitting next to him said. "I couldn't stop her."

Bedard's head swiveled to the old security guard. "Jumped," he repeated. "Jumped you say, Philippe?"

The security guard nodded vigorously. "There was nothing I could do, patrón."

"Who opened the door, so she could . . . jump?"

Bedard asked. "Are you telling me she opened the door of the airplane herself?"

Philippe sighed, clasped his hands before him as if in prayer, and raised and lowered the mass of twisted fingers and fists. "It was hot, patrón, and I opened it to keep her from being sick."

Bedard snapped open a gold cigarette case and removed an American cigarette.

"Is that right?" Bedard put the cigarette in his mouth, waited for Matteo to step forward with a lighter and light it.

"When it is hot in the airplane you open the door?" Bedard looked at the pilot, then back to Philippe.

The pilot sitting at the opposite end of the table looked at his hands and finally shook his head.

The security guard squirmed in his seat, but did not speak.

"What happened then?" He directed the question to the pilot.

"He was playing with her, Commandeur."

"Playing?" Bedard repeated, looking at the security guard, then back at the pilot.

"Scaring her, Commandeur. Philippe wanted her to strip. He told her he would throw her out of the plane if she didn't strip."

Bedard raised a hand to silence the pilot, turned to face Philippe.

"Why don't you tell me the story, Philippe? What were you doing with the girl?"

The old guard shrugged and exhaled a great sigh as he looked up at the ceiling. "I just wanted to see her body."

"You wanted to see her body?" Bedard repeated.

The guard nodded. "I was only playing with her a little, patrón." Philippe used the thumb and finger of his right hand to demonstrate how little.

There was a sound, a human growl.

"But she is dead," Philippe said, holding out the palms of his open hands. "She cannot tell anyone anything, patrón. I will pay you for her." He tried to smile, the salt of his sweat stinging his eyes that he dared not reach for to wipe or dry.

"You will pay me," Bedard repeated flatly. The smell of his skin seemed to ripen with his agitation. "Do you know what she is worth, Philippe?"

Philippe shook his head sadly.

"Fuel the plane," Bedard said to the pilot menacingly. "You will take Philippe to the compound in Santa Marta."

Bedard turned to Philippe. "You will stay in Colombia until the rest of us arrive."

Philippe looked around the room, unsure of himself at first, then a broad smile formed on his face and there was an audible sigh of relief. He leaned forward to shake Bedard's hand, wet shirt peeling noisily from the back of the leather chair.

"Yes, patrón, thank you, patrón."

Bedard ignored the guard's outstretched hand and

rose from his chair. "Wait upstairs," he said to Philippe, and the pilot and the grateful man nearly ran from the room.

When they were gone, Bedard turned to his bodyguard.

"What do you wish me to do, Commandeur?"

"Go with them, Matteo. When you are off the coast of Colombia, throw Philippe from the plane. Then come back to Port-au-Prince and look into this matter of the colonel."

"Yes, Commandeur."

"How soon until the explosives are set in place?"

"We began drilling again this morning. The new man says we will be ready in three days."

"Make it two and put jet-boats in Tiburon harbor. I want them armed and ready to move."

Sherry Moore gripped the arms of her seat as the Air Jamaica flight bounced along the runway, turbines reversing thrust to break the jet's speed. She might have been grateful to know she'd missed seeing the skeleton of a burned-out DC-9 pushed off into the jungle at the end of the tarmac.

"You should feel quite at home, I suspect," Brigham growled, reaching for the computer bag between his feet and turning on his cell phone.

"Home?" Sherry asked.

"The temperature, the goddamned ninety degrees."

She smiled. He was talking about the temperature in Kingston, of course, the stewardess's announcement a minute before. Sherry loved the heat, actually flourished in it, if such a thing were possible.

They taxied for a minute, then coasted to a ramp outside customs.

Twenty minutes later they were streetside and getting into the back of a marked taxi.

"The chapel at the University of the West Indies Hospital." Brigham's face was beaded with sweat, his arms sticking to the dirty plastic upholstery. The radio was blasting reggae. A stick of incense burned from a clip on the dash. The smell was sickeningly sweet.

"Our man will meet us at the hospital chapel, the Mona campus; he says we won't attract attention there."

"What does he sound like?" she whispered cautiously, but the music was so loud that the driver could not hear.

"Jamaican," Brigham said flatly.

"Well, he must be an important Jamaican"—Sherry ignored Brigham's grumpiness—"if he's trying to avoid the press."

Brigham had to laugh. "I think he was worried about you, my dear."

Sherry put her head against the seat rest.

In fact she had been thinking about the press this morning. She couldn't leave her driveway without telephones ringing around Philadelphia and everyone wondering where she was going.

She wore frameless sunglasses and a white baseball cap with the bill pulled low over her forehead. Sherry didn't use a walking stick unless she was alone or on unfamiliar ground, so it wasn't always immediately apparent she was blind. Adding to the effect, she was fit and quite agile on her feet, and while she couldn't rely on it entirely, Sherry was making small advances in echolocation, a means of determining her direction of travel by listening for the returning echoes off objects around her.

The cab dropped them in front of the university chapel. A walkway led them from the street to a trio of great arches and the welcoming shade of a portico.

A man stepped from the shadows when they appeared and extended a hand. "Miss Moore"—he smiled—"I am Inspector Rolly King George."

Sherry also smiled and took the hand. "Thank you for meeting us, Inspector. This is my friend Garland Brigham."

Brigham nodded and grabbed the Jamaican's fist.

"Please call me Rolly," the inspector said. "I have a car at the curb and we haven't much time. There is a woman at the morgue who wishes to see the body and the prime minister herself has asked that she be given access. She is the American woman, Carol Bishop."

"Carol Bishop is here on the island?" Sherry asked, surprised.

"She has been living in the Dominican since her daughter went missing last spring. When she heard on the news we pulled a young woman's body from the water she took the next flight."

Sherry nodded. Everyone knew the Jill Bishop story.

"Is there any chance it's her?"

"Her face is badly marred, Miss Moore, she hit the water at over a hundred miles an hour, but yes, there are physical similarities. Body weight and hair color."

"Does the press know she's here?"

"No, Miss Moore, I took precautions, just as I reasoned I should not meet you at the airport." The inspector sounded apologetic. "It is why I didn't want you to go through the front doors of the hospital. No one knows the body is here, only the people in pathology and us."

"What if it is her?" Sherry asked. "You know what will happen if this is Jill Bishop in your morgue."

Brigham knew what she was thinking, that this was about to turn into a media circus and she had no desire to be caught in the middle.

"You understand, Inspector, that if Mrs. Bishop identifies the dead girl as her daughter the FBI will get involved. There will be nothing I can do here. The FBI won't let me within a mile of her."

"What will be, will be." The inspector nodded. "But you have talked to Helmut Dantzler?"

"Yes, and he wouldn't have anticipated this either. He would never have sent me here if he thought there was a chance the woman might be identified so soon."

"No offense meant, Miss Moore, but I am surprised he sent you here at all. Helmut Dantzler does not strike me as the kind of man that would contemplate the supernatural."

"Perhaps Helmut Dantzler is more complicated than you realize," Sherry said.

"But you are even more complicated, I am told," George said.

Sherry shook her head, smiled. "I don't know what

you heard, Inspector, but I'll be happy to clear up any misconceptions. What I do is very simple. I try to see what someone was thinking about in the seconds before they died. Sometimes I can do this, sometimes not. To be frank, Inspector, I told Mr. Dantzler I wouldn't be hopeful that someone free-falling to their death would be thinking about old memories. I'm not saying they wouldn't, I'm just stating the obvious. I don't know what her state of mind was when she came out of that plane, but one could assume it was consumed by terror."

The halls of the hospital were cool. Rolly King George led them through corridors to an elevator that descended into sublevels. They crossed an entire wing to a door where he asked them to wait. "It is a private waiting room, a chapel for relatives," he said.

He left them there to meet Carol Bishop.

Brigham marched in circles until Sherry made him stop. Twenty minutes later the inspector opened a locked door.

"Mrs. Bishop has identified the body, Miss Moore. It is indeed her daughter," he said solemnly, "and I am sorry you came all this way for nothing."

Sherry was silent.

Brigham stood. "Well, you are about to become one very busy man, Inspector George. We can find our own way out."

The inspector hesitated a moment. "I told Mrs. Bishop you were here in the hospital, Miss Moore. She asked me why. I explained as best I could. She asked me if you would stay a few more minutes so she could greet you."

Sherry didn't know what to say, but she felt Brigham's disapproving eyes on her.

The inspector, still holding open the door a few inches, looked to Brigham and raised a finger. "Please wait. Just a little while longer."

"We'll be here," she said, looking up toward Brigham. "Go and tend to Mrs. Bishop, Inspector."

The door closed and Brigham turned on his heels. "I'm giving him fifteen minutes, then I'm getting you the hell out of here. This whole thing is going to explode into a media extravaganza and you very well know it."

Fifteen minutes later Brigham was still pacing the floor when they heard footsteps and the doorknob turned.

"Miss Moore, Mr. Brigham, this is Carol Bishop," the inspector announced, ushering a woman into the room and pulling the door closed behind her. The inspector stepped back while everyone shook hands.

"Please sit," Carol Bishop said to Sherry. Brigham moved to a corner with the police inspector, letting the women sit next to each other.

Carol put her hands on her knees. "I don't know quite where to start," she said softly. Brigham saw that her eyes were swollen. Her hands trembled, fingernails digging into the skin beneath the hem of her shorts.

"I have two daughters," she said.

Sherry noted that she used the present tense.

"Theresa, my oldest, is in law school at the University of Michigan. Her classes are in session and she's been quite busy before the midterm break. I know Theresa misses her sister, but they were two very different people, Theresa always so serious and Jill so idealistic. She liked art and music, Bob and I were worried that she would drop out of school and join the Peace Corps or something equally stupid." She laughed a little hysterically. "She was constantly taking up causes and raising money for this group or that, volunteering at crisis centers, telethons, walkathons, you name it and Jill did it. She was one of life's optimists. The kind of people who believe they can make a difference. I didn't know until she went missing, and mostly from her sister, Theresa, that Jill was feeling the pressure we were putting on her over school. How silly we were in hindsight. How fucking silly." She stamped a foot hard against the floor and bit down on her lower lip.

Carol Bishop leaned forward in her chair, sunbrowned elbows on her knees, rough hands wringing as she spoke. Brigham thought she looked like a shipwreck survivor that had been found long marooned on some island.

"My husband travels and we don't talk so much anymore." Carol Bishop's look was one of resignation. "He needs to know that I found our daughter, of course, but not this very minute, not just yet. There are other things that matter more to me now. There are things even more important than grieving."

Carol leaned forward, knees close to Sherry's.

"Inspector George told me about you." Carol Bishop made a face. "I mean, certainly I know who you are, but I never expected to meet you under the circumstances."

Sherry held her tongue, not knowing where this was going.

"The FBI hasn't spoken to me in two months." Carol smiled. "I only get excuses from them these days. When I call to ask if anything's changed they tell me the case agent is out of the office. You know how it gets when all the leads go cold. They know she isn't coming back, they know . . ." Her voice got shrill and then faded as tears began to fall. Carol used the back of one hand to wipe her cheeks. "You really can't blame them. I mean, what can they say to me anyhow?"

She thumped the heel of her hand against her knee.

"But I was right about what happened in Santo Domingo. Something bad did happen to Jill in that marketplace. And now that I've seen her lying here looking like she does, I know that something bad was happening every day since."

Carol started to bawl. Brigham pulled tissues from a dispenser and handed them to her.

Carol dabbed her eyes, looked up at the ceiling; her eyes glazed over, she was somewhere else for a moment, not there. Then she cleared her throat and crushed the tissues in a balled fist.

"I know I'm not making myself clear"—she looked at Brigham, then at the inspector—"not making sense to any of you, but you see I can't just go back to the United States and forget all of this happened." She shook her head. "I can't go back to living with what has happened to my daughter. My husband might be able to do those kinds of things. He's a move-along kind of man. He would remind me that we have another daughter to care for, that we have our own lives to think about, he would say that life does go on."

Suddenly Carol grew tense.

"But life doesn't go on for Jill. Someone took that from her and when they did, they took it from me. They were saying that my daughter's life didn't matter anymore. That all those years I bathed and cuddled her and watched her dance and sing and grow into a beautiful young woman, didn't matter. That she was something they could brand with a tattoo and treat like an animal until they were done with her."

Carol Bishop's lips formed a strange smile; she dabbed at her tears. Brigham watched the transformation taking place, first around her eyes, the circles of exhaustion beginning to straighten into hard lines. The look of utter grief was replaced by something more primal.

She squeezed Sherry's hand, her jaw set, resolute. "But they were wrong." Her voice was barely audible, and Brigham, sitting by the air conditioner, found he was drawn forward in his seat to hear her speak.

"I want to know who did this to my daughter and I want them to share my pain. Then and only then will I attempt to go on with what is left of my life."

"Mrs. Bishop, the police can only do—" Inspector George began to say, but Bishop's hand flew up to silence the inspector.

"It isn't always about the law." She shook her head. "It isn't always about books and codes and borders." She looked around the room. "Jill was my daughter, my blood, my genes. My commitment to her childhood didn't end when she walked out the front door of our house and it doesn't end now because we happened to have left the confines of the United States. We are all human beings, for Christ's sake."

She looked at Sherry Moore's face, seemed to study it a moment. "You came here because you thought you could help the inspector somehow. So I have a request to make, a favor to ask of you, Miss Moore. The FBI has had their opportunity. They have done what they could. Now, since you are already here and since you were going to do this thing before you knew who my daughter was, I would appreciate if you would go see her and tell me about my daughter's last moments on earth." She held on to Sherry's hand. "Would you please try to do that?"

Sherry looked her way for one long moment, trying to imagine the woman's face.

"Mrs. Bishop," she started, but Carol reached up and touched Sherry's lips gently with a finger.

"Before you say no, I am begging you, Miss Moore. You must have thought there was at least an outside chance you would learn something from my daughter's last seconds alive. You wouldn't have come all this way otherwise."

She coughed out a laugh. "I'm sure you don't get called every time some young woman is found floating in the Caribbean, which means there is already something I don't know. Something about her triggered a reaction. Something more than a body found in the sea prompted the inspector to call you. You know something I don't. All of you."

She sighed, looked around, meeting all of their eyes. "Don't you?"

"We were taking a very long shot, Mrs. Bishop," Sherry said.

Carol wasn't listening. She was still concentrating on Sherry's face. "It's the tattoo, isn't it? That's what was different about her. The tattoo means something special to you. Isn't that right, Inspector George?"

She turned to him. "Look how my poor daughter was beaten. Just look at her body. What happened to her before you found her? Why was she beaten before they dumped her in the water?"

Bishop sat back, a weary look on her face.

My God, Sherry thought. She doesn't know yet how her daughter died. She is probably under the assumption her daughter had spent many days in the sea.

Sherry looked at Inspector George. "You will be speaking to Mrs. Bishop, I assume? Officially, I mean."

"We haven't talked at all, Miss Moore. There is much to cover."

Carol Bishop looked at them, first at Sherry, then at Brigham, last at Inspector George. "What? What is it? What do we have to cover?"

"Do you mind?" Sherry asked the inspector. "If I tell her?"

"No, ma'am," the inspector said politely. "If you are sure?"

"Mr. Brigham, would you mind waiting outside with the inspector for a few minutes?" Sherry reached out to tug his sleeve. "Please, Mr. Brigham," she said.

Brigham stood reluctantly, George with him, and a moment later the door was closed.

"Mrs. Bishop, I will be frank with you, but I will not share things told me in confidence. I know you have waited a long time for this, to learn what happened to your daughter, and I think you should know sooner than later. But I warn you it will be hard to hear. You must be sure you are ready for this now. Would you like me to call one of the doctors? Perhaps to give you something."

Carol, hands clasped tightly together, rocked back and forth in her chair, "Now," she said. "Please tell me what you know now."

"Your daughter did not die of a beating, Mrs. Bishop.

Nor was she found floating in the water as the news reported. She was seen falling from the door of an airplane off the coast of Jamaica. Inspector George himself witnessed your daughter's death."

Bishop made a sound that Sherry had never heard before, animal-like, a cry of intense pain.

Then Carol tried to stand, but doubled over as if she had been punched in the solar plexus. She went to her knees.

"Mrs. Bishop!" Sherry came off her chair, reaching for her. "Mrs. Bishop, are you all right?" She tried to put her arms around the woman, but the wailing turned to a moan and Sherry heard her body hit the floor. She lay down next to her, holding her, rocking her back and forth.

Carol Bishop, she knew, was still processing the words, was no doubt conjuring images, and the horrible marks on her daughter's body would suddenly be making sense.

"Can you understand, Mrs. Bishop, why I might not be able to help you?"

Carol took a full minute, but then slowly nodded; she was still unable to get complete words out. The noises she made were inaudible.

Sherry waited. Waited until Carol finally turned and she felt the stale hot breath as Carol's face came near.

"Please go see my daughter. Please."

"Mrs. Bishop . . ." But then she stopped midsentence.

The woman was right. She had come all this way. There was no good reason to deny her.

"I'll do it," Sherry said. "I'll do it, Mrs. Bishop."

Sherry helped the woman up off the floor and then to a seat. She rapped on the door and the inspector walked in, thinking Carol Bishop looked catatonic.

"I'd like to see Mrs. Bishop's daughter," she said. "Can you take me while Mr. Brigham looks after Mrs. Bishop?"

The inspector hesitated. "Mrs. Bishop?"

"Yes," she said. "Take her. Take her to my daughter please."

"Of course," he said.

Sherry knew what Brigham would be thinking. That they should have gotten out of here before this turned into something else. Inspector George could hardly be expected to lie when the FBI began to inquire about who had been near the body before they examined it. But there was no leaving this woman without an answer. For Carol Bishop the pain was in not knowing what happened to her daughter.

"Right this way, Miss Moore."

The inspector led Sherry down the hall, opened doors, and guided her to a room.

"She is not well," the inspector said.

"She's not going to be well anytime soon." Sherry shook her head.

"Is there anything I can do to prepare you?"

"Just a chair," Sherry said. "I'd like to sit next to her."

"A moment," he said, excusing himself, and seconds later returned with a straight-back wooden chair.

"Do you want me to stay with you?" the inspector asked.

Sherry shook her head. "I'll be fine alone."

"I'll be right outside then." The inspector backed out the door.

When he was gone Sherry found the edge of the table and sat. It was a stainless-steel table, the cadaver lying level with her face.

She took a moment to be silent, to clear her head. She could still hear Carol Bishop's primal wail; it was not a sound you forgot. Not ever.

It mattered not how many morgues she'd sat in over the years, how many autopsy tables she'd rested her arm against, the sensations, the smells, the apparent sameness was anything but. Every hand was like the first hand she ever picked up. They all had a place in her mind, every one. They all brought a different memory to surface—the little boy in Luray, Virginia, the little girl in Norwalk, Connecticut. Their hands were as different as their faces would have looked. They formed a league of souls in her mind, and the memories of those souls included many of the monsters she held at bay in her cerebral zoo.

She reached across the table, fingers grazing the cool skin of the girl's hip, found a thumb, picked up the hand, and squeezed like Carol Bishop had done in the waiting room.

Then she settled in the chair and waited. . . .

. . . *a middle-aged black man, he was sitting cross-legged on the floor, a machine gun on his lap. He was wearing a dirty black T-shirt and grinning to expose a gold tooth; she saw a field of sparkling lights, she was reaching out to touch them, arms extended, palms open, a warm green wind in her face; she was sitting in front of a cake full of candles, a woman stood behind her, hand on her shoulder; a black cat balled up on a bed; a dome-shaped yellow car; a black man standing over her, he had one brown eye and one white eye that was lifeless; a dark-haired Caucasian woman, she was gaunt, her eyes sunken, hair tangled on her shoulders. She had a tattoo on her face, of a grinning skull wearing a top hat; an olive-skinned woman in a white blouse and gold-trimmed capris, a van, it was pink and full of clothing; the spires of a stone building, a castle-like building . . . in a jungle . . .*

Sherry dropped the hand and jerked back in her seat. "Oh, my God," she whispered.

She put her hands on her knees and bent over, taking deep breaths, the image of the castle foremost in her mind. She was there. Jill Bishop was there. That was the building. That was where Sergio Mendoza had seen the woman in the red room.

There was more, Sherry knew, more of Jill Bishop's memory to see. For the first time in her life, she didn't want to go on with it. She was afraid of what lay before her.

Minutes passed; her heart began to steady, at last, but ever so slowly she reached for Jill Bishop's hand. And took it again. . . .

. . . *a tabletop bar, a pretty young woman facing her, pink drinks with plastic palm trees, a gleaming white ship, a sandy-haired woman in a hammock; bright sunlight, the black man with the gold tooth is crouching now, waving his machine gun at her, she can see blue sky next to him, they are in an airplane, she rises, she is walking toward the man, she steps out into the light and reaches for the dazzling green glitter, something small and white, it is a boat rolling gently in the tide, rushing up to meet her . . .*

Carol Bishop spent a final hour with her daughter, sitting in the same straight-back wooden chair, holding the same cold hand that Sherry had held. She cried until she could cry no more.

She had been thinking about what Sherry Moore had told her.

It was unfathomable that her daughter could have willingly stepped out of an airplane. The only thing left to imagine now was, what had those men done to her to make her want to die? What had they made her do that was so awful she couldn't hang on another day?

Carol put her head in her hands, nails digging into the soft skin of her temples. She groaned again and then the groan turned into a growl.

She wondered what Sherry Moore could do with what she learned from her daughter. The FBI would give no credence to what Sherry claimed she saw. No one would attempt to identify the men her daughter saw or the dark-haired girl with a tattoo just like Jill's. And what about the castle in the jungle? The Bishops had traveled the world over with their children when the girls were growing up. Carol didn't recall ever seeing such a place. Certainly she would have remembered such a building herself, so the memory had to be fresh. Had to be her daughter's alone.

Sherry Moore and the inspector knew more than they were letting on. Carol was certain it was the reason Sherry was brought here. They knew something about that tattoo, but there was something else, something even more troubling to Carol. Sherry seemed different after she walked back into the waiting room. Something had happened in that room with her daughter. Sherry Moore had seen more than she wanted to.

Built of white marble, the Crystal House sat in stark contrast to the dark mountain jungles surrounding Port Antonio. It was a favorite of Europeans, who preferred its austere elegance to all-inclusive resorts full of screaming children and lotion-lathered tourists come to burn in the sun.

Guards stood by the gates at its entrance. It had a spiked iron fence around its perimeter, mostly hidden by jungle from the guests, who today were mostly German. From what Brigham could gather, they were entirely uninterested in the three Americans and their Jamaican friend at a breakfast table.

A blinking green lizard skittered across the dark slate floor, disappearing into the shadows under a heavy window drape. The hotel was dark inside and elegantly furnished. There was a distinct lack of emotion in the dining room, waiters almost mechanically serving breakfasts, busboys in starched jackets moving quietly between tables, silently removing dishes.

The sky had gone gray, clouds forming over the humid jungle on Green Mountain. Brief morning showers were typical before clouds moved offshore and evaporated over the sea, before Jamaica saw another dazzling Caribbean day.

Beyond the front gates Highway A-4 snaked along the jagged coastline, separating jungle from the cliffs that overlooked the green Caribbean. This side of the island was not heavily traveled. It was why the inspector chose the hotel for them to spend the night. It was unlikely that anyone would recognize either Sherry Moore or Carol Bishop.

"Orange juice for the gentleman?"

Inspector George shook his head, deferring to Brigham, who waved away the waiter.

Strands of daylight invaded the teakwood blinds, illuminating sterling pitchers of cream for the coffee and pewter bowls filled with brown sugar cubes. Carol Bishop sat at the table with her face pressed into her open hands. She had spoken little since they left Kingston last night.

Brigham had seen the victims of terrible trauma before and Carol Bishop had all the signs. He thought that she was quite aware of her mental state and was just trying to keep it together long enough to get through this ordeal.

The logical step would be to finish breakfast and part

ways with Carol Bishop and Inspector George. Brigham and Sherry would take the hotel's van to Port Antonio and fly back to Philadelphia. They would be home before the dinner hour.

Carol and the inspector would drive back to Kingston, where they would call the FBI and then announce her daughter's identification. Carol would likely hold a press conference and a flare of media excitement would ensue.

Except that Carol did not want to do that, and Sherry, who had called Helmut Dantzler this morning, knew it. Knew it and sympathized.

Brigham looked at Sherry Moore. He knew what Sherry had seen last night in the morgue. Brigham knew that Sherry could not leave it alone. She wasn't made up that way. Her thoughts were on a body lying eighty miles off the coast of Jamaica in Haiti. She was thinking there were three more days before the voudon man was buried. Before they entombed him with his own last memories of Jill Bishop, and the place she had been held.

A waiter came for the check. The dining room had all but cleared. Busboys were silently crumbing the tables, removing linens. A ray of sunlight pierced the dark room, slicing it neatly in half.

"This thing you know about my daughter," Carol Bishop said. She was looking directly at Inspector George. "I've not pushed you, not any of you, but you've never talked about the tattoo after I mentioned it. You called Miss Moore to come down here because of it, didn't you? So what does it mean, Inspector George? Who put that on her face? Do you know?"

She turned to Brigham. "Are there others out there like her? Is that why you brought Miss Moore here? Do you know where they are?"

No one answered.

Carol scratched at the skin on the back of one hand. "You were hoping to learn something from Sherry Moore, something only my daughter could know. You were hoping she could tell you where she had been, hoping she could describe something familiar. You would only have done that if you already had an idea where to look. If you already had an idea where to start."

Carol looked around the table, regarding each of their faces. "Once the FBI gets here you will be barred from investigating her death any further. I know how things work. I know that my daughter wasn't in Jamaica when she died. She was in international waters and I know that the rest of the Caribbean could care less about some missing girl from Chicago. So how long can you wait for the next girl to fall out of the sky, Inspector George? How many more girls have to die before you get another chance like this? Before some other mother's daughter ends up in a morgue with the devil's tattoo?"

Brigham knew what Sherry was thinking. That the man in the airplane with the gun was sitting down when

Jill Bishop walked out that door. He didn't push her out the door. She jumped of her own free will.

The kidnappers weren't supposed to let that happen; they had made a mistake, and it was only because of that mistake that they found Jill's body. If they hadn't, Jill would be God knows where right now and no one would ever have seen her again. Not to mention that if Inspector George hadn't been the policeman who found her, no one would have known to call Helmut Dantzler at Interpol, who in turn knew what the World Freedom aid worker heard in Haiti last week. Call it what you will, coincidence or divine intervention, it was an opportunity and Sherry would not pass up an opportunity. Not like this one.

"Sherry," Brigham said sternly. He saw it on her face. She was getting ready to leap. "Sherry . . ."

Sherry put a hand on his arm and patted gently to silence him. She turned to Carol. "Mrs. Bishop. Could I ask you to excuse us for a few moments? We'll meet you up on the veranda as soon as we're done."

Bishop looked at the three of them intently. Then she pushed back her chair and stood.

"Do the right thing," she said. Then she left the room.

Rolly King George picked up a fork and began to turn it over with his big hands. A minute lapsed and no one spoke.

"She sees it on your face," Inspector George said, without looking up.

Sherry looked at him. "I'm sorry?" she said.

"Ever since you saw the Bishop girl you have been preoccupied, something's been bothering you. Something you didn't expect to see. Perhaps even something that terrifies you."

George laid the fork down and folded his hands. "Helmut Dantzler didn't tell me the whole story either, did he? He knew more about the death's-head tattoo than he is willing to share and that is why he sent you here. So, Miss Moore. Do you intend to leave me here with Mrs. Bishop and her daughter and no answers as well?"

Sherry took a deep breath and shook her head. "No, Inspector, I don't. Mr. Dantzler asked me to come here because of something I saw a month ago. A man died in a mountain climbing accident in Alaska; at the time a lot of climbers were caught on the summit in a storm. It was believed there were survivors, but there was no way to know where they were, and I was asked to go there and try to help. When I took the dead climber's hand I saw a castle in a tropical jungle. The same castle I saw last night through Jill Bishop's eyes. I saw other things too, a woman being tortured. She had a tattoo on her face. The same tattoo that Jill Bishop wears."

"Why didn't Dantzler tell me this?"

Sherry ignored the question. "At the time I didn't know more than the dead man's name, Sergio Mendoza, a common enough Latino name though we presumed he was a citizen of the United States. The memory of a castle I witnessed when I took his hand could have been a memory from most anywhere in the world. I didn't know who to tell or where to start. Mr. Brigham has friends in our government so I asked him to look into it further. Just to make sure the dead man on the mountain wasn't connected to something they already knew about."

Sherry folded her hands. "It turned out the dead man on the mountain was the son of Thiago Mendoza, Inspector George."

"*The* Thiago Mendoza?"

Sherry nodded. "Mr. Dantzler called me shortly after he talked to you. You can see why, of course. I don't think men like Helmut Dantzler necessarily believe in people like me; it was more out of respect to Mr. Brigham that he did so, but he called nonetheless. But Dantzler knew something else," she said. "Something that made my story plausible. Interpol has come to believe the building I described is in Haiti, Inspector George."

"Why didn't he tell me?"

"He is protecting a source."

"A source," Inspector George repeated, his face contorting. He clenched his fists. "Some blackhearted snitch matters more to Interpol than a dead girl?"

"There was a very good reason, Inspector George." Sherry tried to soothe him. "The source is quite well known; the consequence of revealing it would put countless others in harm's way. If he were to rely on the source's word alone it would even outweigh the good we could do by saving these women. I spoke with Mr. Dantzler last night and told him about Mrs. Bishop's identification. You can imagine his surprise. I also told him what I saw in your morgue. He quickly voiced his desire that we allow Interpol and the FBI to take the investigation from here. But," she said emphatically, "I convinced him there is an imminent threat to anyone still alive in that castle and an opportunity before the FBI gets involved to locate it. The moment the FBI or Interpol approaches the Haitian government with this information, it will leak to the traffickers and any opportunity to save these women will be lost. I told him it is Carol Bishop's desire not to contact the FBI if there is something we can do to help first."

"Tell me," the inspector said curtly.

"A child in Haiti overheard her father talking about a place where women were being caged in the cellar of a building, women bearing the tattoo of Baron Samedi on their faces. This child told a humanitarian aid worker, who in turn contacted Interpol. You understand the ramifications of such contact from a nongovernmental organization."

George nodded, watching her.

"Two days later the child's father was killed and dumped in his village. A piece of paper was found in his mouth, a name was written on it. The child had no idea where her father was working, and Haiti is a big country."

Inspector George sighed, looked at the ceiling, eyes fixed.

"You can see Helmut Dantzler's dilemma, Inspector. When the FBI comes here, they cannot be told about this dead man in Haiti. To do so would be to compromise the nongovernmental humanitarians, one of Interpol's most valuable sources. Even if the FBI knew and believed the story, they have already tried and been denied access to Haiti to search for Jill Bishop."

"And what do you propose we do, Miss Moore?"

"The body in Haiti has not yet been interred, Inspector George. If you could stall identification of Jill Bishop another day, I could go to Haiti and attempt to reach this man before he is buried. If I could spend only a minute with him, we might learn where these girls had been. If we can cite a location, the government of Haiti could no longer ignore us. They would have to act because we could hold them accountable in front of the world."

The inspector laughed. "The whole world is going to listen because a blind woman told them so?"

"No, Inspector George." Sherry leaned forward. "Because Carol Bishop told them so."

The inspector looked at Brigham, then back at Sherry. "Explain?"

"Can you think of anyone in the Caribbean who can

attract more international reporters at a press conference than Carol Bishop? The world would focus entirely on what she said and on what Haiti's new president was going to do about it. They will barely care about how she came across the information. Once she says she was in Haiti and received information about this castle, they will be committed to act under international scrutiny."

Inspector George seemed to be contemplating the possibility.

"Except that everybody is forgetting just how dangerous Haiti is," Brigham interjected. "How can you even consider going there, Sherry? The country is virtually lawless."

"I need to do this, Mr. Brigham," Sherry said.

"He is right, Miss Moore," the inspector said. "If you were caught, the police would of no help to you. They might even turn you over to the traffickers."

"We won't be caught if we do this right now, and it is an opportunity law enforcement might never have again. No one is expecting us. No one knows about the child who overheard her father or the aid worker who sent the note to Interpol. No one knows that her mother identified Jill Bishop last night in a morgue in Jamaica. Two women traveling as tourists, we'll waltz in and out of Haiti and they will never know we were there."

"Y-you and Carol Bishop!" Brigham stammered.

"We take a bus from the Dominican. There aren't any terrorists trying to get into Haiti. Do you think they look at the passports of every white woman who crosses the border? They're up to their ears in Christian volunteers and nongovernment aid workers. People from all over the world are coming and going."

Brigham frowned. There was no stopping her now, he knew.

"The FBI will not be happy about delaying Jill Bishop's identification," Brigham said to the inspector. The argument was weak and Brigham knew it. He also knew what Carol Bishop would have to say about the matter. From what he'd heard so far, she'd jump in with both feet.

Brigham folded his arms.

Rolly King George studied Sherry's face. "I could state we have yet to determine a cause of death and that we are awaiting scientific evidence regarding identification. It would buy another day, but no more, Miss Moore."

She turned to Brigham. "If Carol Bishop wants to do this, we will need to leave for Haiti this afternoon."

Brigham nodded grimly. "And what of me? You want me to wait here and worry while the two of you are in Haiti?"

"We'll get a room in the Dominican Republic tonight and take a bus in to Pétionville in the morning. In Haiti we'll rent a car and be back in twenty-four hours. Really, Mr. Brigham. The fewer we are and the less we make of all this, the easier it will be. If bells are going to go off at a customs border crossing, it would be when a retired

United States Navy admiral's name is entered into their computer. Border policemen aren't going to check on a blind woman and her companion, no matter what their names are. Right now it is best I get upstairs and tell Carol Bishop what we know. It she's in, we'll need to get moving." Sherry stood. "Will you lead me, Mr. Brigham?"

Carol Bishop was adamant, as expected, about going to Haiti with Sherry.

Brigham found a *New York Times* and said he'd be in the air-conditioned lobby until they were ready to say good-bye. Sherry was beginning to think she'd made a mistake bringing him to Jamaica. She knew she had put him in an awkward situation and she knew that she worried him unnecessarily. It was the last thing she wanted to do, considering she brought him to Jamaica to cheer him up. She felt as though she'd need to make it up to him somehow afterward.

Sherry heard voices coming across the terrace: Rolly King George and Carol Bishop circumambulating the swimming pool. They were talking about an autopsy and how to handle her daughter's remains.

George sat down at the table with Sherry. "You are right about entering Haiti on the bus, they are careless checking passports at border crossings, but I checked and there is only one bus a day. It leaves Santo Domingo at noon tomorrow and arrives in Pétionville at 6:30 P.M. I called Helmut Dantzler and he has arranged for a

Colonel Deaken of the Haitian police to meet and escort you to Tiburon. No one checks outgoing flights, so you will be safe flying out of Port-au-Prince when you return. I will meet you with Mr. Brigham when you land back here in Kingston."

"We can trust the policeman?" Sherry asked.

"The colonel is reliable, Miss Moore."

"Then thank you, Inspector," Sherry said.

"May God go with you," he said.

Sherry met Brigham in the lounge before they departed. His mood was dark and there was nothing she could say that would change it.

"You have your cell phone?" he growled.

"Of course," Sherry said. Years before she had switched to a carrier with satellite coverage at Brigham's suggestion. The phone was invaluable to a blind person, especially in the kinds of places Sherry had been prone to visit.

"You have me in speed dial?"

"Yes," she groaned, like an overprotected child.

"I want you to listen to me, Sherry. Just listen, okay."

"Yes, Mr. Brigham, I am listening," she said.

"If anything seems at all wrong, anything at all, if you are the slightest bit uncomfortable about anyone or anything going on around you and you aren't free to talk, I want you to dial my number and hang up when it rings. You have GPS. I'll be able to find you."

Sherry nodded. She knew this was a serious conversation to Brigham and she didn't want to give the impression he wasn't taken seriously, though she was sure he was being overly dramatic.

"I will be fine, Mr. Brigham. There's going to be a policeman with us. What could go wrong? We'll be in Tiburon harbor tomorrow night and back here by noon the next day. I promise you, though. If anything is out of the ordinary, I'll call. In fact I'll call you when we reach Tiburon just to let you know we're safe. Deal?"

Brigham grunted.

"Please," she said. "Relax, Mr. Brigham. Enjoy the weather. Get into the ocean. Get a drink and watch the girls."

She took his hand in both of hers. "I'll be back in no time."

He nodded and she kissed him on the cheek and said good-bye.

The setting sun's light caught the face of Louis XIV, sitting horsetop in Place Bellecour. A tall rigid man carrying a leather satchel crossed the square, joining an American wearing a sports coat over a polo shirt.

"Graham, it's good to see you again." Dantzler extended a hand. "How was Saint-Exupéry Airport?"

"More like Tel Aviv every day," Graham said. "I miss the innocent days when there were no machine guns in terminals. You heard about Mogadishu?"

"A thousand dead and counting," Dantzler said.

"The European Commission should be concerning themselves about complicity in war crimes, or perhaps they think they are immune," Graham said. "The security adviser told their representative in Kenya the Ethiopians were violating the Rome statute."

"And the Red Cross is reporting the worst fighting in fifteen years. How do they keep doing this?" Dantzler waved a hand through the air. "Funding war criminals as peacekeepers. Doesn't anyone feel stupid down there?"

He stopped and squinted at the dying sun. "A warrant officer named Aleksandra Goralski was on assignment for the Polish National Police when she went missing in the Baltic harbor of Gdansk six months ago."

"Routine assignment?"

"Not at all. She was with the Polish Central Investigation Bureau looking into a corruption allegation about a customs commissioner."

"Jesus," Graham whispered. "That could be it. Do you have enough handwriting to work with?"

"Three words isn't much, but they're looking at it now. She has plenty of known handwriting from the police department they can compare it with."

"What can I do?"

"We've identified the ships that were in port when Warrant Officer Goralski went missing. I was hoping you could take a run at them."

"You're thinking if DEA might connect one of the ships to the Mendoza cartel?"

"DEA, ICE, FBI, I don't care who it comes from," Dantzler said.

"What about Bishop and Moore?"

"They're in the Dominican Republic, crossing into Haiti tomorrow at noon by bus."

"Do you see problems?"

"They're going to Haiti, aren't they?"

"What's the scenario?"

"Tourists bound for Tiburon harbor. It's a well-photographed location, quite beautiful, I'm told. They'll be in Pétionville outside of Port-au-Prince around six thirty P.M., which puts them in Tiburon by midnight, seven P.M. our time. You'll be back in Washington then?"

"I'm on the red-eye," the CIA man said.

Dantzler nodded. "I wasn't comfortable with them traveling alone, so I asked our contact, Colonel Deaken with the Haitian National Police, to meet them. He wasn't happy about Carol Bishop entering Haiti. He said it would cost him his job if he was connected to her."

"He must have considered the possibility that Jill Bishop was in Haiti."

"I'm sure the entire Haitian government did, but they weren't about to invite the FBI in for a look around while Bush is scolding Préval for getting into bed with Castro and Chávez. I'm sure the Bishop girl is still a hot topic in the palace."

"But he agreed?"

"As long as his name doesn't come up in any investigations. He'll meet them tomorrow evening in Pétionville and drive them to Tiburon himself. They should return before noon the next morning."

"Did you tell him how Jill Bishop was found—about the airplane, I mean?"

"He doesn't need to know."

"Well, I feel better, I must admit. It wouldn't do you or me any good if something were to happen to Carol Bishop in Haiti."

"The airplane that Jill Bishop came out of, nothing new?"

Graham shook his head, reaching for a handkerchief from his back pocket and blowing his nose. "I looked at the surveillance photos again, plenty of runways and DC-3s in the jungles, but nothing we haven't seen before. You know what air traffic control is like there."

"What if Moore pulls a rabbit out of the hat and they find a castle. What are we going to do then?"

"I don't know," Graham said, "but you've seen Carol Bishop on CNN. She pulls no punches. If they find anything she will not let us sit on it, not for a moment."

"Maybe we made a mistake calling in Sherry Moore."

"We" meant "he," Graham knew; Dantzler was the one trying to appease Admiral Brigham. How could he have known that Sherry Moore would insist on going to Haiti from Jamaica? She was just as headstrong as Bishop. The two of them together were the virtual powder keg ready to blow. "Too late for that, Helmut, admonish me later."

"You said you were looking for possible links to the Mendoza cartel."

Dantzler stopped and set his valise on a wall, opened it, and took out a thick legal envelope. He removed a file folder and began to read. "Patrick Dupont's great-grandfather made a fortune off rubber plantations in Haiti during the Second World War. The son was educated in the States and moved to Rio de Janeiro with his mother after a divorce. The old man left them a small fortune, enough to open successful nightclubs in

Ipanema, and this was long before the tourist boom of the sixties. The son still owns the original clubs—they were gold mines then and now—but he's also laid claim to a significant percentage of Brazil's private clubs, sex tourism destinations. I don't need to tell you Rio de Janeiro's rank in human trafficking."

"Dupont still has ties to Haiti?"

Dantzler nodded. "Properties. A villa in Pétionville, an estate west of Jéremie. We can't put him with Mendoza, but he has traveled to Haiti a few times this year."

"Who else?" Graham asked.

"ICE agents found two Canadian women in a crack house in Calakmul, Mexico, last year." He replaced the envelope and took out another, shook out the documents. "The women were kidnapped while backpacking in 2002. Typical story, rape, heroin addiction, they were forced to prostitute in brothels in the Yucatán Peninsula. They were found when Mexican nationals shot up the house looking for a kidnapping fugitive. Each of the girls had a red chili pepper tattooed on her breast. It designated them property of Angel Ochoa, the methamphetamine kingpin in Belize."

"Haiti's connection?"

"Ochoa networks meth through a company in Les Cayes that purports to export native art. So do a lot of other South American dealers. He's got a house there and a hangar for his Beechcraft."

Dantzler opened another file from the envelope.

"Former Tonton Macoute commander, suspected drug and small arms courier, named Jean Bedard."

"Tonton Macoutes," Graham repeated. "Papa Doc's secret police."

"Very bad man," Dantzler said. "Bedard has a glass eye. Remember the Bulgarian informant mentioned a one-eyed man in Burgas?"

"Go on," Graham said.

"Bedard's primary residence is in Colombia, near Barranquilla and Mendoza's estate, though he still has property in Haiti. He made tens of millions during the Duvalier years. His legitimate business is coffee and produce, but he's all over DEA's intel files on cocaine trafficking."

Dantzler handed Graham the envelope and closed the valise.

"All right." Graham sighed, tucking the envelope under his arm. "I'll see what I can do with them. Talk to you tomorrow."

"Tomorrow." Dantzler nodded. "Let's hope we all get through tomorrow."

22

The room was dark and heavy with cigar smoke. Brocaded drapes tied with golden sashes framed a vista of sun-scorched foothills. Bedard looked out over the Mornes, then down at the guards by the helicopter on the lawn of the compound. His neck was heavily bandaged and he'd picked up the habit of touching his throat each time he talked.

The chairs were tooled mahogany, covered with calfskin from Argentina and inlaid with gold. The Polish girl, Aleksandra, sat behind him on a leather divan. She was naked, hunched over, eyes barely open. Her hair and body were clean but black and blue, broken blood vessels nearly hiding the grinning death's-head tattoo on her cheek. She turned her head to look up at him, eyes hollow, glassy pupils large as dimes.

Bedard looked at her battered face and then pushed an intercom button by his knee.

"Yes, Commandeur?" The woman spoke in French.

"My bodyguard will be joining me for dinner."

"Oui," the woman said obediently.

Bedard looked down upon the shadows of the mansion's many spires.

There was a knock at the door.

"Commandeur?"

Aleksandra turned her head to squint at the man entering the room. She grinned foolishly, her mouth partially open, gums black and bloody. When she closed it again her lips shriveled around her mouth. She looked down at her naked body, shaking her head from side to side.

"What did you learn?" Bedard asked, putting two fingers across his Adam's apple. His voice was hoarse and low. He had been worrying about the FBI coming to Haiti ever since Jill Bishop was found at sea. Worried that once her body was identified, the Americans would convince Haiti's president to allow FBI investigators on the island.

"Interpol wants the colonel to escort two women to the village of Tiburon. They are both Americans."

Bedard's eyes widened. "FBI?"

Matteo the bodyguard shrugged. "I don't think so. Colonel Deaken says he is supposed to escort them to Tiburon harbor and back. The visit sounded unofficial, he said, but one of the women is Carol Bishop."

Bedard closed his eye, touching his throat lightly. "So they know."

"It would seem, Commandeur."

"Why Tiburon?"

"They want to visit the dead man Pioche."

"Which means they also know he was here." Bedard pounded the windowsill.

"If they knew, Commandeur, the body wouldn't matter to them."

Bedard nodded. "Perhaps they are looking for evidence. Something from the body, or maybe they want to question the widow. They are looking for something to lead them here. Who is the other woman?"

"Her name is Sherry Moore."

"She will be a forensics person, an FBI scientist," Bedard said. "When will they be here?"

"Late tomorrow night."

"Tell the colonel to do as they ask. We will meet them in Tiburon and remind the colonel that his wife and daughters are still our guests, if he needs further persuasion."

There was a knock at the door before it opened. A servant carried a tray to a table and placed the tray on the white linen. Food was dished, wine was poured, candles were lit, and the servant was gone.

Bedard walked to the dining table and picked up a glass of wine.

"Our last ship is approaching the Caicos Islands from Ukraine. It will meet a Colombian fishing trawler and transfer the women at sea."

"And then?"

"She will dock in Port-au-Prince, the hulls will be scorched and the ship and her papers will be turned over to a captain from Venezuela. Funds for the remaining nine vessels will be transferred to a Cayman account."

Bedard looked around the room, taking it all in. He would not miss Contestus. No more than he would miss the land he was born in. He had no regrets. Bedard had been a man for his time, a man for Papa Doc Duvalier's time. His edict, as simple as the dictator's political agenda, was to use the power of superstition and terror against the people. Plunder the nation's wealth, shock dissenters into obedience. He had been judge, jury, and executioner all wrapped up in one.

Now Papa Doc and Thiago Mendoza were in their graves. There was nothing left of Haiti for him.

Bedard walked to the divan, leaned over, and gestured to the girl. Aleksandra flinched, then looked up, trying to focus. She managed to use the coffee table to support her upper body and crawl off the couch to her knees.

"Eat," he told his bodyguard. He lifted his glass and drank from it, wine dribbling down his chin, staining the white bandage a bloody red.

"I'll join you in a minute."

SANTO DOMINGO, DOMINICAN REPUBLIC
The air conditioner was malfunctioning in the old Airbus A310. Hacking coughs ensured that a percentage of the ninety-odd passengers onboard were going to come down with a virus. Then everyone's luggage was

held at Las Américas International in the Dominican Republic at the insistence of a drug-sniffing dog.

When Sherry arrived at the Renaissance she knew immediately why Carol Bishop had chosen it. The public areas were busy. Marble walls echoed the mélange of languages from all over the world. There were Germans, Japanese, French, and Swiss. They moved in waves between the smells of eateries and perfume shops, casinos and spas. There was a rush of energy in the resort, bell captains calling out to cabs and pushing noisy luggage carts, car doors being opened and closed.

People who came to places like the Renaissance wanted nothing but to drink and gamble the week away. They wanted nothing of the world's bad news, and the hotel staff was trained to insulate them from it. No one would give them a second look in a place like the Renaissance. If it was supposed to be hiding, it was hiding before someone's very eyes.

Sherry parted with Carol at her tenth-floor room.

She showered and lay down on the bed, thinking how she'd let Brigham down. She knew of course he didn't approve of her going into Haiti and was only somewhat mollified when he learned the police colonel would be meeting and escorting them across the country. Brigham was the only person in the world whom Sherry would allow to dote over her, and that was because it was far more about pleasing him than her. Now she felt as though she'd abandoned him after talking him into coming along with her in the first place. Brigham had classes tomorrow. He would have to make special arrangements to have them covered. If only he was capable of relaxing and having fun.

Sherry smiled.

Fun . . . What a strange thing to think, but Sherry had never associated the word with Garland Brigham. They just didn't seem to quite go together. Brigham could be said to be content or even delighted, but never to be having fun.

Her thoughts led her to wonder what Brigham's former life in the navy was like. He'd retired only months before she moved into the house next to him, a stone behemoth on the shore of the Delaware River. He had obviously distinguished himself in the navy—you didn't make admiral quietly—but how she had no idea. She knew almost nothing of his life before retirement. It was difficult to imagine another side of him, a boy who drilled and bunked with other men and women, then a man in charge of whole navy fleets. He must have made friends who were important to him over the years, more than just his monthly breakfast club that he referred to as his old man's club.

When he invited her to the rare holiday party at the university, she would always find him in the library or out on the patio with a cigar, just about anywhere he could avoid the crowd. He might have commanded fleets but he was hardly what anyone might refer to as a mover and shaker. He was far too subtle for that. So then how had this quiet man ascended the ranks without being noticed?

She was nervous about going into Haiti. For all she had tried to make it sound harmless, she understood the gravity of the situation. Carol Bishop might not be so rational. Carol, who was driven entirely by thoughts of her daughter's last days, would have stormed the very building her daughter had been held hostage in if she had a clue as to where it was. Sherry's motivation to enter Haiti was more about the guilt she'd have to live with if she didn't. It would have been too easy to walk away. To let Interpol use Jill Bishop's body to try and find its own way into Haiti. Except that no one was going to do that. Not anytime soon. Certainly not in time to save lives.

It was ninety-two degrees when Sherry and Carol Bishop boarded a bus bound for Haiti. Sherry, in a rare reversal of character, made it obvious that she was blind, using her cane and Carol's arm way too much. Sherry wore a visor that was pulled low to conceal her forehead, and her long chestnut hair was braided into two unflattering pigtails. Carol Bishop wore a shapeless dress, with pockets, maps, and a cheap drugstore camera visible to anyone who looked. She had applied gobs of white zinc to her nose and cheeks, and her face was all but covered with a floppy straw hat. They looked the part of tourists, stumbling blindly wherever their passports took them, oblivious to any dangers around them.

The bus barely stopped for a minute at the border crossing; one policeman made a show of studying the driver's manifest while another yelled "Papers!" as he walked up and down the aisle. Papers were waved in the air, the two policemen got off the bus, and then they were moving again. Nothing was going to stop them now, Sherry thought. They were really going to do this.

Six hours later they were approaching the capital city. Haiti had the atmosphere of a country on the verge of civil war, alleys teeming with paupers, mobs roaming the sidewalks and streets.

They departed the bus and found Les Bonnes Nouvelles, a boutique hotel on Rigaud Street in Pétionville. Inside, Carol led them to a smoky pub with a dozen antique tables.

The room was nearly full. There would be doctors and volunteer aid workers, teachers and engineers. There would be reporters and diplomats and no doubt arms dealers and drug smugglers and cash couriers, and greedy politicians.

Carol scanned the room for anyone overly interested in them, but found no one. Not the well-to-do Africans with their whiskeys and Cuban cigars, not the white-haired grandma with her cigarette and plastic bag on the table in front of her. Not the sleek young Italians with their first-year-intern smiles. Not the smarmy middle-aged American wearing a Panama hat or the trio of Europeans with long cigarettes, one of them pressing his briefcase against the table leg with a shoe to ensure it never moved.

A man entered the bar through the lobby door of the hotel. He was dark-complexioned, in his mid-thirties, dressed casually in designer jeans and jeans jacket over a Miami Dolphins T-shirt. He looked around the room, then at their table in the corner. The man started making his way toward them.

"He's here," Carol whispered, rising to her feet.

"Colonel Deaken?" she asked softly, putting out a hand.

Deaken nodded, shook the hand, and walked to a seat in a corner facing the door. A fire exit behind him had a sign across it: SANS ISSUE.

"Mrs. Moore?" He reached for Sherry's hand.

"Miss," she said.

"I know of Mrs. Bishop," he said tiredly, "but you are?" His voice was friendly enough, but the question seemed abrupt.

"I'm a spiritual friend of Mrs. Bishop's."

"Spiritual," he said, looking at her oddly. "Like a priest or a minister."

"Something more mystical, I would say."

"And you want to meet the wife of the murdered man found in Tiburon."

"We were hoping to convince the dead man's widow

to let us pay our respects to the body," Sherry clarified. "As you know, this man might have seen Mrs. Bishop's daughter before he was killed."

"Our people are mostly voudon, Mrs. Bishop. If the body is being cleansed by a priest, they may not let you near it."

"We can at least convey our regrets to the widow."

"Yes," he said. "I told Interpol I would try.

"I'm sorry, Miss Moore," the colonel said hesitantly, "but you have a problem with your sight, yes?"

"I do," she said, cheerfully. "I am blind, Colonel."

Something told Sherry he already knew.

The colonel clasped his hands together. "The village of Tiburon is to the extreme southwest. There is one road to it from Les Cayes that follows our southern coastline. It is susceptible to mudslides and washouts this time of year, but the government keeps it maintained for the most part. President Préval has made a pledge to the advancement of safe tourism in Haiti." He hinted at sarcasm. "If we leave now we will reach Tiburon before midnight."

"Just let me use the ladies' room and make a call," Sherry said.

23

Aleksandra sat in the dirt, staring at the wooden door of
her cell. She was alone now. All the other cells were
empty.

They would kill her soon. She knew what the man
drilling holes was going to do. She had seen the demoli-
tion of bridges and caves in Afghanistan when she was
still in the army. She knew too that Bedard was enjoying all this.

The day she had arrived at the castle, Aleksandra had
managed to disarm one of Bedard's guards when they
were pulling her from the truck. She'd gotten an arm
around the man's neck and shoved the barrel of his pistol under his chin, and was backing away from the others toward the fence when Bedard stepped past his
men.

The others were immobilized, rifles wavering, not
knowing what to do.

Bedard simply pulled his pistol and shot the guard
who was shielding her. As the weight of the dead man's
body slipped from her grasp, the others raised rifles and
Bedard walked up to her and took the gun from her
hand.

Aleksandra counted that moment as the biggest mistake of her life. She should have shot him. If she'd known then what she knew now, she would have emptied the clip in him and gladly sacrificed her life doing it.

Bedard had her taken to the red room afterward, the first of many experiences in the chair in the months to come. The more she hid her pain, the more he seemed to enjoy torturing her. It became a contest of wills. A challenge of who was in control of the situation. He vowed to her then and there she would die a slow death. That he intended her to suffer the knowledge that he was master and he alone would choose the time and place she would die. She knew he enjoyed the idea of letting her think about the explosion.

As a young woman she could not have imagined this fate. None of them could have. It was too much to believe that men could be so evil.

She remembered the day Bedard shot the man in green pants and left him to die outside their door. Poor Jill Bishop had not known what was going on. Aleksandra was terrified that they were going to kill them both. But Bedard had read the note with her name on it—before he stuffed it in the dead man's mouth—and took her to the red room and strapped her to the chair. And he raped her every orifice with an electric cattle prod until she passed out.

She remembered the fiery sting of ammonia swabs stuck up her nose, her burning eyes. She remembered the unwelcome feeling of regaining consciousness, she knew that what awaited her above this plateau of semi-awareness was not good.

Then something felt as if it had detached from the center of her being, and it came rising through her pain-racked body toward her head, collecting all the good in her before it took flight and this thing she imagined was her soul, the best of her memories and talents and deeds.

Bedard shook her, laid his ear to her lips, thinking he might at last have gone too far. But the thing rising through Aleksandra was not her soul, it was her spirit, and with every ounce of remaining energy she lunged and sank her teeth into his neck, tearing flesh to get at his carotid artery.

Bedard managed to pull himself away in time, but she took meat and plenty of it. The one-eyed man stumbled away from her. She could sense his alarm, hands to his throat as he went for the door. It was an hour before he returned, his neck completely wrapped in heavy gauze. He had brought vise grips with him and she remembered screaming as he shoved harsh ammonia swabs up her nose and then began to take out her teeth one by one. Bedard did not want her to pass out again. He would not let her miss a moment of the pain. After that, Aleksandra was no longer allowed to stand in Bedard's presence. He made her crawl on all fours like a dog everywhere she went. He had given her to all the men in the compound. He told her he knew she wanted to die, but he was still master of her fate.

She was weak. She could only eat bread soaked in water.

But Aleksandra was still alive and Bedard was still wrong.

She did not want to die. She wanted to kill him.

It would have been so easy to let go. But every time she considered it she thought about Jill and the red-haired girl on the ship and all the other women who had endured this cellar. She knew there were bodies here too. She remembered the nights the trucks had come and gone. She had heard the women's whimpers and soft voices from the air vent in her cell. She had heard them being brought into the cellar and she had heard their screams from the red room. But she also remembered the nights when the trucks came and there was nothing but silence. The men unloading at the door, carrying their burdens deep into the recesses of the old castle's foundation. The next day the guards would come with bags of lime on hand trucks.

Whatever had prompted the traffickers to abandon this place, she couldn't know. Not for sure. But she had a feeling that young Jill Bishop's kidnapping had much to do with it. The backlash of Bishop's disappearance might have been more than the traffickers anticipated.

It was a small consolation, she thought, the traffickers would only move to another location, but she wished at least that Jill might have known she was responsible for closing this horrible compound down.

Aleksandra looked around the cell and thought about the explosives being placed throughout the cellar. She worried for her friend Jill, but at the same time was glad that she was gone. At least the young girl would live to see another day.

Route National 2 was a timeline of Haiti's prosperity. The evidence of good years, when housing and utilities were being built for the people, and the bad years, when construction came to an abrupt halt. All along the highway the treeless land was dotted with half-completed houses, all of them occupied by desperate-looking children. Women washed clothes where mules drank from aqueducts; open gutters along the road flowed with raw sewage. Roadwork itself had been funded, then abandoned, following revelations of corruption; the skeletons of old machinery rusted in their tracks, scavenged for every hose and gauge and lever and pipe that could be pried away with a board or crowbar.

Colonel Deaken seemed distracted; he was a man going through the motions, Sherry thought, was not really there in spirit. They were only minutes from Pétionville when he suddenly had to get out of the vehicle to make a call. Perhaps it was official business but Sherry couldn't help but wonder what Deaken had to say that couldn't be said in front of them. Soon afterward, he began to question Carol Bishop about her daughter.

When Carol told him the girl was dead in a morgue

in Jamaica, he was clearly surprised. He hadn't known. No one had told him. Then he asked them about their stay in the Dominican Republic the night before. He wanted to know if anyone had accompanied them to the border and was waiting for them on the other side.

Sherry in the backseat was thinking about Brigham, suddenly wishing she'd been more sensitive to his concern for her safety. She didn't like it when people handled things or thought for her or tried to protect her, and she knew that in being defensive of her independence, she might also have been ignoring his valid warning.

Sherry folded her hands in her lap, body rocking in the back as the jeep encountered potholes.

They say when you lose something you gain something else, lose a sense and gain another, or at least that another might become more acute. Sherry had a thing for people's vibes, or so her friends always said. She could pull them out of the air like text, and she was wondering now what it was that was bothering her so about Colonel Deaken.

When he asked them to turn over their cell phones, Sherry knew.

". . . was clear in my conversation with Interpol that neither of you would be permitted to communicate with anyone until you were back across the border. This was for my sake, because I was taking a risk in meeting you."

Sherry didn't buy it. Not for a minute. Something was wrong.

This time she listened to Brigham.

The road to Morne Mansinte was as primitive as in the days it had been forged to haul cannons up the mountain. Packed dirt and shell, it was little wider than a modern SUV, with an incline from sea level to 3,000 feet in just under two miles. There was nothing to protect a careless driver from the eroding edges that would send a vehicle plummeting to the bottom of a crevice.

Not that the road to Morne Mansinte was heavily traveled by vehicles. Mansinte was a destination for the sick and the dead, a ramshackle community of primitive shacks owned by coffin makers and grave diggers and the parish houngan, who lived next to the cemetery.

Hettie Baker had rarely visited Morne Mansinte since marrying Pioche, though her ancestors had lived in the harbor for two centuries and had never taken a remedy but those prescribed by a houngan. It was Pioche's wish that their daughter receive an education and the advantages of foreign missionaries and aid workers like the ones World Freedom sent into the village. Pioche had often repeated his desire that they would one day send Yousy away from this island of death and desperation.

Pioche was the exception to Haiti's predominantly

unskilled population. He was a graduate of the State University of Haiti and one of a handful of Haitians chosen by Reynolds Metals to learn strip mining in the southern peninsula in 1979. The bauxite mines folded in 1986 and Reynolds moved out, leaving Pioche unemployed, but, as a skilled blast engineer, he found work from time to time.

Pioche would likely have continued to earn a decent living—even by Haitian standards—operating heavy equipment for foreign interests in Haiti, but Pioche did not want his daughter growing up in the dangerous streets of Port-au-Prince or Cap Haitien or Les Cayes. He wanted to raise her as far from the political turmoil as possible and Tiburon harbor, the seaside village of his wife, Hettie's, ancestors, was about as far from civilization in Haiti as one could get.

Pioche's fear of mobs and bullets wasn't all he wanted to protect Yousy from. He wanted her to concentrate on what lay beyond the shores of Haiti. He wanted her to break away from the tradition of superstition. He wanted her to realize there were other worlds to explore, and he wanted her to understand the world as a whole before she attempted to understand and identify with her heritage. So Hettie raised Yousy as a Christian while Pioche drove the countryside in search of work. He was a hardworking man, took any job he could find, many of them menial. Hettie knew he had sacrificed dreams of his own to see that his daughter would not struggle as he had always done. She accepted the few days a month she got to see him, and true to his wish made sure that Yousy reached Port-à-Piment for a Jesuit education. And she tried her best to shield Yousy from the old ways and the old beliefs, though she herself wasn't a convert. She still believed in voodoo.

She could still see Pioche sitting on their bed with his father's picture on his lap or playing with Yousy or leaning over the open hood of his old pickup truck.

But then Pioche was murdered and someone left a voodoo poppet on his body and now there was no one to save his soul but the old houngan of Morne Mansinte. Hettie had worried plenty about whether or not Tam-Tam Boy would even agree to Pioche's cleansing after all the years of avoiding him, but there had been no choice but to ask him. This was not something she could bring to the Jesuits' door. The Jesuits would not understand the power of the poppet, would not believe that Pioche's soul could be enslaved by a bocor for all time.

She looked out the window. The harbor was green and the waters lapped gently on soft white beaches. Neighbors would have normally come and gone by now; there was always something to eat in Hettie's cottage, corn porridge and fried plantains, salted fish and beans and rice. Not everyone had the extra money Pioche managed to provide for her to put food on the table, but Hettie's neighbors hadn't been as inclined to stop by as when Pioche was alive.

Of course the reason was that in Haiti when people

were murdered their bodies didn't get returned. Most were left in the streets or disposed of to deprive the victim's family of a burial. Whoever had killed Pioche and dumped his body in front of his house had wanted to send a message not only to Hettie but to the entire village. Whatever Pioche had seen or heard that was enough to get him killed was also enough to buy anyone else their own bullet and poppet. Hettie knew that her neighbors were reluctant to be around her because she was the person most likely to know Pioche's secrets.

Etienne, her cousin's young boyfriend, didn't care. Etienne sold wild plantains in Port-à-Piment and drove Yousy to the Jesuit school when Pioche was not around. He had been good enough to put Pioche's body in the back of his little pickup truck and take him up the mountain road to Morne Mansinte, where the houngan consented to cleanse it of the curse. Each night for nine nights the houngan communed with Pioche. In three days Pioche would be taken through the gates to the cemetery and laid at last in holy ground, behind the protection of Papa Ghede's black cross.

Hettie knew that Pioche wouldn't have approved of her taking his body to the old houngan. But Pioche couldn't have known he'd end up dead with a poppet on his chest or that his body would be thrown in front of his door as a warning. Pioche would have wanted Hettie to do anything she could to protect herself and Yousy from harm, and he must surely know now that Tam-Tam Boy had laid hands upon him in his temple, that there really was more to the old man than meets the eye. How else could Tam-Tam Boy have known about Amaud's photograph if he hadn't spoken to Pioche himself?

This wasn't what she'd wanted, it wasn't what Pioche wanted, but then Pioche got himself killed and now she had to think for both of them; she had to protect Yousy and get her to the United States once she was certain that Pioche's soul was safe.

She looked out the window.

Etienne would be dropping off Yousy very soon. It was her first day back at school since Pioche's body had been found.

Hettie had made corn pudding, her daughter's favorite meal. She hoped that they would soon have a new beginning, hoped that once Pioche was buried they could begin to reclaim their lives.

Evenings had always been a time for them alone. Yousy liked to recount her day with the Jesuits and show Hettie the marks on her school papers that Hettie didn't understand. Sometimes she would teach Yousy to sew or Yousy would read to her or play music on her radio. Sometimes they would walk the beach and Hettie would tell Yousy about nights with her own mother walking the beach or sitting under the stars.

She didn't know what to expect of her tonight. Yousy was different from most thirteen-year-olds—older, but not in the way of city-raised thirteen-year-olds wearied by poverty, not because she had been driven to forage and become a caretaker for younger siblings like so many barely old enough to take care of themselves. Yousy's wisdom was in her eyes; she seemed to understand things at times that were not yet apparent to Hettie. Yousy, for instance, was far less interested in the voodoo poppet found on Pioche's chest than in the paper stuffed in his mouth. Hettie thought it curious that she had kept it and, though she couldn't know for sure, felt certain Yousy had shared it with her friend Linda, the aid worker from World Freedom, because Linda had endless questions about where Pioche had been working before he was killed.

Hettie stepped onto the little terrace Pioche had made behind their cottage and swept the sand away with her broom. Pioche was always bringing bricks and things home from job sites and adding little improvements to their cottage. Pioche had been the best thing about Haiti, Hettie had always believed, the most wonderful thing the island had ever given to her. Haiti wouldn't be the same without him. And with Yousy in America, what would be left?

She wondered how long $4,800 would last Yousy in Miami.

"Mom." The door opened and Yousy walked into the cottage.

Hettie turned to see Yousy and the thin brown dog following her through the door.

"Yousy, you mustn't let that dog in the house."

"Chaser is behaved, Mama."

"You've named it!"

"It's a she, Mama."

"Dogs don't belong in houses, Yousy."

"They do in America," Yousy said dispassionately.

Hettie didn't answer. There was no answer to a girl who lost her father a week ago.

"She is very smart, Mama, do you want to see her sit?"

"I want to see it out of here. And what would people say if they saw a dog come into our house, Yousy? I'll tell you what they would say. They would say those Bakers think they are like royalty giving roof and food to a scavenging mongrel."

Hettie sat down heavily next to Yousy, pulled the big hairpin Pioche had made of whalebone from Yousy's hair and watched it fall to her daughter's shoulders. She hadn't stopped wearing it since the day Pioche was murdered. The dog looked up at both of them, tail wagging, eyes moving between them. "Of course we haven't seen a neighbor all week so maybe we shouldn't care what they think," she added tiredly.

Yousy's face softened. It was the first expression of any kind that Hettie had seen all week. Hettie put her arms around the girl and held her as the dog looked on. "We're going to be all right, Miss Yousy," Hettie said. "We're going to be all right, I promise you."

She pushed Yousy away and looked into her eyes. "Your father was a very good man, Yousy. More special than you could ever know."

Yousy began to cry and Hettie pulled her to her shoulder. "No more tears, my Yousy, no more tears now. Pioche will rest peacefully soon and when his spirit rises in a year and day, we will take it with us to Miami, what do you say?"

Yousy looked up at her, looked in her eyes for the truth, and when she saw it she smiled. "Really, Mama?"

"Really," Hettie said firmly, "but you mustn't talk about it. Do you understand how important that is? How important when I say that you must tell no one? Talk is bad in Haiti. Bad things happen to those who talk."

Yousy nodded.

Hettie smiled down at her, and stood.

"We must get ready to visit your father soon, but first I will check with Etienne to make sure he will take us tonight. You promise me you will stay in if I let the dog be with you?"

Yousy nodded. "I will stay in," she said. "I promise."

Yousy picked up a tattered copy of *Time* magazine and lay down next to the dog, using a lime green cassette player for her pillow. The cassette function had never worked, but Yousy caught FM waves from the Dominican and Jamaica and sometimes Cuba when conditions were right.

The dog was cute, Hettie thought, cute and smart and playful; it was the kind of thing Pioche would have approved of. Hettie had first seen it under her sleeping daughter on the brick terrace the first night she returned from delivering Pioche's body to the houngan. The dog had been hanging around their door waiting for Yousy to wake each morning and now today after school.

This wasn't the time to take anything else away from her. Let the neighbors talk. She was sure they talked enough as it was.

Morne Mansinte was as dissimilar from Tiburon harbor as night was from day, Hettie recalled—as all villagers surely recalled—her first trip to Mansinte as a child and the terror that accompanied that steep climb to the cemetery. To a mere child what lay above the serene ocean harbor was dark and mysterious. The bags of bones and magic spells, the row of wooden coffins leaning against the cemetery fence, sometimes waiting for bodies yet unknown. As children they used to compare the lengths of coffins to their size, but any laughter as they played the game veiled a fear that one of the coffins was really their own.

The road hugged walls of volcanic rock that twisted upward. Etienne inched the old Toyota carrying them and Yousy slowly up the mountainside.

"Do you know what I heard today?"

"No, Etienne, but I know you will tell me." Hettie looked out the window.

"There is a story . . ." He hesitated.

Hettie smiled weakly. There was always a story in Haiti. In other lands they called it the grapevine, in Haiti they called it telejaw. For a country widely lacking electricity and telephones, word managed to travel quite efficiently. Rumors moved on the tongue of every truck driver and merchant, social workers and nuns and policemen and missionaries. It went down every road and across every mountain until what was said in the east was known by nightfall in the west.

"The lady who cooks for the Jesuits, Mrs. Lambert, her son works for the drug police in Port-au-Prince."

Hettie nodded, eyes on roots clutching at the mountainside above them.

"He is in charge of maintaining their computers." Etienne nodded, hands gripping the vibrating wheel. "His boss called him today and told him to look up the name of a woman. She was on a passenger list coming by bus to Haiti from the Dominican Republic. He said the woman was on the Internet. She is like a mambo from the United States. A white mambo."

"Speak plainly," Hettie said, "and keep your eyes on the road."

"She touches the dead."

Hettie looked at Etienne.

He shrugged. "I am only telling you what Mrs. Lambert said."

Hettie looked up to see a basket of bones hanging from the limb of a mapou.

The mapou are sacred trees in Haiti, and the spirits of ancestors are believed to dwell in their roots. The few that were left standing in Haiti the villagers feared to burn. Offerings to the spirits are commonly tied to their branches.

The truck passed beneath other trees, straw haversacks of rotting fruit, empty bottles of rum, hardened sugar candies, pieces of colorful cloth, seashells, and pictures of saints and past presidents pasted on cardboard.

"And what can she do when she touches the dead?" Hettie tried not to sound curious.

"She knows what they are thinking."

"She talks to them?"

Etienne shrugged. "She holds their hand, he told Mrs. Lambert. He said she is blind."

"Blind," Hettie whispered, immediately thinking of Tam-Tam Boy, who also held hands.

Etienne nodded. "Crazy, huh? What if she is coming to see Pioche?"

"Etienne," Hettie said, shocked, "why would you say that?"

Etienne shrugged. "She is coming to Tiburon, Mrs. Lambert said. It is what was written on the customs form."

Hettie's heart skipped a beat.

Near the craggy summit of Morne Mansinte, the road snaked away from the sea, skirting boulders through hollows of dense jungle growth and saplings growing out of the stumps of felled trees. The road beneath the shantytown was wide enough for a single car, so Etienne had to pass the path leading up to it and park near the gates to the parish cemetery.

It was a lesson of the Caribbean ancestors that the dead were as vulnerable to hurricanes as the living. No one wanted their family's bones washed to sea with the bones of pigs and goats, so cemeteries were placed in the cradles of mountains.

Etienne looked at the crude gates to the cemetery. Few visited the bodies within, caring less that the graves were attended than that the bodies remain behind the magic of the black cross and beneath the earth where they belonged.

Pioche would have had none of this, but Hettie still believed. The soul spent a year and a day in dark waters, then it could be reclaimed by ritual—at a price— by the houngan and put in a bottle called a govi. Later, if she wished, she could release Pioche to join the ancestors in the cosmos, as the bones and flesh were now released to occupy the natural world, roots and rocks and rivers.

The obligation to a soul was a serious undertaking in voudon. Souls left to wander the earth might bring illness and disaster to a family. The struggle for Pioche's soul to rest would be over in days; he would be able to pass by the crossroads and Hettie could begin to prepare for the day when she would purchase Pioche's soul and release Yousy from this place forever.

They walked along the road to a well-worn path, climbing the hillside to the outlines of shanties.

Hettie could smell boiled meat and the decay of rotting carcasses. There would be two sacrifices at Pioche's service tonight, both a chicken and a goat she had bought as offerings to the spirit of Papa Ghede. But Pioche was not the houngan's only concern this day. The parishioners of another village were here; a small crowd had already gathered around the temple.

The temple—hounfor—was decorated with flags of red, yellow, and green. A bucket of pink water sat at the edge of the pavilion, which was open on two sides but covered with a thatched roof. A toy plastic boat hung from the ceiling. Someone had put the torn vinyl seats of a car in one corner and a stand-alone ashtray stood before them. Drummers in red shirts and blue jeans and hounsis in white dresses circled a boy on the floor. Hettie and Etienne joined the villagers from Morne Epine, who watched as Tam-Tam Boy pulled a corncob plug from the neck of a decapitated chicken and sprinkled blood over the feet of a crippled boy, which had been tied together with black ribbon. A moment later Tam-Tam Boy knelt in front of the boy; arm extended, searching for his head until he found it and drinking from a bottle of rum, he stared at the roof with his milky white eyes and then leaned down to face the boy and spit the rum upon his face.

Hettie backed away, leaving Etienne with the gathering, and retreated to the clearing's edge, where Pioche lay in his open coffin. He didn't look or smell so much like Pioche anymore, was already beginning to leave this world, she thought. His hair was collecting dirt and loose grass, his skin bloated and stained with paint and blood and the houngan's magic oils meant to keep the bocor away. She looked at the hole in his stomach that had leaked his intestines into the street for all in the village to see.

She was worried about the white mambo Mrs. Lambert's son had said entered the country. Her whole life had changed in the course of a week because Pioche had seen something he should not have, because Pioche's heart was too big to turn his head away and to mind what business was his own.

Was it only coincidence a white mambo would be coming to Tiburon harbor?

She thought about Yousy. Yousy had always preferred the company of Linda, the World Freedom worker from America, to the children of her own village, and reading to hide-and-seek, or listening to English radio stations instead of playing kickball on the beach.

Hettie remembered the night Pioche told her what he had seen in a cellar where he was drilling to place explosives. Yousy was playing her radio that night, her music filling the small house and out the back windows; they'd whispered on the terrace, except that when they got up to go back inside, Yousy was not there. Not lying by her radio.

Pioche had run outside and found her sitting on the beach in the dark, just beyond the terrace where they had been talking. He'd wanted to admonish her for spying on them, but when he asked her if she heard them talking she had said not. Hettie knew he wasn't sure. Hettie knew that he was worried about what Yousy might have heard.

And now that Hettie had heard the story about the uniformed men in jeeps she was worried, too, about something that had been bothering her since the day Pioche's body was found.

Why had Yousy's American friend Linda been so insistent about where Pioche had been working?

Had Yousy overheard Pioche's story after all?

Had Yousy placed them in danger without knowing it?

Graham paced his office in Langley, Virginia, as a phone rang in Lyon, France. He snatched it off the cradle.

"Helmut?"

"What have you got?"

"One of the ships in Gdansk when Warrant Officer Aleksandra Goralski went missing belonged to Jean Jasmine's fleet. DEA boarded it a couple of years ago in Caracas when he went down for distributing cocaine. It was later sold to a straw corporation, but DEA says it was definitely Jean Bedard's and Jean Bedard had ties to the Mendoza cartel."

"How did Bedard operate?"

"He exported goods from Central and South America, stuff like bauxite, soybeans, and mahogany, also his own produce and coffee from Haiti."

"Going to?"

"Mainly Bulgaria and Russia on the Black Sea. He brings back farm tractors, small engine parts, and appliances."

"Which translates to drugs trafficked east and women trafficked west," Dantzler said.

"And everything hubbed out of Haiti to places like South and Central America," Graham added.

"Which fits the Bulgarian's story last year. Women imported to South America from ports on the Black Sea. Bedard was the Tonton Macoute commander, right?"

"The same. I got aerials of his compounds in Colombia and Haiti, but it's this second one that's interesting, Helmut. It's in the mountains of de Cartache, in jungle about thirty kilometers north of Tiburon harbor. The ruins of an old cathedral converted to a mansion, but it's got these balustrades. It looks like a fucking castle, Helmut."

"Lord Jesus, what have we done? Have you raised the colonel yet?"

"I've been calling him for an hour and still nothing. I got a security officer from the embassy to try to find him through local channels. There is no one at his home or office. The police weren't very helpful; they say that colonels make their own schedules."

"What's your take?"

"He may have been compromised."

"My God," Dantzler said. "How did we manage to let civilians into Haiti? Does this castle or whatever look active?"

"It's active. Security fencing, vehicles on the property, there's a helipad on the lawn."

"Why hire a blast engineer? You see any new construction going on, forest being cleared?"

"None, but the original cathedral is historically documented. It was built above a marble quarry used to construct the interior in the 1700s. The whole side of the mountain is hollow under it."

"He's getting ready to bring it down."

"It's all we can guess."

"Then we have a time issue, too. Can you get Ambassador Sanderson to the palace?"

"Already made the call. I'm expecting her any moment."

"She's not going to be happy we have people in Haiti."

"Christ's sake, Helmut, they're not ours. Tourists go there every day."

"Yes, tourists, and one would question their judgment, too, but I don't think Carol Bishop and a psychic investigator will qualify as tourists. You're going to have to tell the ambassador about Jill Bishop and how she was found and why Carol and Sherry are in Haiti. Ambassador Sanderson has got to convince President Préval to send troops to Bedard's compound and now."

"Well, if you can possibly imagine how little I look forward to that conversation, imagine how well Garland Brigham's going to take it when I tell him we can't reach the escort."

Sherry had checked in with him just before leaving Pétionville, a little over thirty minutes ago. Ten minutes later Graham called to say Interpol had not been able to reach Colonel Deaken for the last two hours and that a structure like the one Sherry Moore had described in both Denali and Jamaica had been located less than twenty miles from Tiburon. It was owned by a former commander of Papa Doc's secret police.

Brigham, furious, had had the bad feeling ever since. This was exactly the kind of thing that happened when people went off half-cocked. How could they be so stupid, inserting civilians into hostile territory with an unknown entity for support? How could he have witnessed it all himself and done nothing? Was he getting senile, for Christ's sake? And Sherry, how stubborn she could be while leading him around by the nose; support me, support me, she liked to say. Civilians, he thought. Fucking civilians.

He was just about to dial her number when his phone rang. Once. No more. He looked at the number on the screen, then at his watch, feeling his heart pound in his chest. He crossed the hotel's terrace to a deserted balcony and dialed a number. It was 7:12 P.M. There were five more hours before she reached Tiburon. If she reached Tiburon.

Beyond the jagged coastline overlooking highway A-1, a beautiful wooden schooner glided toward Port Antonio; she had three sails and towed a rubber skiff in her wake.

"George," the inspector answered.

"Something's happened. They're in trouble. Your boat is fueled?"

"Use the hotel's courtesy van. Two miles down the road to Frenchman's Cove, the Bertram sportfisherman, she's named *Zuben'Ubi*, you can't miss her. But I'm still forty minutes away."

"I'll need it," Brigham growled. "I have calls to make."

The men had talked after the women boarded their flight to the Dominican Republic yesterday afternoon. They talked about boats—Rolly King George was terribly impressed when he learned that Brigham was a retired admiral—and they talked about politics and the dangers for women going into Haiti alone. Brigham had told Rolly King George about the signal he had arranged with Sherry Moore. They agreed that if anything were to happen, they would never be able to fly into Haiti and reach Tiburon in time, even if they could get past customs and God knows what else lay in store. But Tiburon harbor was on the near western coast of the island, only three hours by sea. If they could get to Tiburon harbor, Brigham had told the inspector, the Bertram sportfisherman was large enough to accommodate the second part of Brigham's plan.

Sherry's unease about the colonel continued to build after he insisted on taking their cell phones. She wasn't completely convinced they were in trouble, but Brigham had been adamant about erring on the side of caution. She had dialed his number and let it connect on her lap behind the driver's seat before she hung up and turned the phone over to Colonel Deaken. She had no idea what Brigham could do if she was in trouble, probably there was little more he could do than call the American embassy, which would cause a lot of political consternation over Carol Bishop's being in Haiti.

In retrospect, she should have come to Haiti alone. She should have told no one what she was doing. She could have hired a car to take her to Tiburon and back. She could have tried to reason with the dead man's family on her own; someone in Tiburon had to speak English. Someone had to be willing to help her.

"What do you see?" Sherry asked.

Carol looked silently out the window. They crossed an arched bridge; a boy was wading through water, hands full of net, a rope to a wooden rowboat clenched between his teeth. Several middle-aged men wearing only shorts sat on the bank smoking cigarettes and drinking rum, pointing at the boat, telling the boy what to do.

"There are buses and pickup trucks with canopies over benches bolted to the bed; they are taxis, but the people call them tap-taps. When you want to get off you tap against the side of the truck," Carol explained. "We are behind one now, a bus painted red and yellow— someone sprayed graffiti across the side."

"What does it say?"

"*Bondye si bon,* God is so good."

"There are houses?"

"They are plastered and mostly windowless. There is a white man painting a garage full of chairs, missionaries. You smell the market?"

Sherry smiled and nodded. It was impossible not to smell the market.

"There are murals on the walls. Haitians like color, yes, Colonel?"

The colonel nodded mechanically.

"A procession of women in light-colored dresses, something religious, no doubt, everything in Haiti is religious. There is a fire ahead." Carol leaned forward, craning her neck to see from the opposite window. "An old car and tires, smell the rubber? The smoke is black. Some men are chasing a dog with a stick."

It took four hours to reach the town of Port-à-Piment. They passed marshes that reeked of methane gas, rolling brown hills that looked like the badlands of the American Midwest. There were treeless plains and standing green water swarming with clouds of black mosquitoes.

The doors of the homes in Port-à-Piment were splintered by hammers and boots from police raids long past. Bullet-pocked walls were crumbling to reveal magazines and old newspapers used to form the plaster. The stench of human waste in the open gutters followed them everywhere. Houses in the southern peninsula had twice been underwater from Hurricanes Noel and Dean; the sewers ran free and wells would have been contaminated.

Carol Bishop sat next to Sherry, wondering if Jill had been on this very road. It was quite likely, she thought, there were only two main roads that extended to the ends of the island, one north and one south.

She remembered Jill as a tiny girl on her lap in the nursery of their home in Chicago. She remembered a girl in pigtails on a porch swing, on a log tube in Disney World, holding her hand at her grandmother's funeral.

Out the window she saw a smiling girl in a filthy dress playing with a hula hoop and two boys swatting with sticks at the roof of a car buried in the mud. Others only stared at the traffic, taking particular interest in the white women in the jeep going by.

Port-à-Piment had more than its share of ramshackle churches and missionaries. Old men stood in the doorways talking to old women with wet eyes. There were tents and signs and crosses planted everywhere. All the world's religions seemed intent on converting the destitute population, and indeed the people of Haiti were transformed to Catholics and Baptists and Mormons for a day. They got their candy bars and hot dogs and marshmallows, sometimes clothing from collection boxes around the world. But when the sun began to set they were voudons once more. Voodoo was the only constant in their lives. Only voodoo had never criticized or subjugated or abandoned them.

"Incredible," Carol Bishop said.

"Haiti?" Sherry asked.

"It's utterly sad."

"We will fuel in Port-à-Piment if either of you needs to relieve yourself," the colonel said.

The streets were quiet under a three-quarter moon, trees wilted from the scorching afternoon. They passed between blue and yellow homes, watched by big eyes behind small hands that were curled over banisters of second-story porches. Stray dogs roamed deserted streets; the smell of the sea was heavy with fish.

They stopped at an old Texaco station and saw a military truck parked off to one side. The bed of the truck was crowded with solemn-looking men wearing black. Two of them were inside the garage.

The last stretch of highway to Tiburon hugged the rugged coastline. To their north was a rock wall that formed Morne Mansinte, to their south the glassy black surface of a moon-splashed sea. There was no traffic on the road in either direction, but Carol Bishop kept turning to look over her shoulder. The truck full of men bothered her. They weren't policemen, she knew. Was she mistaken or had the colonel nodded to one of them while he was fueling the jeep?

An hour later they were there, the breathtaking harbor, a field of stars that stretched from mountain to sea. Carol described the moonlight ripples, the masts of small wooden boats gently rocking in the surf. The village was dark and shaggy with thatched roofs. Torches flickered at the water's edge as fishermen speared pan fish.

The jeep turned into the village, its headlights lacerating the serenity. The colonel braked at the end of a street, jumped from the vehicle, and began to hammer on doors. Candles were lit behind curtains. A few electric lights came on. Sherry could hear unintelligible voices, the colonel's loud rebukes.

After almost twenty minutes passed, the colonel marched back out of the shadows, pulling himself behind the wheel, and jerked the jeep irately through a three-point turn to head back to the main road, where they continued west half a mile and turned up the side of the mountain.

He was out of character, Sherry thought. His impatience seemed less about helping them to locate the family than apprehension. He did not seem like a man in control.

The sea quickly fell away behind them, headlights wavering between the mountainside and a black bottomless void to their right.

Carol looked back once more in the direction of the

coast and this time saw the pair of tiny headlights eight or ten miles behind. Someone was coming from the direction of Port-à-Piment, where they had just fueled.

"They are at the dead man's cleansing," Colonel Deaken said into his rearview mirror. "The houngan's temple is behind a cemetery on the mountain. We will be there any minute."

The sparse lights of Tiburon on the coast were dizzying from the height of Carol's passenger window. The road had many switchbacks and blind curves. It climbed through wisps of fog to an eerie, treeless summit. Sharp silhouettes of the jagged rocks poked through, pockets of lingering condensation.

A large black cross appeared before them, posted between squat thorny trees. Horned skulls hung from the bare branches.

"What are they?" Sherry heard Carol ask.

"Goat heads," the colonel interjected.

"Their skulls, they are hanging from the trees," Carol explained to Sherry.

The rotted wooden gate of a cemetery came up on their left. There was an arch over it and crude tombstones and crooked stick crosses behind. On a hill behind the cemetery was the silhouette of a shantytown. Behind the ramshackle buildings was the orange glow of a fire. Smoke on the fog was bitter and acrid. The sound of drums permeated the night.

Half a dozen battered cars were parked in a clearing.

"We will have to walk in from here," the colonel said, swinging the jeep around and parking next to them. "There is a path over there." He pointed in the direction of his headlights before he turned off the igntion.

An old woman walked out of the darkness. She was holding a smoldering cigarette in a hand with two fingers. She looked at them a moment, then started down the road, vanishing into the night.

Sherry exited the vehicle and Carol took her arm.

They followed the colonel to the path and climbed it toward the shanties. The drums beat steadily in the distance, Sherry could make out voices now.

There were coffins leaning against one of the shanties, one painted black was five feet tall, the other no larger than a baby.

"I can see it now. The temple," Carol told Sherry. "It's a wooden structure, but there are only three walls. There is a pole in the center of the floor, people are sitting outside on the dirt looking in. There is a body on the floor, a man's body, and he is naked but for underwear. An old man is kneeling in front of him. He is wearing blue jeans and a red shirt. He has a red kerchief around his neck."

The drums stopped. The people turned to look at them, a few wandering away, escaping into the shadows.

"Tell me more," Sherry urged.

"The walls of the temple are painted light blue like a robin's egg, there are murals drawn on the walls, a large black eye looking down from the heavens, a child wearing a crown, fish, and colorful dancers. There is a big black man with no face who holds the earth in his hands. There are flags everywhere, colored patches of cloth tied to the trees, to the posts and frame of the building, all different, some green, some red, some yellow."

"Who is this man?" the colonel barked, the heels of his boots striking hard across the wooden floor of the temple.

"Pioche," the old houngan answered. "His wife"—he introduced a heavy-set woman sitting next to him—"and his daughter; and who are you?"

"Colonel Deaken, Police National," he retorted.

"It's him," Sherry whispered. "Pioche."

Carol squeezed Sherry's hand, biting back tears.

"We must be careful, do you understand? We don't want to scare them."

"Yes," Carol answered. She understood well.

"I've brought someone to look at this body. It is police business," the colonel barked. "Move away."

"Let him stay," Sherry interfered. "I want him to help me."

There was a moment of silence, the colonel shrugged as if indifferent, then turned and marched away.

"He's blind," Carol said in awe. "The old man. He can't see."

"That should make it easy." Sherry smiled and squeezed her hand.

Bodies parted as Sherry walked forward. "How far is he?" she asked.

"Ten feet. The ground is level in front of you." Carol stepped forward and pivoted Sherry's shoulders. "The houngan is straight ahead—the body is lying horizontal in front of him."

Sherry walked straight and confidently ahead as the crowd continued to part for her. She could smell the sweat, the rum and tobacco, the decomposing body in front of her.

Sherry spoke first. "Tam-Tam Boy?" she asked.

"Kisa," the old man said cautiously.

She had a fix on him now, stepped forward several feet, and knelt on the floor, edging forward until her knee found the side of Pioche's lifeless body.

"My name is Sherry Moore."

"What do you want, ooman?"

"I came here to learn something from you."

Tam-Tam Boy turned his face upward in the general direction of the ceiling.

"Dere is no ting to learn here." He shook his head.

Sherry leaned forward and whispered. "There are things you know."

Carol watched the colonel leave. He was on the path leading back to the cars.

"Tricks," the houngan said. "You want a charm, a spell. Dis," he said angrily, "is a funeral, ooman."

"I know," Sherry said softly. "I need to know what he told you."

"He be dead, ooman," the houngan snorted.

"But you hear them speak, don't you?" Sherry said quickly. "They talk back to you, don't they?"

Tam-Tam Boy smiled. "You tink me a fool."

"Quite the contrary," Sherry said. "I talk to them too."

The old man sighed tiredly, looked about, seemingly ready to stand. A sheen of sweat over his face glistened in the light of the fire, a stubble of gray beard against his crinkled black skin. He leaned forward suddenly.

"You talk to the dead," he said contemptuously.

There was every possibility the houngan was a fraud, Sherry knew. Or that he actually believed in what he did, both encouraged and empowered by these people's superstitions. There was also a possibility that the houngan was telling the truth. Who knew that better than she? How many people had doubted her over the years? Not that it mattered. The purpose of her visit was to lay a hand on the body, that was the goal here, and to achieve it she needed to keep the houngan talking.

"In truth, they do not speak to me," Sherry admitted, "but maybe you can understand what I'm saying. If I touch them, if I hold their hand, they show me pictures of where they have been, of what they were last thinking. I was hoping you would tell me what this man told you, or maybe it is possible you see the pictures, too."

"I am blind," he said contemptuously, starting to rise.

Sherry could smell rum on his breath, the hint of spicy cologne.

"As am I," she answered.

The old man stopped, his milky dead eyes meeting the barrier of darkness between them. He sat back down. "Please," he said. "Sit."

Sherry carefully lowered her body.

The houngan reached across Pioche's body to touch her face, his fingertips finding her cheek. Sherry leaned forward, letting him trace her nose, then Tam-Tam Boy flattened his hand and covered Sherry's face. He spread his fingers across the mounds and valleys, her nose, her chin, her forehead, her eyes.

"I am sorry to interrupt you, Tam-Tam Boy," Sherry said. "I am sorry to interfere with this man's funeral, but time is important and I have come to ask a favor."

"Which is?" the old man said.

"I need to know where this man was when he died."

There was a long moment of silence.

"Take him hand," he told Sherry.

Sherry found it quickly, bloated and cool, skin loose but oily, not dry; something had been used to preserve his body.

She squeezed it gently.

. . . a young girl was lying on a lumpy mattress, her long luxurious hair was pinned behind her head, the pin was ivory white and carefully carved by hand in the

shape of a fish; a stone wall through a path into the jungle; an old wooden door, it had a viewing pane; the face of a young woman, she was Caucasian and her hair was dark and matted. There was a tattoo on her cheek, a skull wearing a top hat; an old man in front of a statue, he was wearing a straw hat; a young blond woman curled in the dirt; a kitten floating down a stream on a raft made of palm fronds; a pack of ciga- rette papers; a heavy-set woman in red shorts; a black man with one white eye; the spires of an old stone ca- thedral; the man in front of the statue again but he is framed in blue, it is a picture and he is taking the back off, the picture is crammed with money; a ladder in a stone walled cellar, holes drilled into the mortar in the walls; the black man with one white eye has a gun; blood on the toes of his boots; his hand touching the bottom of the old wooden door, painting a bloody streak with his finger; nothing more . . .

"He was killed by a one-eyed man," she whispered, letting go of the hand.

"Yes?" the houngan said tentatively.

"He was thinking about a young black girl, she was lying down."

"Wit long hair," Tam-Tam Boy interrupted. "She use some-ting to hold her hair in di back of her head?" He listened carefully.

"A hairpin," Sherry said. "It was white, long, with a sharp point at one end, carved like a jumping fish."

"Him saw a cat," the houngan said.

"On a raft made of leaves," Sherry said.

"Dere is a picture."

"Of a man in front of a statue."

"Di frame is yello," Tam-Tam Boy lied, cocking his head to the side.

"No, it is blue." Sherry smiled, catching him. "Does his wife know what is behind it? Behind the frame?"

"Her know." The houngan smiled. "I told her tell no one."

Sherry reached across the body, touching the houngan's shirt, finding his hand. "The old castle," she said. "Can you tell me about it?"

"It is evil," the old man said solemnly.

"I have seen it before," Sherry said. "It is where this man was killed, isn't it?"

The houngan hesitated. "Contestus," he whispered at last. "It is north of here."

Sherry let out a deep breath. "There is a cellar beneath it, do you know?"

"A quarry," Tam-Tam Boy said. "For mining marble."

"Who lives there?"

"Tonton Macoutes," he said contemptuously.

Sherry could barely hear the words.

"I don't understand."

"The boogymen," he said. "Do not go there, ooman."

Sherry nodded, squeezed the old man's hand. "We are the same, Tam-Tam Boy," she said. "You hear and I see."

Tam-Tam Boy leaned closer, whispered softly, "I tell

dem what I see. Dem like to hear their loved ones speak."

Sherry smiled. He really was just like her.

"Thank you," she said.

"You are welcome, white mambo." Tam-Tam Boy got to his feet.

Carol saw Sherry stand and turned to where the colonel had disappeared over the hillside.

Something was wrong. She felt it. Carol stepped forward toward the building, calling Sherry's name.

Then she heard the engine, the sound of an approaching truck, and it was moving fast. People began to run toward the trees, there was a clamor of metal from the parking lot, tailgates falling down, men shouting orders, shapes appeared on the path by the shanties, you could hear their boots pounding, the rattle of small arms on slings.

"*Kisa ou vie?*" the old houngan shouted.

Carol grabbed Sherry's arm, but Sherry pulled away, reaching to help the houngan out of the temple. "Run," she yelled to Carol, but by then the soldiers were upon them.

Sherry and Carol were seized and pulled away from the building, each placed on a chair in handcuffs.

Carol watched in horror as a dark man with one eye approached and pulled a pearl-handled automatic pistol from his holster. "Her"—Bedard pointed at Hettie— "and the girl. Take them both."

Soldiers ran up and put the women in chains.

"Him, too," Bedard shouted, pointing at the dead man, and two more guards ran to carry away the body of Pioche.

Tam-Tam Boy looked at Bedard with his cloudy white eyes. *"Kisa ou vie,"* he repeated.

Bedard put a bullet between them.

"You're serious."

"As a heart attack," Graham said. "I told him I had already called Ambassador Sanderson and that she was on her way to the palace to see President Préval."

"And Brigham said what?"

"He told me not to do another thing. I mean he was just sizzling, Helmut. He actually used those words, verbatim, like I was some little kid. I said, 'All due respect, Admiral,' and the phone went dead. He hung up on me. Ten minutes later I get a call from Senator Metcalf, chairman of the Armed Services Committee. He tells me to stand down and wait for further instructions from my director. The director, Helmut! I've never had a conversation with the director in my life."

"What the hell is going on down there?"

"Hey, I've never even heard of anything like this. You can raise hell from your side of the pond. I'm not doing another thing until I hear what the director is going to say."

"I thought we were lucky enough to run down the missing policewoman from Poland in a week's time.

That and connect her to a ship from Haiti. What in the hell more could anyone expect?"

"I'm just saying, this Sherry Moore is a close friend of Brigham's and Brigham is pissed."

"What do you think he's up to?"

"All I can say is what I've heard around the watercooler, that maybe Brigham keeps a hand in DEVGRU."

"DEVGRU?"

"Navy Special Warfare, the old SEAL Team 6 that wasn't supposed to exist."

"Jesus H. Christ."

"If what they say is true, Helmut, Brigham's armed with the Joint Special Operations Command and four teams of alpha-grade SEALs who are autonomous from the regular military."

SOMEWHERE OFF THE CAYMAN ISLANDS

When she dreamed, Katya saw yellow butterflies. They were Russian butterflies or, more exactly, Caucasus Mountain butterflies, and behind them she saw her parents' home on the snowcapped peaks of Mount Elbrus.

The Caucasus region was a virtual melting pot of biology, of bison and wolves and leopards and eagles, of Muslims and Christians and Buddhists and Jews. She should have stayed there. She should have appreciated the simplicity of her life. Appreciated the sun and the moon and the wind and the rains, the true elements of existence that had forever influenced her ancestors.

But she had not. She had run away with a foreigner, an ecologist from Switzerland who came to photograph the leopards. He had pictures of exotic places and he told stories and knew many languages. He was funny and he was interesting, which was everything that her life, her parents' life, and that of the other mountain farmers, were not.

Their relationship lasted only to the Black Sea resort of Sochi; the ecologist confessed he could not take her home with him, he had a wife, but she was smitten with adventure by now; she had seen palm trees and beautiful botanical gardens, Greek architecture and the gleaming hulls of ships on a startling blue sea. Even her severe asthma had seemed to suppress at sea level. There was no going back to the life she once knew.

She spent a few nights in a hostel with summer camp students who had come to learn tennis at the academy. She visited cathedrals and museums. She sat on sandy beaches and drank vodka with a man who promised he could get her a housekeeping job on one of the cruise lines. And when it came time to interview, she used a landlady's iron to press her wool dress, brushed her hair a hundred times, and arrived early for her appointment. But it was not the chief cabin steward who showed up to greet her. It was a man with a handgun.

She spent that night in the hull of a freighter with girls who had been kidnapped in Taganrog and all the while more girls were loaded into the hold at the harbor at Sochi, all with stories like her own.

The air was bad from the beginning, but a fuel leak at sea would send her into asthmatic spasms. Katya, when she wasn't fighting for air, fought to sleep, to dream in the rumbling hull of the ship. After days at sea all her questions about what had happened were reduced to one. Katya wondered if heaven had yellow butterflies.

The captain of the *Anna Marie* nosed his trawler beneath the hulking bow of *Yelenushka*, looking up at the rails where men were dropping lines and readying a battered metal life basket. His crew of four tied off against the freighter's lines, then sat bobbing in the dark sea off Haiti while the women were being readied.

When they came down, they came two at a time. The captain had them put below in the empty ice hold. It took an hour and fifteen minutes, but all of the women survived. The *Anna Marie*'s crew untied lines and pushed off, letting the forty-foot trawler drift away from the hulking freighter. Ten minutes later the captain checked his radar screen, started his engines, and headed for the coast of Colombia.

CIA HEADQUARTERS
LANGLEY, VIRGINIA

"Helmut."

"Hold on, Graham. I need to close the door."

Graham cradled the phone to his ear, waiting. He had been staring blankly at his desk ever since his conversation with the director two hours before. It was one of those conversations you couldn't quite remember afterward but you knew had monumental implications. Especially the part about straying dangerously close to violating state's sovereignty in Haiti.

"I'm afraid to ask," Helmut said.

"I got a call from a friend before the director came to see me. My source tells me Ambassador Sanderson is inside the palace in Port-au-Prince."

"And?"

"President Préval was already waiting for her. He told her he had talked with Washington and that the FBI was putting together a forensics team to send to Port-au-Prince in the morning. He's agreed to send guards with them to Bedard's compound."

"Just like that," Helmut said.

"Just like that. The ambassador hardly said a word."

"So who softened Préval up—was it Senator Metcalf?"

"Actually, my source said that President Préval told the ambassador he talked to the White House, but if you think that's strange, listen to this. Préval put a lockdown on all of western Haiti. He ordered all police field commanders to their stations. Then he closed the airports. Nothing comes or goes from Haiti for the next twelve hours."

Helmut didn't know what to say. "What about Colonel Deaken?"

"Officially missing. The palace sent national security guards to his house. His housekeeper said his family hasn't been home in a week, since about the time the explosives engineer's body was dumped in Tiburon and your office contacted the colonel for his help."

"Ah, Jesus," Helmut said. "Why is Préval restricting access to Haiti and letting the FBI in?"

"He's not letting the FBI in for twelve hours either," Graham said. "The lockdown is universal. No one comes or goes from Haiti until noon tomorrow."

"Why in God's name would President Préval order that?"

"Why would the Senate Arms Committee order the CIA to stand down? Want to wager a certain retired admiral is in the middle of all this?"

CONTESTUS
HAITI

Sherry could hear men shouting above the thrum of a generator, a high-pitched whine somewhere in the catacombs of the ancient cellar.

"What do you see?"

"The walls are stone and dirt."

"What else?"

"Bags, cloth sacks of something, men with guns. They are waiting for something."

"What did they do with Pioche's wife and her daughter?"

"Next to us," Carol said, sitting on the floor, her hands wrapped over her head.

Carol's voice was strained. Sherry knew what the

woman was thinking, that her daughter had been here.

Sherry stood at the door. "How far away are the men?" she asked, trying to distract her.

Carol got slowly to her feet, looked out the viewing pane.

"Forty, fifty feet," Carol said, again collapsing to the floor. Sherry heard the noise rising from within the woman; she turned to hug her and Carol moaned, her mouth pressed against Sherry's shoulder. The tears weren't for herself, Sherry knew. Carol was thinking her daughter might have shared this very cell. And here she had spent a summer, with her mother on the other end of the island.

Sherry thought about Brigham just then and was thankful he was not here. He would have preferred it the other way around, she knew; Brigham was like that, he tried to be protective of her, and she had never made that an easy responsibility. They would only have killed him, too.

Of course Brigham wouldn't let this go away quietly. Interpol would try to capitalize on what they learned, would try to do the right thing, but Sherry knew they shared information in a secretive world. She had no doubt as to their intentions, but Sherry had struggled through countless challenges to have some purpose in this life. She wanted to be an example for others. She did not want to become a casualty in a clandestine war.

Brigham wouldn't allow it, she was sure. He would

do everything in his power, use every bit of knowledge at his disposal, including what he knew about Madame Esme's humanitarian organization, if it helped him get to President Préval. Failing that, he would go public.

Sherry only hoped that he would succeed, that their story would be told. She wanted the world to get a glimpse of what she had seen. She wanted CNN to show what caged humans looked like. She wanted those six o'clock sound bites to provoke reflection on what it must be like looking out from within. Knowing that dreams of love, motherhood, and success were all gone, that their lives, the only lives they would ever have, had been sacrificed to amuse and profit strangers.

Car doors slammed faintly. Sherry turned and looked to where the sound was coming from. She put a hand up, found an air vent. "Can you see out there?"

"Lights outside," Carol sobbed. "Trucks."

Sherry heard voices. Footsteps fading into the recesses of the cellar. The whine of the drill stopped.

Sherry heard men talking. The voice of the leader, the man who had shot the old houngan, was disquieting in a way Sherry could not describe.

The man speaking to him sounded British. They were talking about electrical loads and flashovers, but the voices were too distant, and the sobbing of the women around her too loud, to hear specifics.

Then the leader's voice was coming back toward them, speaking Creole now, moving closer to their cell.

"Open it," he ordered someone.

Sherry heard the rattle of a metal hasp, the creak of hinges as it opened.

Hands grabbed her arms and pulled her out in the open.

She could smell rancid breath. The man measured six, perhaps seven, inches taller than she.

A hand took her hair and wound it around the fist. She could feel his eyes on her body. She could smell the odor of his skin as he leaned close. Suddenly he jerked her head back and dragged her by the arm and hair across the dirt floor and removed her wrist restraints. Then Bedard said, "Bring the mother out, bring all of them. Line them up on their knees."

Bedard took a cigar from his shirt pocket and lit it while the women were being brought to him.

Sherry could hear them getting close, perhaps only ten feet away, before they were made to kneel facing her.

"So you are the girl's mother." Bedard left Sherry standing there and walked toward Carol Bishop. "The American crusader," he said mockingly.

Carol looked up at him with disgust, muscles tightening in her legs. She looked ready to spring headfirst, but Bedard grabbed her throat and squeezed, watching her face go blue. "You will die soon enough, woman, but first I want you to see how easily a person can be broken. Your daughter was easy," he sneered. "You should have seen her perform. She didn't even beg."

He pushed her away, back to her knees. Then he

walked down the line, past the others, lifted Aleksandra's hair, and let it fall over her battered face. He leaned over and took her head in his hands and jerked it to face the others, grabbed her nose and chin and pried open her empty mouth. "See this. This is my work." He smiled. "What do you think?"

The dead man's widow screamed and Bedard back-handed her jaw, sending blood and spittle over Carol's face.

Bedard stepped away from the kneeling women, looked over his shoulder.

"Take off your clothes, Miss Moore," he yelled. Sherry's face showed no expression. She did not move.

Bedard turned to face her. "If you do not, I will take them off myself, or perhaps I will go to the child first. Would you rather I start with her?"

Sherry's mouth tasted like metal; panic-inducing adrenaline flooded her bloodstream. Until now she had been presented with no opportunity to resist. She'd had guns pointed at her since she'd been taken from the houngan's temple. Her wrists had been bound.

She took a deep breath from the abdomen. Wait, she coaxed herself, for God's sake don't panic.

Sherry was hardly defenseless, she knew martial arts well, but protecting one's self was not about the imme-diacy of a response. It was also about opportunity. She knew she had to fight down what her mind and body were screaming for her to do. She could not flail out and overcome the odds, no matter how physically capable. She needed to know more about who and what was around her. She needed the perfect moment.

Sherry kicked off her shoes, unbuckled her belt, and unzipped her shorts, tugged them off her hips, and let them fall to the ground. She heard men speaking in Creole, three of them, to be certain. Two were distant, near the corridor leading to the outside, or so she gauged. The other was closer, within striking distance.

They were all enjoying this. This was something they had seen many times before, had likely participated in.

Bedard concerned her most. She could feel his eyes on her. She could sense his lust, his hatred.

She undid the buttons of her shirt and let it fall off her shoulders. She took a deep breath. This would have been a lot easier if the young girl were not here. She might have had options then. Or maybe she would have done as all the other women did here. Try to live for another moment, another day.

The captain of the *Anna Marie* stooped to crane his neck beyond the ship's wheel. There was a light in the sky to the north. It seemed to be growing, shimmering on the wet windshield of the cabin.

He rummaged through rags and sundry tools, found binoculars in a hatch, and trained them on the light.

One of the crewmen came into the cabin behind him and shut the door.

"What is it?"

The captain shook his head.

The light continued to grow on a cloudless palette of stars. It wasn't heavenly, he knew, nor was a second light now becoming visible on the horizon. There was another ship out there.

In twelve years of smuggling, the *Anna Marie* had never been boarded. The police and military were fixated on the go-fast boats, which had been highly successful outrunning them. Fishing trawlers weren't immune from the drug interdiction cops, but the ones that were targeted had been linked through informants to cocaine. The *Anna Marie* smuggled bodies, not drugs, and her name had not yet come up on law enforcement radar.

Two more crewmen entered the cabin, pulling automatic rifles from the hatches. The lights were converging in front of them, bright as small moons.

The captain turned the wheel in a reflexive but futile gesture. Then they could hear the *whop* of a helicopter coming toward them across the open sea. The helicopter's floodlights came on as a machine gun fired and hot orange tracer rounds rained upon the dark water off their bow.

The superstructure of the coast guard cutter was now visible in the captain's glasses. She was a big one, he thought, eighty, ninety feet, and she would be armed with cannon and torpedoes. He put the binoculars down and barked an order to his crew as the helicopter descended over the cabin of the *Anna Marie*.

The crew put down their weapons, opened the double doors over the hold full of women, quickly stepped away, raised their hands to surrender, and waited for the cutter *St. Louis* to come alongside. Above them the Jayhawk helicopter's crew looked down in wonder. The open hold was packed full of women, every one of them staring up into the blinding lights.

30

CONTESTUS

HAITI

Men in black flight suits huddled over a black-and-gray
satellite image, topographical features of a coastline il-
luminated in laser-green light. Their attention was being
drawn to a mountain ridge. There was a series of small
outbuildings by a cathedral, the perimeter of a security
fence traced in red.

"Five-knot winds from south-southeast." The leader
met each of their eyes. "If your body begins to plane in
free fall you're going to sail off target. Every foot matters, gentlemen."

The men nodded their understanding.

The blacked-out KC-130 Hercules was silent at
35,000 feet, releasing the five high-altitude chutists
into chilled unbreathable air over western Haiti. The
men dropped like shadows into the night, oxygen
masks linked to personal tanks on their chests,
Heckler and Koch .45-caliber pistols in black shoulder holsters and 5.56mm SCAR light combat rifles
strapped across their backs. They plummeted an as-
tonishing six and a half miles before deploying the
square black plumes of their canopies. The men were

virtually invisible as they floated above the spires of the ancient cathedral and dropped within the security perimeter.

Metcalf landed on his feet at the edge of the outbuildings. In less than a minute he heard the others hit dirt; all but one dropped their harnesses and used their radios, making telltale clicks over the closed frequency to signal they were okay.

The last man to land drifted northwest of his target, was still inside the perimeter but dangerously close to the fence and foundation of the cathedral. He was still trying to extricate himself from a coil of barbed wire inside the fence when one of Bedard's guards, who just happened to be standing there, shot him.

A hundred feet away and behind the foundation walls, Sherry in bra and panties stood listening to the sound of Bedard's boots in the dirt. He was waiting for her to strip; had started toward her, and she flexed her right hand, knew that if needed she could make her second finger go rigid. Tucked slightly beneath the first, it was called the spear hand and it was deadly to an opponent's throat or eyes.

"All of it!" he screamed again, but then they heard the rifle shot.

"Guard them!" Bedard yelled, as he ran from the cellar.

The leader of the parachutists also heard the shot. It was an ominous sound and explained the missing signal from one of his men. He pointed in the direction of it and nodded, watching two of his team members split and head toward the entrance to the quarry. He removed a rectangular box from his backpack—small, about the size of a loaf of bread—and found the switch that activated a pin-dot red light. He buried it under vegetation and slipped the rifle off his shoulder, motioned to the remaining members of the team, and they moved forward, beginning to work their way through the outbuildings toward the foundation of the cathedral.

"Bring him," Bedard shouted, enraged.

Sherry, still standing in her underwear, heard men laboring under the weight of a body. A moment later they dropped it at her feet. She heard the man moan; he was alive.

"I think you know something you are not telling us, Miss Moore."

She didn't move and he slapped her. Sherry remained expressionless and he slapped her again.

"Perhaps then you will tell us one more fortune before you die." Bedard reeked of fear and aggression.

Sherry heard the hammer snap back on Bedard's pistol, then an explosion deafened her right ear. Through the ringing she heard screams from the women kneeling not ten feet away. She prayed no one would move, that no one would dare to run.

Bedard grabbed her and threw her facedown on the

dead man. His belt buckle jabbed her stomach; his clothing had heavy zippers and snaps, the coarse ballistic shoulder holster. Her face was against his chest, her right arm over his collarbone. It was wet and warm over the bullet hole above his heart. She could feel her panties soaking up the blood from the shot he'd taken in the hip when he was still outside.

"Touch him, you bitch." Bedard's voice was low and cruel. He pulled back the hammer on his gun once more.

Sherry grabbed the dead man's right hand with her left. She lay there upon him. He was warm and ever so human, she thought, catching a *flash of light and then hands reaching out for him, she saw light in the jungle, the entrance of a tunnel; a man to the right was holding an antiquated Kalashnikov, the man to his left, there were three in all, now was carrying a radio; the tunnel was lit by strings of bare lightbulbs, the walls were a combination of rock and smatterings of luminous marble reflecting in the light; a woman, herself, in white brassiere and pale blue panties; a man with a dead white eye, dark-complexioned, automatic pistol, a .45-caliber Colt in his right hand; a man's face, streaked dark with paint, his face was large and chiseled, his eyes pale green; a younger man with red hair, a map, the sparkle of moonlight on black sea; the silhouette of jagged coastline; a dark-haired woman in a hospital bed, she was smiling, holding a crying baby smeared with blood; spires of a cathedral; bare feet of the nearly naked woman; his own hand shaking in front of his face; thumbnail scratching dirt; nothing . . .*

Sherry tried to think. What did she say to Bedard? He would kill them all anyhow.

Bedard grabbed her arm and pulled her to her feet. "Who is out there?" he shouted, gun to her head.

A cell phone rang. Bedard snatched it from a pocket. "What?" he screamed.

There was a long moment of silence as he listened. His face must have registered alarm because someone came forward.

"Commandeur?" a man said.

Bedard's voice was different, somehow shaken. "The palace has ordered all police commanders to their stations."

"Martial law?" the man asked.

"I do not know," Bedard said. "They have been instructed to account for their men, Préval has closed the airports. Nothing flies in or out."

"What do you wish, Commandeur?"

"Get the helicopter ready. No, first get that detonator for me."

"The engineer, Commandeur?"

"Kill him. Just bring me the fucking thing."

Gunfire erupted outside the cathedral. Bedard ordered men to respond. The shooting continued outside, then a mighty explosion rocked the ground.

Smoke poured into the cellar. It was chaos after that, automatic weapons fire, but now it was from within. Bedard's remaining guards sprayed the entrance, Sherry heard them shouting in Creole, but she thought there were fewer of them now. She thought they were taking hits.

Bedard grabbed her once more, wrapped an arm around her neck with inhuman strength, and pivoted her in the direction of the fire. She could feel the heat of his body against her. She went rigid.

The firing suddenly stopped.

"Let her go," a man shouted in English. Sherry turned her head, surprised. She sensed the smoke was clearing.

Bedard backed her into the corner, his men on both sides. "I am taking your blind woman," Bedard said. "Matteo," he screamed over his shoulder. "The detonator!"

"Let her go or you die," the American said calmly.

Sherry heard footsteps running; someone came up behind them and handed something to Bedard.

Sherry felt him slip the pistol back in his holster.

"Perhaps I will kill us all." Bedard raised his arm over his head. "We are surrounded by explosives."

Sherry let her head fall forward, chin to her own chest. She wondered if she could get hold of his gun. It was right there in the holster on his right hip.

"You're not going anywhere," the man said again. Sherry had already matched a face to that voice. A face she had seen only minutes before, in the final few seconds of the dead soldier's life. A face she had once imagined on a mountain called Denali.

She knew she shouldn't have been surprised by the calm in Metcalf's voice. He had not come all this way to lose. Metcalf would not show emotion.

"Put down your weapons, you fools," Bedard snarled. "Put them down or you all die."

"Barrage radio interference," Metcalf said evenly. "Or maybe you would understand it as random frequency blocking."

"Babble," Bedard mocked.

"Not babble," Metcalf said calmly. "Your signal has been jammed. Your detonator is worthless. Kill them."

Rifles cracked from the area of the cells, bodies fell around them with no return fire.

"One more chance," Metcalf said.

"Fuck . . ." Bedard managed to get out, but then he lurched sideways as a bullet struck his shoulder, half spinning him with Sherry still in his arm. She filled her lungs and snapped her head back, striking Bedard's bandaged throat.

He did not let go, but it was enough for Sherry to use his weight and momentum against him, her knee sweeping his left leg until he fell rolling on his back. She felt his arm moving for the pistol, but something heavy landed on him, pinning him down, and Carol Bishop yelled, "Die!" as Aleksandra drove the point of Yousy's bone hairpin through his good eye.

Rolly King George sat in the pilot's chair on the flying bridge of his Bertram, water lapping softly against the side of the boat, sky above a virtual dome of tranquil stars. They were afloat off the coast of southwestern Haiti. It had been thirty minutes since they'd gotten word the KC-130 Hercules had dropped men over Contestus.

Brigham was below in the cabin, speaking on his cell phone with someone in the United States. He had been communicating with someone ever since they left Frenchman's Cove in Jamaica almost four hours ago.

The cabin door opened and closed below, and George heard the handrail rattle as Brigham began to climb the ladder to the bridge.

"Take us in, Rolly," the retired admiral said. Brigham stood behind, his hand on the inspector's shoulder.

"They'll meet us on the beach in Tiburon harbor."

"All of them, sir?"

"All but one," Brigham said throatily, looking out at the random spray of stars on the horizon. These were emotions the admiral hadn't experienced for quite some time, the love and fear that a brotherhood of arms never talked about. And then there was Sherry Moore. She was all but a daughter to him. His wife had died. His parents and siblings were all gone. Sherry was all he had and he was ever so glad to have her back.

Captain Metcalf loaded the women and his soldiers into one of the trucks on the compound. There was no plan to take any Haitian citizens off the island until Hettie begged them to. She had but one request, that they stop at her shanty in the harbor long enough for her to retrieve something.

Brigham and the inspector watched as the truck's headlights appeared and stopped momentarily in the village. They did not expect resistance; even the Haitian policemen were to have been recalled to their stations and should pose no threat. But Inspector George had brought arms for both and they were ready to defend themselves if need be.

In only minutes, however, it was Captain Metcalf who ran the front tires of a truck into the salt water and jumped out, unloading men and women from the back. Brigham was over the rail and running to meet Sherry. The soldiers carried the body of their comrade aboard, then Pioche's body, as Carol helped Aleksandra along behind. Hettie, with Amaud's picture under her arm, held Yousy's hand as Rolly King

George helped them through the gate in the transom.

Then a small creature came darting across the beach and Yousy screamed, "Chaser!" as Hettie pulled her away. Metcalf leaned over the side of the boat and scooped up the dog as Rolly King George eased the Bertram into deep water.

Sherry sat in her sunroom overlooking the Delaware, Christmas music playing softly on the speakers. The house smelled of pine from two live trees and countless wreaths.

She'd hired a local florist to decorate.

She wondered how many years it had been since the old house hosted a Christmas celebration. She knew nothing of the former owners, but it had been more than a decade that she'd been here. More than a decade since a red ribbon or anything remotely like it had festooned the front door.

Why, she couldn't say, but it had never felt right to her before. She couldn't say she had memories about Christmas; from before the age of five she remembered only flashes of her mother and the beach in New Jersey.

This year was different, however. This was a year of new hope and new promise.

Brigham poured himself another glass of port. Sherry, holding a dark bottle of beer, had decided to spend the holidays with lagers.

Brigham seemed to have a new vigor about him, a playfulness that she hadn't witnessed in a long time.

Perhaps, she thought, the holiday cheer was contagious.

"Carol Bishop called this morning."

"Really." Brigham rested his glass on a knee.

"She says Hettie is going to night school. She wants to get her GED someday."

"Bravo," said Brigham.

"And Yousy is starting seventh grade."

"What about Carol?" he said kindly.

"She loves having them. She credits Yousy for finding her daughter's killers."

"So she should. They need anything?"

"Hunh-uh. They're living in their apartment over the garage, she said it's twice the size of their home in Tiburon."

"We should send them something. A ham, a turkey."

"Will you handle that, Mr. Brigham?"

He smiled. "My pleasure."

The doorbell rang.

Sherry looked at Brigham. "You expecting anyone?"

"Not me." Brigham put his glass on an end table. "Are you here?"

"As long as it's not the press."

"Lord, I know that much, Sherry."

She smiled.

Brigham left her there, feeling the warmth of the winter sun through the plate glass wall that faced the Delaware. He'd said it was snowing earlier, would snow again before midnight. By the weekend there was supposed to be a foot of white stuff on the ground. She didn't even mind.

"Sherry, guess who's here?" Brigham said.

"Miss Moore," Metcalf said politely.

She swiveled her chair toward the door. "Captain?" Sherry smiled, thinking she hadn't smiled this much in years.

"I can't believe you're here," she said, knowing that for once she wasn't doing a great job of hiding her emotions.

"I hope it's not a bad time."

"Heavens, no," she said. "Mr. Brigham, would you please get our guest a beer, or something stronger, Captain Metcalf?"

"A beer is fine, but please call me Brian."

Sherry nodded, beaming. "I didn't know how to reach you, to thank you again, Brian. Mr. Brigham said you were out of the country."

"Briefly," Metcalf said.

There was a moment of uncomfortable silence.

"You knew about this?" Sherry turned to Brigham. "That the captain, that Brian was coming today?"

Brigham said nothing.

"You never cease to amaze me, never."

"So I was told that you're ready to go downhill skiing, Miss Moore."

Sherry looked at Metcalf, perplexed.

"My friend the ski instructor, he has been working with the blind for several years at a resort in western

Pennsylvania. It's not Vail or Vermont, but I told the admiral it's a great place to learn."

Sherry looked straight at him, nodding her head slowly, question mark on her face. "Uh-huh," she said slowly. "Is there more?"

"Uh, actually yes," Metcalf said, eyebrows raised like question marks at Brigham. "I have some, well, I managed these days coming up, you know, some time off."

"To go skiing." Sherry grinned.

"Yeah, well, I mean, it takes two skiers to get you down, one on either side of you. I could be the second, if that was all right with you," Metcalf said shyly. He looked at Brigham and shrugged.

"And when exactly are my lessons to be?"

"Uh, the day after tomorrow?" Metcalf said tentatively. "You don't know about any of this, do you, Miss Moore?"

Metcalf's face began to redden.

Sherry shook her head. "You've made reservations?"

"Two rooms at a bed-and-breakfast near Fort Ligonier, four-day lift passes for Seven Springs Resort. The admiral didn't tell you?"

Brigham rose and picked up his bottle. "Well, you kids work out your plans, it's time for my nap and I'm sure you can entertain yourselves."

"Nap?" Sherry made a face. "It's dinnertime, Mr. Brigham."

"Nap," Brigham said firmly.

He chuckled and was gone.

My dearest Eva,

I cannot begin to tell you the wonderful things that have happened since arriving in Burgas. Who could have known what lay beyond that endless sea of grapes in Romania? I thought we knew all there was to know about life. I imagined I was the luckiest girl in all of Cotnari.

Do you know how little money I left home with last month, my "wedding" savings, and yet in three short weeks I have doubled it. There is more to life than marrying a Lepushin and farming dawn to dark.

Grigori, my new friend, has been paying me to model. And no, it's not what you think. I wear clothes and lots of them. He photographs for a fashion designer based out of Italy. Oh, Eva, you would love him. I told him how beautiful you are and he said I should send for you immediately.

I know it was you that was always accused of having a wild streak, and me that everyone thought so levelheaded. Well, let me tell you from a level head, pack your bags and get here as fast as you can. Grigori has booked passage for me to Italy in eight days. He says if you are as beautiful as I described he'll throw in passage for you as well and *you* will get to meet the designers personally. He says we will be rich within a year.

Eva, I am staying at the Mirage on Slaveikov Street, Room 1221. Be there by Wednesday, my friend.

Destiny awaits us.

ACKNOWLEDGMENTS

My agent, Paul Fedorko; my editor, Colin Fox; and all the talented people at Simon & Schuster who make my work look good.

Cindy Collins, the none-too-subtle voice over my shoulder. Barb, for that very first read.

ABOUT THE AUTHOR

George D. Shuman grew up on a cattle farm in the Allegheny Mountains of southwestern Pennsylvania. He worked in a steel mill before moving to Washington, D.C., where he joined the Metropolitan Police Department, from which he retired a lieutenant after twenty years of service. For the next decade Shuman held executive positions in the luxury resort industry, in both Montauk, New York, and Nantucket, Massachusetts, and was a member of the prestigious International Association of Professional Security Consultants.

He has since returned to the Laurel Highlands of Pennsylvania, where he resides and writes full-time.

He has two grown children, Melissa and Daniel.

Turn the page for an exciting preview of
George D. Shuman's
newest Sherry Moore Novel

Second Sight

Coming in hardcover from Simon & Schuster

Attached to Sherry's head were a profusion of colorful electrodes, each connected to tubes that snaked their way into somber-looking machines. The gurney was stainless steel and felt cold through her flimsy gown. She had the sense she was in a station, about to depart on some futuristic trip.

The light flashes from the migraines had been getting worse, not better.

She was beginning to see colors as well, bright purples, reds, and orange. Ophthalmic migraines were common, Dr. Salix told her, and many people reported shapes and colors similar to what she was seeing. It was caused by blood vessel spasms behind the eye. People who suffered cortical or cerebral blindness such as herself might still be candidates for migraines because it was whole brain injury, not just damage to the occipital lobes, that prevented her from seeing. In other words, it takes all components of the brain to see and whole brain changes that might have altered the order of the delicate nerve systems might also permit vision behind the iris.

Sherry was convinced she was reacting to the radiation she'd absorbed. The only question for her right now was whether or not she was the same person that she had been before New Mexico. What effect did the radiation have on an EEG of her brain and thus her ability to read the memories of the dead?

"We want to perform some tests before we get started," Dr. Salix said, looking down at her.

Getting started meant bringing in the cadavers.

"You remember the strobe? You've done this before. We're going to move the machine over you and see how your brain perceives the light."

Sherry nodded.

"If you sense something, if you feel anything—pain, nausea—I want you to signal me by raising a hand. Otherwise lie quiet and I'll let you know when we're done. Are you ready?"

She nodded and wheels squeaked as a machine was rolled into place.

Something snapped in the hollow-sounding room, a switch, she thought. She felt a vibration and then it was as if there was pressure against her eyes, but she saw no light.

She heard a metallic noise behind her, someone was moving to her left.

"It's on?" she asked, but was quickly countered with a *shhhhh*.

"Just your hand, Sherry. Look, don't listen."

She wanted to see something, anything, so badly. She wanted an answer for what was happening to her. And if she couldn't give them an explanation by seeing lights she at least wanted to return to the state she had been in all these years. Blind.

The switch snapped off and the machine was wheeled away.

She could feel warm tears streaking down the sides of her cheeks. "I didn't see anything."

Someone laid a hand on her shoulder. "Which is not important," Salix said. "We're bringing in the first of the bodies now. Once we get her alongside you, I'll need your right hand. Are you doing okay?"

Sherry nodded.

Someone dabbed her cheeks until they were dry.

This part was familiar. More than two decades familiar. Her very first experience with a corpse had been as a child. A roommate in the orphanage in Philadelphia had swallowed a lethal dose of rat poison. It took years to understand what she had seen in that moment holding the dead girl's hand. Years more to accept that it was going to happen every time she touched the dead. That it was now a part of herself.

She wasn't the only skeptic during those early years and she certainly wouldn't be the last. How did you accept that you are a freak of nature? Or as Mr. Brigham, her best friend and neighbor, liked to say, a very special human being?

Well, there was special in this world and there was *special*. Could someone, much less her, a blind woman who had retrograde amnesia due to a childhood head injury, really exhibit aptitude for reading people's minds? In time it became impossible for the medical community to ignore what she appeared to be doing. They wanted to have their own look at this freak from Philadelphia.

Then came the psychologists and neurologists and on it went until a young biologist from the University of Calgary in Alberta suggested she wasn't clairvoyant at all. He believed, instead, that electrical anomalies in her damaged brain somehow enabled her to connect with the dead person's central nervous system through the profusion of skin cell receptors in the human hand. Her brain then used the deceased person's neurological wiring to reach their short-term memory in their frontal cortex. She was actually seeing the last visually encoded memories of what the deceased person had been thinking about in the final seconds of their life.

Once she got past the macabre of holding hands with the dead, Sherry found fulfillment in what she was doing. Helping murder victims find their killer. Setting straight someone's last moments in life. Locating missing persons. Helping find artifacts lost to antiquity. She had seen images that would lead investigators to crime scenes. She had a purpose in life—perhaps even a responsibility.

But it wasn't always easy.

Sherry's mind recorded the collage of human memories that assailed her when she was touching a hand, including countless seemingly mundane events in a person's life, not important to anyone else, but special enough for them to remember in those precious few seconds before death. Residual memory, Sherry called it. Everything that happened before the power went off and the brain recorded its last thought. They had become her memories now as well, those remnants of a life . . . a particularly beautiful sunrise, a smile on an old woman's face, a child's teddy bear, a grandfather's cane. Memories were both God's gift and God's punishment, it seemed. You didn't want to live with them and you didn't want to live without them.

The gurneys were pushed together. Sherry's hand was lifted and laid next to the cadaver. She found the fingers quickly, a small hand, delicate. There wasn't anything to be done after that. Sometimes the response was immediate; sometimes she drifted into it like a dream. It had never taken more than a few seconds and even now she saw . . . *the lights in a child's bedroom, no, it was a ward, some kind of a hospital ward and it had bright colors and murals painted on the walls.*

She saw parents sitting with their children on the floor. Shelves and boxes and baskets in the corners were filled with plush toys and games and books and videos. Nurses wore pink and blue and yellow scrubs with a hodgepodge of prints that included stars and moons and nursery rhyme characters. There was an ice cream cart in the hall outside the door. There was a girl in the bed next to her and her head was shaved and she was playing a video game in her lap.

She saw a nurse leaning to pick up a Popsicle stick next to her bed and she reached out to touch her, but her arm was too short, her fingers too weak to stretch. She opened her mouth but no sound came out. She felt as if she were trapped inside her body—capable of understanding, but not of getting anyone's attention.

She wanted that girl in the bed next to her to turn and

look at her, to see that something was wrong. She moved her eyes toward the ceiling, and then the wall and the window and to the bathroom door before going back to the girl.

Right there, just a foot away, the red button on the call harness. She only had to mash it with her thumb and nurses would come running.

She felt odd, like someone had ahold of her arms and legs and now they were pulling her inside of herself, folding her up like a piece of luggage, and with every minute that passed she was recessing deeper and deeper within until the clown lamp began to dim and the girl in the bed next door faded to black. . . .

Sherry let the hand go and sighed.

"You had an event?"

Sherry nodded, a tear streaking the corner of one eye.

She hated the labels people tossed around over the years. Yes, she'd had an "event." *Is everybody happy with that? Just another dead girl, yeah. Just another event.*

"Did you see anything different?" Salix asked her. "Vision, quality of vision, anything we haven't talked about before?"

Sherry shook her head. "What about you?" she retorted.

Salix grunted loudly and moved to Sherry's shoulder. "You know I won't look at the EEGs for a few more days, Sherry. I want to compare your brain's activity against some of your earliest base examples. This is really important."

Salix had been working with Sherry for years. He

knew not to treat her like a patient, but then again he didn't know what else to do but study her tests.

"We're looking for velocity changes, Sherry. Changes in the speed your cells release neurotransmitters. Perhaps even chemical changes in the hippocampus; I can't determine much until I have it all in front of me. We'll know more later."

"What if the results are different from before?"

He laughed softly. "I can't really say it will tell us anything new," he said. "You know that, but be patient." He patted her hand. "Let me do my job and be patient. We'll do one more cadaver today and talk about where to go from here."

She nodded grimly. It was all just a crapshoot, she knew. They didn't know what they were looking for; and even if they found something, they wouldn't know what to do about it. And she couldn't blame them. She was no different than the twelve thousand epileptics in Philadelphia who for reasons beyond the ken of science had electrical storms in their brain. It wasn't a matter of matching up the color-coded wires and then everything was all right again. No one had an owner's manual for the brain.

A few minutes later, a second gurney was wheeled into the room. She heard the wheels pivot into position and then the cart was pushed alongside hers. There was a moment of activity as the nurses and assistants reset something on the equipment wired to Sherry's brain. Then someone pulled back the sheet over the cadaver and she got a whiff of decay.

She thought about that machine in New Mexico just then. How stupid those people had been to steal a radiological machine and start prying apart interior canisters. Stupid or just woefully ignorant. She could imagine that poor child in their morgue eating bread from a table dusted with radioactive powder. Breathing it into her lungs as she lay in her filthy bed. She'd heard they found the mother and father inside the trailer, both dead in the living room. The son was found in the desert, miles away, behind the wheel of his pickup truck. There was an X burnt into the skin of his forearm.

And then there were two Indians who had been at the table. They'd carried a capful of the blue powder back to the reservation and showed it to the children. Twelve more—some in the public school—came down with the flu in a week. Everyone who touched the men's clothes was infected.

In the end, the incident claimed fourteen lives. Twenty-eight others survived with an undetermined prognosis.

Salix took her hand and quickly bridged it to the next gurney, placed it gently across the cadaver's hand.

It was a man's hand, the skin was slack—*did the room temperature suddenly rise?* He was an older man, she thought, seventies, perhaps eighties. The fingers were long but the hand itself was narrow, infirm as if the muscles had atrophied. Whoever he was, his hands had not been active for some time.

She closed her own hand around it and then her

eyelids, aware of the wire harnesses pressing against her shoulder . . .

She was in a room with white walls, a projector behind a hole in a wall was showing a grainy video of a child running naked between two thatch-covered huts; three dark-skinned women wearing cone straw hats were sitting nearby under the shade of a palm tree. One of them was stirring something in a bowl. Another's hands appeared to be flailing in animated conversation.

Suddenly the child stopped and pointed at the sky. A moment later there was a blinding white light. The child stood in perfect silence, as if the world had suddenly come to a halt. The women and the child turned black against the white background, as if you were looking at a negative of the image. Then a hurricane-like wind obliterated everything with sand and debris. When the wind was gone there was no village, no child, no women, no tree, nothing but flames that licked the bare earth.

He was sitting at the end of a long wooden table. There was a gun in front of him, within reach. He looked at the door and then at the dusty light coming from the projector through the hole. He turned and saw a dirt road on the wall. He was looking over the hood of an open-top jeep. There was a woman on the road in front of him, young, she was wearing a khaki-green uniform with Red Cross patches on the sleeves. Her shoes were missing. Her legs were spread wide and staked open, her arms out from her sides as if on a cross. A hand grenade was pinched between her teeth, a string tied to the handle and the handle to the neck of a water buffalo standing over her. The jeep stopped, the buffalo stepped away, and she could see hands waving in front of the lens, gesturing for the animal to stay still. The buffalo shook its big head and snorted, went down on its front knees as if to pray and then sprang sideways, leaping into a gallop. The string came taut and a red mist replaced the medical corps woman's face.

A bead of perspiration ran down Sherry's cheek; she could feel sweat forming on her scalp, itching under the hair. *God it was warm.*

There was a metal box at the far end of the table, slits for air vents on top and a round white gauge on the left front side. There was black mesh cloth covering two cones facing him. They appeared at times to be vibrating. He turned his head to look at the door. "can't . . . on, can't . . . on." Sherry started to say it out loud: "can't . . . on, can't . . . on . . ." *Someone was looking at him through a glass observation window in the door, a man with a white hat, and there was smoke rising around his face, distorting his features. He was smoking a pipe.*

"Help me," he called to the man behind the door.

Sherry's lips continued to move: can't . . . on, can't . . . on, can't . . . on . . .

He looked down at the gun in front of him. His hand moved toward it as his eyes darted back to the white dial. "Can't . . . on, can't . . . on . . ."

He saw a man in a fishing boat with an open cabin. There were rectangular wire cages in the stern tied to dozens of battered cork buoys. He saw the man kneel and reach into the hold and come up with a rifle and start shooting at him.

There was a grinning soldier, American, sitting at a crude wooden table in a room. There were enemy soldiers all around him. A rifle pointed at his head. There was a gun on the table in front of him, just like the gun on the table in this room. He picked it up and put it to his head and pulled the trigger and his head jerked sideways and he fell to floor and the soldiers were smiling at the camera and laughing.

Five, ten, fifteen, twenty, twenty-five, thirty, twenty-five, twenty, fifteen, ten . . .

There was a dirigible floating just above his head—it was massive—approaching a tall steel tower. There was lightning and the dirigible caught fire and exploded in a ball of flame. People were falling from everywhere, charred black people, and the people on the ground were catching on fire as the debris fell.

He looked away from the wall and tried not to watch, but voices kept telling him not to turn away, voices not from the cone-shaped objects or the hole in the door but from in his head, his own head, and they would not let him look away.

There was a young girl. She was wearing a sailor's cap and red lipstick. She was wearing a white shirt tied above her stomach and red pedal pushers. She was smiling at him and waving and a friend, another brunette, ran up next to her and was pushing an elbow in her side.

He forced his eyes down. Something was burning his skin on the arm of the chair. The gun on the table had a cylinder and he could see the ends of the shiny brass cartridges in the chambers. It was a six-shot revolver, double action; it had no safety, required no effort but to point the barrel and pull the trigger.

Thirty, twenty-five, twenty, fifteen, ten . . . there were wet spots on the table next to the revolver, beads of perspiration that had fallen from his cheeks. He didn't want to watch the girls on the wall, he didn't want to know what the shadows coming up behind them were.

There were marks on the table by the gun, grooves cut into the wood, the scars from someone's thumbnail that had been carved into the wood. He put his thumbnail in one and rocked it back and forth. His fingers were only inches from the revolver, it was shiny and he wanted to pick it up, pick it up and end it all . . . ten, five, zero, thirty, twenty-five, can't . . . on, can't . . . on.

It was dawn and he was awakening from sleep. He was covered with mud and lying on his side on the ground. There was an open-bed truck with the rear end facing him. It was full of corpses and next to the rear tire soldier helmets had been stacked. Next to the helmets were web belts and canteens and gas masks. A man wearing rank and chaplain corps insignia was putting his hands on each of the bodies. He rolled to look away, then he looked down, pulling a green, leather-bound journal closer to his body.

Can't . . . on, can't . . . on, can't . . . on, can't . . . on, can't . . .

"Sherry?" Dr. Salix shook her shoulders roughly. "Sherry!"

Her eyes fluttered but remained shut. Sherry could hear his words, but they were far, far away. Suddenly she saw something pink, blue orbs floating in space, dark caverns that oddly reminded her of a nose and she felt as if she were falling through a soft warm light and that the light would protect her. She was aware of the old man's hand. She could still feel the energy coursing between them. It wasn't over.

There is a riddle, she thought, *something she must solve*. "Can't . . . on, can't . . . on," she repeated, thinking it would be dangerous to say anything else, to say the wrong thing.

"Sherry, it's Dr. Salix."

"Monahan," she said suddenly. "Thomas J., private, first class, serial number 7613779 . . ."

"Sherry! Sherry Moore, I want you to focus on my voice. I want you to concentrate on the date. Tell me what day it is."

"Can't . . . on, can't . . . on . . ."

"Sherry," he said sternly. "Tell me what day it is. Think about the day."

"Thanksgiving." She began to falter. "Can't . . . on, can't . . . on . . ."

"Sherry, you're in a hospital. You are in Philadelphia. Do you remember Philadelphia, Sherry? That I'm Dr. Salix?"

She shook her head no, distrustful.

"Sherry!" he said, turning and pointing toward the ceiling. "Somebody give me some light!" he yelled and one of the technicians turned on the overhead surgical spots.

He thumbed open one of Sherry's eyelids and she let out a bloodcurdling scream.

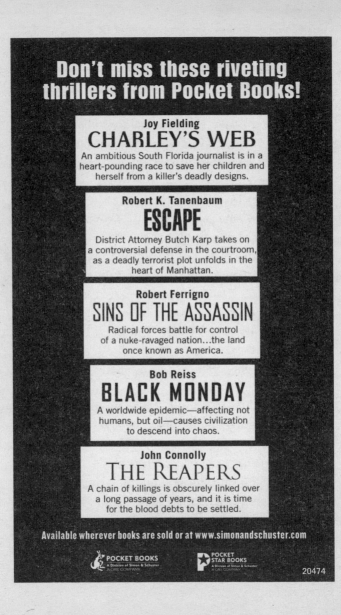